ALEXANDRA BRYCE

teacher

PINNACLE BOOKS   LOS ANGELES

TEACHER

Copyright © 1981 by Marianna Birns

An original Pinnacle Books edition, published for the first time anywhere.

First printing, January 1981

ISBN: 0-523-41012-3

Cover illustration by Norm Eastman

Printed in the United States of America

PINNACLE BOOKS, INC.
2029 Century Park East
Los Angeles, California 90067

Aggie Hillyer is a schoolteacher at the newly integrated Arcadia High in the small factory town of Avalon, Florida. It is populated with characters, some of whose lives are as narrow and limited as the boundaries of the ghetto she teaches in.

VANCE—the handsome, married football coach who is in constant sexual pursuit of Aggie. He and the male faculty members establish a "pussy kitty" to be settled on the first to make it with Aggie.

MURIEL—an overbearing old maid who is both Aggie's superior and nemesis—a woman whose only security lies in following the rules.

BECKY—a preacher's daughter and a victim of his incestuous advances, for which he punishes her.

FERNANDO—an award-winning teacher whose two great loves are his radical gay activist lover, and teaching.

PRIDE—a teenage pimp who manhandles his prostitutes (Aggie's students) and brings the walls of Arcadia High tumbling down.

BOB—a handsome young cop, a widower and Aggie's lover, protector, pot-supplier and playmate.

SHEILA—a 15-year-old whore who runs for Homecoming Queen.

To Michael and all my other kids

Teacher

1

A bright pink sun peered through silver skeins of Spanish moss like a blushing virgin from beneath her bridal veil. Cypress trees stood knee deep in the muddy shallows of the Avalon river, and the tar-slick highway, still slippery with the heavy mists of morning, glowed in the heat of another steamy Florida day.

A sleek white Corvette burst upon the landscape, blaring an accompaniment from an overamplified sound system.

On the far side of the river in the commercial district, the cannery woke to the invasion of the day shift, creating a traffic jam on the business arm of the Southbound 41. A locomotive converged on the crossing, hauling in another load of citrus to feed the machines that processed orange juice for the breakfast tables of the nation.

The Corvette raced the train across the trestle that spanned the river. It cleared the crossing as the warning signal flashed and clammored, slipping under the descending guardrail and outdistancing the engine laboring under its ponderous load. The 'Vette sped past factories already darkening the morning sky with smoke, and warehouses where rats as big as alley cats feasted from the trash bins overflowing with rotting fruit.

The woman behind the wheel turned sharply into a side street, lined with endless acres of cinderblock structures known as the Projects, then came to an impatient stop behind the flashing lights of a school bus bearing the legend AVALON COUNTY PUBLIC SCHOOLS.

Ms. Aggie Hillyer took a last, lingering toke of a neatly clipped roach and snubbed it self-consciously in the ashtray before returning the boisterous greetings of several youngsters congregated on the curb.

2

The yellow monster swallowed them up, belching gas fumes as it lumbered awkwardly on its way.

She could see the clock tower rising bleakly above the palms as she followed the bus onto Eastern Avenue. She considered pulling out of her lane to pass till she spotted several police cars standing a conspicuous vigil under the trees. "Christ," she muttered under her breath. "You'd think the President was visiting . . . at the very least."

As the buses lined up to disgorge their cargo of children, the DJ on the FM was playing an old 60's ballad by Crosby, Stills, Nash and Young.

The tune took her back to another time, another place. She was a schoolgirl, experiencing New York City for the first time. And there was a boy . . . her high school sweetheart.

About the time she left to study art in the city, he'd turned down acceptances to several perfectly respectable colleges to enlist in the Marine Corps. While he was being trained in the ways of the warrior, she was becoming an aggressively active passivist. But they continued a relationship for a while in their letters, the last remnants of their puppy love.

The weekend he completed his training, Aggie packed a valise and boarded a bus at New York's Port Authority terminal, headed, by way of Atlanta, for Beaufort, South Carolina. She'd never been south of the Poconos till then.

Steering her high-powered car down the highway, she remembered her first view of the alien, steamy South. Acres of red clay soil unrolled beyond the windows of the bus, Negro field hands gathering the last of the crop, tar-paper shacks by the side of the road—a bleak, anonymous landscape.

It was 1962. James Meredith was trying to get into the University of Mississippi. The names and places failed to register as anything more than newspaper headlines. Interesting . . . and aggravating. It was all too distant, too remote, to make a real difference in her own life.

She was already enrolled in a good college. And her grade on her last Art History exam was more real, more relevant, than James Meredith's crusade for equal educational opportunity.

There was no direct bus route to South Carolina then.

3

So Aggie sat and absorbed the view, while the Greyhound rolled steadily southward.

It was in Atlanta that Aggie first saw a segregated restroom.

"Where you goin'?"

Someone grabbed her arm as she was about to push through the ladies room door. The speaker was a plump, pleasant-faced girl in a beehive hairdo.

"Isn't it obvious?" she said with a New Yorker's reluctance to speak with strangers.

The woman's name was Dottie. Born and raised in Georgia, she gave Aggie a crash course in deportment south of the Mason Dixon line.

"White ladies use the *other* facility," she said. "It's a good thing we're both headed for the same place. You need someone to watch out for you."

They boarded a northbound bus out of Atlanta for Beaufort, but the bus was already half full.

Aggie preceeded her new friend up the aisle of the bus and, seeing no empty seat together, opted for two vacancies across the aisle from one another. She was about to swing her weekender onto the luggage rack when Dottie's indignant exclamation stopped her dead in her tracks.

"What are you doing? You want people to think you're white trash, girl?" asked Dottie loudly enough to be heard by all aboard. "You don't plan to sit the whole way next to that there niggah, do you?"

Shocked and mortified, Aggie gaped open-mouthed at Dottie, unable to answer.

A young woman about her own age sat staring out of the window. She turned, her black face void of emotion. For an instant, she simply stared at them. Everyone on the bus stared, but no one said a word.

Then the girl in the window seat got up and pressed past Aggie, to assume another seat in the rear of the bus.

"That's where the likes of her belong," said Dottie, unwrapping a homemade lunch of fried chicken and corn bread. "The back of the bus."

It was Aggie who now sat staring silently out the window.

"Have some chicken," said Dottie. "I want you to get a

taste of that famous Southern hospitality while you're down here."

The word had been mandated by the black-robed pundits in their cloistered tabernacle—and the word was *integration*. Now into the teaming masses of black and brown came the fair-haired, well-fed sons and daughters of the polite folks who lived on the north side—the right side—of town.

Aggie flipped the lid down on the ashtray where the smoldering roach lay wilting and pulled into the parking lot. There, inside a ten-foot chain-link fence that encircled the compound, a huge, black mountain of a man guarded the gate with a clipboard in his hands.

Ezekial (E-Z) Jordan, Dean of Boys, ex-linebacker from Alabama, made a notation on his tally sheet and approached the car. "Where you think you goin', Missy?" he drawled, as a grin of recognition split his ruggedly handsome face.

The blonde in the oversized sunglasses hit the brake, hard, and brought the car to a sudden stop by his side. "Reporting for duty like the rest of you wage slaves," smiled Aggie.

"Well, I don't know 'bout that. This heah lot's just fo' teachers, Missy. You don't look like no teacher to me," he teased, exaggerating the honeysuckle drawl of the southern Black. He bent his massive frame and leaned against the low-slung car. Sweat beaded his face and his shirt clung damply to his ample chest.

"I come equipped with the optional trim package," she beamed.

"And one of the classiest chassies ever to roll by these tired ol' eyes," he laughed. "Summer agrees with you, Aggie," he said, running a gnarled finger over the back of her sun-stained hand where it lay idly on the steering wheel. "You get a little bit blacker and a lot more beautiful ev'ry time I see you."

"I'm trying to pass." Aggie laughed, shrugging off the compliment. "I suddenly feel like a member of the visiting team. I see a few new faces in the crowd," she ventured, glancing back toward the police cars.

His face clouded over. "Yeah! Ain't that a bitch. Just

5

watch yourself with that stinkweed you favor. Hey, we may need this gate for emergency vehicles. We plan to close off the rest of the campus after the tardy bell in order to monitor the access of the press and other 'potentially disruptive factors'." He smiled. "Why don't you park behind the gym on the Driver's Ed lot. Somebody'll be out there all day."

"We gonna have trouble, E-Z?" she asked him apprehensively.

"We got trouble, honey," he answered, straightening to his impressive height. "Whenever you get the cops on campus you got trouble just lookin' for a place to happen. But if anybody bothers you, you just come and get me." He winked and reverted back to his jive-talk drawl. "I would jus' lo-o-ove to be your personal bodyguard."

"Hey, E-Z," she teased. "Tell me somethin'."

"Hey what," he responded, leaning into the car again.

"Is it true what they say about black men?"

"You owe it to yourself to find out, girl," grinned E-Z, "now get out of here, you loose-lipped lady libber. The show's about to start without you."

A hot pink '57 Chevy convertible sounded an impatient blast from its horn behind her. Aggie spotted the chubby, mustachioed face of Fernando Gomez in her rearview mirror and shot him a "bird" without turning around.

"Shame on you!" yelled E-Z slapping the fender of the 'Vette as Aggie dropped the car into gear and peeled out with a screech of rubber on the hot pavement.

Gomez, plump and breathless, caught up with her on the stairs.

"Did you think I didn't see that obscene gesture?" he panted, trotting to keep up with her on the stairs. His Cuban accent was still heavy, almost a caricature.

"Nandy," she gushed in reply, stopping only briefly to plant a quick kiss on his balding pate. "How lovely to see you again."

"You American women," he puffed. "You're all too fast for me."

"The final word on the entire gender from the lips of Arcadia's jet-setting profess-air," said Aggie, mischievously mimicking his accent. "How was your summer abroad this year, my dear?" Her high heels clicked on the cool granite floor. The corridors were already filling.

6

Gomez conducted summer tours through Europe for an organization called American Youth Abroad. It seemed to fulfill two of his most ardent passions—travel and kids, and every fall, when school resumed, Gomez came back to Arcadia armed with a new collection of amusing anecdotes of the trials and traumas of conducting a couple of dozen American teenagers through the hostels and high spots of the continent.

"Same ol' shit with a new smell," he sighed. "One of my kids gotta hol' of some hash. We nearly left the Louvre without him. I was counting noses on the bus and I came up one short. I say to myself, 'Fernando, we got trouble.' The other kids tell me about the dope, I think for sure he got busted. I go back inside. I find him stoned out of his head, sound asleep laying in the lap of a statue of a reclining nude. I didn't know whether to hug him or hit him. I was just grateful I didn't have to call his folks in America to help me bail him out of jail. These drugs, Aggie. Everybody is trying to kill some kind of pain inside. I jus' don' understan'."

"As long as it all turned out OK," smiled Aggie, unwilling to debate the subject.

"Wait," he wheezed. "You don' know the half of it. So I get home and find out Randy has quit his job. I say, why you quit, you have such nice position. You know, he work for the airline, he get me good fares. So I get it out of him they fire him. 'Cause . . . well, you know. Somebody find out about him and . . ."

Gomez faltered, searching for the words.

"You mean, about being gay?" she asked unabashedly.

"Shhh," he whispered, almost comically, as though the word would hurt if said aloud.

"That is the least of it. Now he carries signs and marches in the streets and lectures me about my obligation to stand up and declare myself to the world. 'Coming out of the closet,' he calls it. Aggie, you know I been savin' for years to bring my mother out of Cuba. This year, I think they finally let her out. Can you imagine? She come here and fin' out my roommate is my . . ."

"Hey, Hilly!" yelled a young voice from the crowd. "How ya' doin', Señor?"

With smiles pasted nonchalantly in place, they ap-

7

proached the office, exchanging amenities with friendly and familiar faces.

"She fin' out about me and Randy, she drop dead on the spot," asserted Gomez. "Me and Randy, we have a lover's spat the night I came home," he wheezed dolefully. "We're still not speaking."

"Nice to hear everything's going so well for you," said Aggie, shaking her head as they made their way through the final leg of locker-lined hallways.

"It will be good to get back to work," he smiled sarcastically. "Compared to my other life, I am really looking forward to some peace and quiet."

"You've *got* to be desperate," smiled Aggie. "In case you haven't noticed, this is *not* going to be your typical school opening."

"Maybe if we pretend we don' notice," he laughed, "it will go away."

"I don't think we'll get off that easy, love," smiled Aggie woefully.

Above the faculty attendance sheet in the main office, someone had posted a warning in neatly typed red caps: TEACHERS ARE ADVISED TO REFRAIN FROM COMMENTS AND CONVERSATION WITH OUTSIDE PERSONNEL THAT COULD BE CONSTRUED AS INCENDIARY OR MISLEADING.

"I guess that means we don't have an opinion till they give us one," mused Aggie aloud.

"Listen, Aggie," said Gomez with alarm. "Did you read the paper this morning?"

"Read the paper?" she scoffed. "I'm not even awake yet. I don't come alive until my morning dose of caffeine enters my bloodstream. What was in the paper?"

"They burned a cross on the lawn of the superintendent of schools. They had a picture of all these guys in sheets. It was really scary."

"Don't tell me they still do that shit down here?" she asked incredulously.

"I wouldn't have believed it either," said Gomez. "The local citizens are very upset about this busing business."

"When they see that it can work, they'll come around," she answered him optimistically.

8

"Yah, hay," sighed Gomez. "I know. We shall overcome."

"Well, we'll keep trying," answered Aggie.

"If I advocated brotherly love," he groused, "it would only be misunderstood."

"If I had your problems I'd lay low for a while, too," she laughed. "I don't plan on making any waves this year. I've pledged myself to keeping the peace with Muriel this season."

"Good luck to us both," said Gomez, heading back into the crowd. "See you later, my darling."

Gomez waved a chunky hand and disappeared as Aggie pushed open the door of the faculty lounge.

The tiny room with its shabby time-worn furniture overflowed with an animated congregation of teachers. No air conditioning relieved the smoky, breathless air in the crowded room.

"Aggie," said a fat lady munching a glazed donut. She burst through a wall of tightly packed humanity. "Have you heard? There's still no agreement on our contract!"

"Betty, you're incredible. How can you think about contracts at a time like this? The campus is crawling with cops and reporters, and the tension is so thick you can feel it on your skin."

"That's no tension, that's prickly heat." She stuffed the last of the donut in her mouth. "I get it every summer. Listen! It's time we all go down to your room to paint signs. We need some attention in the paper. We're gonna get the shaft for sure. They're not even gonna give us a cost-of-living increase. Christ, we ought to be getting combat pay. This is gonna be a hell of a year."

"I'd really hate to be accused of taking advantage of a potentially volatile situation, sweetie. The public is nervous. The kids are always hyped when they come back from vacation. We've got enough to do," answered Aggie.

"Is this the same girl who used to tell me stories about carrying protest banners through the cold hard winters of New York? Why can't you muster some enthusiasm for our cause?"

"Because I know better," said Aggie adamantly.

"Well," said Betty, licking her fingers with a smacking

9

sound, "I think we're missing a golden opportunity. Now they're asking us to monitor their experiment in race relations. It's just not gonna work, regardless. They just keep asking more and more of us, and give us nothing. We're at the bottom of the national pay scale, and the cost of living rising so fast, why, I filled my gas tank this morning. Thank God for credit cards. However," she added, "I may have to remortgage the house when the bill comes in."

"Yeah, I know," mused Aggie. "I wonder how much it costs to fill all those school buses. Wouldn't it be nice if they gave us the money to get some of the things we need for the kids?"

"Screw the kids," snapped Betty. "Wouldn't it be nice if they gave *us* the money? Aggie, we need full support! What happened to that crusading spirit of yours."

"I redirected it when I discovered the system was more vulnerable from within. You wouldn't ask me to blow my cover, would you?" Laughing, she pried through the crush of bodies to the coffee machine and rifled her purse for some change. Wouldn't it be nice, she thought, if the wages stretched a little further, if so many teachers didn't have to moonlight as midnight checkers at the all-night A&P, if the budget stretched just a little bit further to accommodate the expanding class roles.

Betty followed, undaunted, pushing her plump body through the throng. "Well, damn it, Aggie, aren't you gonna do *anything*?"

"Sure, I'm gonna get some coffee and open up my room. Listen, it's a futile fight. It's true, back in the good old days, I carried signs and fought for causes. I saw my friends maced and clubbed and jailed, and still I hung in there. I really believed we could change the world. But when all the commotion was over, nothing had really changed at all. Except, a few of us had police records and drug habits, and a few of us were dead. So here we are, with all that crap going on outside, and you want to go out there and ask the public for a raise?"

"That's the point, Aggie. If they can find the money to buy buses and drivers and gas to bring this trouble to our doorstep, they can find the cash to pay us decent salaries," fumed Betty. "Or they can just keep their kids where they came from."

10

"If trucking kids around this town will bring understanding and an end of fear," she said, "I don't mind giving it a shot."

"Is that a firm no?" asked Betty, beligerently.

"We're teachers. We should teach them what they need to know in the classroom, not in the streets," said Aggie, popping a quarter into the coffee machine. She withdrew a styrofoam cup of dark, hot liquid and left the lounge with relief.

Muriel Peterson, chairman of the art department, stood hall duty as Aggie approached with her cup. She had been Arcadia's only art teacher until an increased enrollment warranted hiring a second teacher two years ago. Now she rode herd on Agnes Hillyer—a department of one. She'd spent the last two years making it eminently clear to all concerned that Agnes was not her choice for the job. Bo Callaway overruled Muriel's objections and hired Aggie because he liked her tits. The first time he'd encountered her in the hall she had to jog his memory. She was certain he'd hired her before he'd ever seen her face. He didn't know he had hired himself a dedicated professional, nor did he really care. Bo had spent his fallow youth on the football fields of Texas A&M ogling cheerleaders, and it was common knowledge that if you wanted to work at Arcadia, it was imperative you be an ex-jock or a broad with boobs. Muriel was neither. She'd just been there forever . . . preceding even Bo's tenure as principal.

"Good morning, Agnes," Muriel's greeting was noticeably cool.

"Good morning," Aggie answered. "Muriel, my mother gave me that name to honor her belated, beloved mom, but not even my mother calls me Agnes." Still a bit high, she was reluctant to let a downer like Muriel dampen her day. "Don't you think we could start this year on a more informal note?"

"It's your informal approach to the way we do things here at Arcadia, Agnes, that concerns me. You're aware, I'm sure, that page thirty-six of the Faculty Handbook contains a paragraph expressly forbidding food or beverages in the classroom."

"No," laughed Aggie, incredulously. "I wouldn't have known that, Muriel."

11

"And, naturally," she continued, "I needn't remind you that the public eye is on us."

"Of course," she said, remembering her pledge to keep the peace. That bitch has a ramrod up her butt, thought Aggie as she deposited her cup, still full, into a swing-top garbage can. "Always nice talking to you, Muriel," she said as she escaped to her room. She inserted her key with a sense of possessive familiarity. This was *her* turf, her own domain.

Aggie's art room was an enormous afterthought to an antique structure whose rate of decay had long overtaken a chronically ill-funded effort at preservation. Huge chunks of missing plaster had exposed several wood shorings where her students could amuse themselves observing the cancerous growth of a colony of termites. Oversized, curtainless windows with transoms that only opened with a pole hook looked out on the traffic of Eastern Avenue and the porn shop that had once been a gas station. Scarred slate chalkboards lined the front wall. Old Mr. Farley, the janitor, had made a half-hearted effort to clean them, and they were empty now, pregnant with a story yet untold.

There was a rat once that came to water at the perpetual puddle under the sink. His usually inopportune appearance always elicited mass hysteria in the room. After the rat repeatedly frustrated old Mr. Farley's attempts at capture, the kids started rooting for the rat. They named him Van Gogh and booked their bets in the bathrooms between classes.

One day Van Gogh left some pellets on the project of a young man with a flaring temper who snuffed him out with a single blow of the pole hook. A visible stain on the woodwork was all that remained to commemorate the spot where Van Gogh had met his messy demise.

At the front of the room a desk intended for the teacher was covered by a big brown paper cutter that squatted there like a toad. Thirty-two mismatched chairs, their undersides dotted with brittle wads of old chewing gum, stood upended on eight work-worn tables whose surfaces bore the engravings of students past. Above the blackboard hung a limp, yellowed rendition of the Stars and Stripes and the Cyclopean eye of a clock that gazed mutely from the wall, poised to mark the passage of time doled out to

12

the minute. The time was near. The hands of the electric clock slid silently into place.

A bell began tolling the Genesis, and they answered the summons. A swarm of adolescents converged on the site, raising the decible level to an overload. They came individually or in clusters, joyous or nervous or afraid.

A thin boy in tight orange trousers and white lace entered, miming a disco hustle to the inaudible strains of the shirt-pocket transistor plugged into his ear. His silent gyrations resembled the movements of an apoplectic duck.

Two young lovers still entwined like summer vines embraced in the far corner of the room.

"Hey, Ms. Hillyer, I'm back," yelled a kid in a surfer shirt swinging in on his crutches. "Did ya miss me?"

"You're all I thought about!" she said. "What'd you do to the leg?"

"Is this my room?" came the query from the door. "I can't find my room."

Still on the launching pad and already crashing, she thought as her tongue turned to cotton in her pot-parched mouth. My kingdom for a cup of coffee. She produced a key and inserted it into the lock of an old-fashioned Dutch door.

SUPPLY ROOM—KEEP OUT, read the sign on the door, decorated with bats and tombstones and a laughing skull. The kids called it the Cave.

She fumbled with the lock till it gave way, but only the bottom half of the door swung open. Annoyed, she ducked under the door. Like sneaking into a pay toilet, she thought, flipping on the lights to illuminate a small, windowless storeroom. Have to get ol' Farley to look at that door.

One small corner among the crates served her as an office and hideaway. It was her sanctuary, the only place in the building she could be alone with her thoughts.

Man, it stinks in here, she thought, getting her first whiff of the musty air.

An electric coffeemaker, its interior patterned with hard water rings, stood empty now on top of an ancient, ceramic kiln, thick with cobwebs and dust.

Moving two large, heavy cartons, she carefully deposited her handbag in one padlocked cabinet, then began,

13

from her perch atop the precarious pyramid, to rummage through another. Band-Aids, Kleenex, a few pink packets of artificial sugar, a half-empty box of tampons, a handmade ceramic mug with TEACHER inscribed in childlike script—she inventoried the contents of the cabinet, knowing she had disposed of any remaining coffee at the close of the school year last June.

Beneath the half-closed door in the classroom beyond, she could hear the raucous sound of a couple of dozen voices, each competing to be heard above the rest.

"Aha!" she said aloud, raising a sorry-looking tea bag that had somehow escaped its wrapper. A cup of tea will have to do, she thought.

"Hey, Hilly," came a familiar voice from beyond the Dutch door.

Pete Santini, gangling arms hugging tightly folded knees, came rolling under the half-closed door on a skateboard.

"Pete," she smiled, looking down as he spilled and righted himself at her feet.

"Hi, teach!" Pete Santini's smiling face gleamed with perspiration. His lean, angular frame was encased in the usual blue denim topped by the T-shirt he had screened in her class the previous year. It bore the impression of a black hand.

An Italian joke, he'd explained, a veiled reference to his Sicilian ancestry. On the back of the shirt he had screened another hand—this one with a raised middle finger. Pete was particularly proud of that shirt. "It's an expression of my philosophy," he said, when challenged on the propriety of the message. "An exercise of my right of free speech. When I'm gone, man—fuck 'em." Around Pete's neck hung a gold St. Christopher medal and a solid brass roach clip on a leather thong.

"Pete! What are you doing here?" asked Aggie, descending the stacks to hug him.

"I talked Richardson into letting me be your lab assistant first period." He slung the skateboard across his shoulder. " 'Cause of the art club! Ol' Richardson's a marshmallow," he said. He shook his head at the thought of the rotund guidance counselor. "I'm all yours for homeroom and first period, you lucky lady."

"Pete Santini rolled his butt out of bed early to organize

14

his sadistic gang of brush-wielding pranksters, huh?" she asked, incredulously, referring to the art club she sponsored.

Last June's elections had put the art squad's leadership into the capable but irreverent hands of Santini, the finger, who'd renamed them Hilly's Hellions. They were a high-spirited group, dedicated to the perpetuation of the pride and tradition of Arcadia High, especially during the football season. The Hellions became notorious for blitz raids on the opposition. It was not uncommon for the rival team to discover the night before a game that their school walls and precious artifacts had been freshly painted with Arcadia's red and gold.

"Not really." Pete flashed his boyish smile to charm her. "I was hoping I could talk you into springing for a couple o' Big Macs before class. Is that an offer you can't refuse?"

"Better than that," she laughed, ditching the tea bag. "You've saved my life. I was dying for a cup of coffee when you came in. By the way, how do you plan to get there?"

"In a hot white 'Vette?" he asked, trying to charm her again.

"Not this time, Pete. Dean Jordan's gonna be guarding the only open gate once the tardy bell rings."

"Not to worry," he said, patting the skateboard affectionately, "I'll use my own wheels."

"Pete!" she called after him as he ducked under the door.

"Yeah?" he poked his head in, upside down.

"Don't waste time. They're closing off the whole campus right after homeroom."

"Gotcha!" Pete mounted his skateboard and disappeared.

2

Aggie watched them enter, noting the disparity of sizes—young men and women poised eagerly on the threshold of adulthood, or peeping hesitantly from the edges of innocence.

Another bell sounded. She took a deep breath, licked her lips, and stepped through the door to meet her class. A denim-uniformed conclave of adolescents had crammed themselves into every crevice of available space.

"S'pose you put that away now," she said, addressing the kid with the headset.

"Huh?" he yelled without missing a beat of the tune he alone could hear. Dozens of small braids anchored with brightly colored plastic barrettes bobbed from his scalp as he moved.

Aggie pulled his ear plug. "Turn it off!" she shouted.

He inserted a finger in his ear, feigning injury.

"I'm sorry. I didn't mean to shout. Please take a seat so we can begin." She took her place at the head of the class.

"Hey-ey! You da teachah?" he asked, in a rich ethnic accent, looking her over approvingly. "All *rah't*!"

"I'm *Ms. Hillyer*," answered Aggie pointedly, turning around to write her name on the board, but the dust ledge contained no chalk. Looking around for a trustworthy face, Aggie dispatched a freckled young girl named Nancy to the Cave, aggravated with herself for forgetting the chalk.

There was a poker game in progress in the back of the room, and an overendowed early bloomer in a fuschia halter perched on a table top polishing her toe nails.

"Your attention, please," demanded Aggie with all the authority she could muster. Sudden silence swept the room. Playing cards and toenail lacquer disappeared.

17

Like a Medusa with seventy eyes, they riveted their collective gaze upon her. She knew they were checking her out.

She stood perspiring before them, wondering if sweat rings were forming in the armpits of her new silk blouse. "I want to welcome you all back," she said, surveying her audience. "I'll be your homeroom teacher this year."

A wolf whistle, shrill and shocking, sounded from somewhere in the back of the room.

She experienced the chilling fear known only to those whose livelihoods depend on performing for a crowd, but the smile on her face never wavered. The loneliest spot on earth is center stage in a packed house, thought Aggie. Well, if I'm opening to critical acclaim it's for all the same wrong reasons. Time to flex some mental muscle if I'm gonna win this game of Show and Tell. "OK, knock it off," she said sharply.

"I hope in the course of the year we'll spend together, that it will be unnecessary to impose a great many rules, that we can all work together in harmony, in an atmosphere where decency and common sense prevail. I expect each of you to respect yourself and others in this classroom, to be trustworthy and responsible for your own actions. But make no mistake who's the boss."

A paper airplane sailed indolently through the heavy air.

"Ladies and gentlemen," said Ms. Hillyer quietly. "The next person who challenges me in *my* classroom will find himself out on his ass. Now let's cut the crap and get down to business." This time she got their attention.

She began to distribute the stack of garbage on her desk—schedule cards, student handbooks, all the usual first-day busywork . . . and one sheet mimeographed on bright yellow paper that was unfamiliar to her.

" . . . complete the form with name, age, *race* . . . " she instructed, embarrassed suddenly by the word. God, why didn't you make all your children the same shade and spare teachers this humiliating bodycount? Aggie queried silently. "Please check the appropriate box with an X," she said, passing out the Ethnic Information Forms.

"What if you a mutt, teach? What if you don't know who your old man was? Do you check 'em all?" The questioner showed a gold tooth as he smiled a pernicious smile, enjoying the reaction of his audience.

Several students needed pencils and Nancy made another trip to the Cave. "How can you come to school without a pencil?" asked Aggie of no one in particular.

YOU WILL NOW RISE FOR THE PLEDGE OF ALLEGIANCE

The public address system suddenly spluttered to life overhead. Aggie recognized the amplified voice of Martha Barnes, the principal's secretary.

AFTER WHICH YOU WILL REMAIN STANDING FOR A MOMENT OF SILENCE.

Martha, a birdlike, hyperactive little old lady, had been at Arcadia for as long as anyone remembered.

I PLEDGE ALLEGIANCE TO THE FLAG OF THE UNITED STATES OF AMERICA

An inadequate breeze wafted through the open transom, and the stiff old flag merely nodded.

AND TO THE REPUBLIC

Outside in the shade of the sun-scorched palms, Aggie watched a cop wipe the sweat from his face. A young man who looked like a truant student perched idly in the back of a van on which were stenciled the call letters of the local TV station.

FOR WHICH IT STANDS. ONE NATION

A car pulled up in front of the one-time gas station, and the purveyor of porn opened his store for the day's business. Just another day.

UNDER GOD, INDIVISIBLE

Another bus pulled up, belatedly. The young reporter hopped down from the van, anxious and ready.

It had been a nice neighborhood once, where mostly working people lived in the modest two-story houses. Then the neighborhood began to disintegrate with creeping blight. The only whites left were the ones that were too old or too poor to move.

WITH LIBERTY

The Supreme Court in its infinite wisdom threatened to withhold federal aid from schools that were composed of more than seventy percent of either Caucasian or combined minorities. Predominantly ethnic Arcadia, which de-

19

pended heavily on that aid, was importing Anglos from suburbia to increase its ailing white blood count.

AND JUSTICE

The locals weren't thrilled. Nor were Avalon County's boys in blue standing riot duty in the summer sun as the bus, filled only to half capacity, deposited its nervous cargo on Arcadia High School's ancient stoop. The cops blocked the reporter from the bus as the students hurried into the building.

FOR ALL.

The intercom died. The compulsory moment of silence dissolved when someone belched aloud.

The room began to smell of body odor as Aggie took roll.

"Adderly."

"Yo."

"Brown."

"She ain't comin'. Her papa won' let her come to no niggah school."

Bo Callaway, Arcadia's principal began his customary opening day speech over the PA system before she'd even finished roll call. There was a different tone to his rhetoric. It seemed infused with an implied threat, his Texas-tinged voice competed with the wheeze of an ineffectual window fan.

"I sincerely hope that we may all work together in an atmosphere of friendliness and mutual understanding to carry forward the highest traditions of Arcadia High School, and to eliminate any condition unworthy of our finest achievements," he concluded. "For each of us, for all of us . . . for Arcadia."

Aggie, who needed to use the restroom, began glancing anxiously at the clock.

"Can we leave?" someone asked.

"Till we get instructions to the contrary, we'll wait for the bell," she said as Martha Barnes's disembodied voice droned on.

ACCORDING TO BELL SCHEDULE NUMBER TWO, PAGE TWELVE, OF THE STUDENT HAND-BOOK, HOMEROOM WILL BE EXTENDED FROM THE USUAL TEN MINUTES TO TWENTY-FIVE, NE-CESSITATING THE REDUCTION OF CLASS PE-

RIODS FROM THE NORMALLY ALLOTTED FIFTY-FIVE MINUTE INTERVALS TO FORTY-NINE MINUTES EACH. THAT IS, ALL BUT PERIODS FOUR AND FIVE WHICH ARE LUNCH PERIODS.

When the bell finally rang, the room emptied remarkably fast for a capacity crowd. There wasn't time to navigate through the mile-long mob between her classroom and the faculty lounge. Aggie, annoyed, distastefully opted for the girls' room down the hall.

A cramp grabbed her kidneys as she pushed open the swinging door.

Once in a doctor's waiting room, she had read an article about the high incidence of kidney and bladder disease among professional educators. The article attributed it to a higher rate of alcoholism, but Aggie was certain it was from just holding it—there was never enough time nor an accessible faculty toilet.

The bitter sweet scent of Marijuana tickled her envious nostrils, then the stench of urine overwhelmed her. Two young girls wearing too much makeup vied for space before a small, fly-specked mirror. The stained tile walls were much like those of a New York subway, and one of the stalls was missing a door.

A buck-toothed girl Aggie recognized as a senior named Cocoa dropped something out of the open window as she entered, but the sweet scented smoke hung fragrant in the rancid air.

There was no toilet paper, and she was forced to fish some Kleenex from her purse. On the door of the stall someone had written in black felt pen "SCHOOL SUCKS!"

Back at the Cave, she found Pete, seated on a carton, munching a Big Mac. On another carton he had laid out her breakfast, a freshly made cup of instant coffee, and her change.

She expressed her thanks. "I was beginning to worry about you. Did you have any trouble?"

"Nah. We Santinis don't sweat the heat."

She lit a cigarette.

"Those aren't good for you," said Pete.

"How can you sit there with a roach clip hanging

around your neck and tell me with a straight face that cigarettes aren't healthy?" asked Aggie.

"Then smoke a joint," he said nonchalantly. "At least pot makes you feel good. What do you get from a cigarette but a scratchy throat?"

"I don't think that my store carries that brand."

"I can get you all the dope you want," said Pete.

"No, thank you" she answered emphatically, hoping she sounded convincing.

"You oughta try it. You're the one who always told us not to form our values by what other people say or think. If you ever got on marijuana, I'll bet you'd *never* want another cigarette."

"There is a difference, Pete. Cigarettes are legal."

"They shouldn't be. They're lethal. You never heard of anybody dying from an overdose of grass? My mother O.D.ed on cigarettes. She died of lung cancer."

"Pete, I'm sorry. I didn't know. You never said . . ."

She butted out the cigarette.

"It's OK. It happened a long time ago. I was just a kid. I hardly remember her. But my pop says she was very beautiful and very artistic. That's probably where I got it. I like to think she woulda been a lot like you."

"You've got a lot of talent. You could be an artist, if you just take it a little more seriously. It could be a career as well as a hobby."

"No, it couldn't."

"Don't be so negative," she said. "I have faith in you."

"It's not that," said Pete. "I'm my father's only son. He expects me to take over his lumber yard when I get outta school. It probably pays a lot better than art."

"It probably does," she said.

She finished her hamburger.

"Oh shit, I almost forgot. I stopped by the gym and picked up a schedule for the new season." Pete swallowed the last of his cheeseburger and slurped the dregs of a Coke through a straw.

"That was efficient of you," answered Aggie, brightening over the information. "First game's a week from Friday, right?"

"Yeah. We've got to set up the game ribbon screen and design a new pennant pretty quick," he said. "The season's gonna get off to a fast start. We're playing Jefferson, last year's league champs."

"I'll give you all the help you need. Just let me get through today."

"There's something else," he said fumbling in his pocket and extracting a rumpled, dog-eared envelope. "Coach asked me to give you this."

She hastily took it from him and carefully opened the note.

Dear S—M, it began.

Vance MacCarthy often teased her about what he called her sadomasochistic tendency of self-denial, but he refused to abandon his futile assault. Nor would she have it any other way, though it was difficult in his presence to consider a merely platonic relationship with the handsome football coach.

"Pretty hot stuff, huh?" asked Pete.

"What?" Aggie flushed as she looked up at him.

Pete smiled slyly. "You just lit up like a movie marquee on Saturday night." He deposited the refuse of their junk-food banquet in a metal bin. "I'll leave you to your privacy. Later, Hilly!" he said as he split.

Aggie grimaced and read the brief note again:

"I'll buy lunch if you let me eat you for dessert.
                                    Hopefully, Mac."

3

"Isn't it any good?" Vance MacCarthy's voice was a trill of Irish tenor with the soft-edge consonants of the Deep South.

"What?" asked Aggie, covering her momentary embarrassment with a pretense of inattention. He had caught her staring at him.

He spoke again. "This is the last time you're gonna get treated this good, Sadie Mae. That's a 75-cent lunch you're leavin'."

His eyes were the color of—what? The ocean? No, no, greener. Aggie'd seen the sea in all its colors and infinite moods, but never had it displayed the green of Vance MacCarthy's eyes.

A shaft of sunlight from the window at his back illuminated his blond head like a halo.

"My inquiries were directed at your apparent lack of appetite, Ms. Hillyer," he said emphasizing each word as one would for a rather slow child. "What's wrong with the spaghetti?"

"Oh, nothing's wrong with it," she lied, looking down at her plate. Pasty white strings of starch wallowed in a lumpy orange liquid from which grease escaped to congeal on the edge of the plate. "It's just that I ate a Big Mac for breakfast."

"You should've waited for the real thing," he smiled, shoveling another forkful of the sloppy stuff into his mouth. Blond stubble caught the sunlight like flecks of gold dust along his chin as he chewed. "How'd you get ahold of a cheeseburger in homeroom?"

"One of my kids went out for it," she answered. "Muriel made me dump my coffee this morning and I couldn't wait

25

for lunch." Sweat trickled down her belly as she watched Mac's mouth.

"The wicked witch of the South still ridin' your pretty little ass, Sadie Mae?" he asked, sucking a strand of spaghetti across his lips and flicking his tongue suggestively.

She laughed self-consciously and dropped her eyes, but the image of Mac's face and body lingered on the insides of her eyelids. Mac wore the amber T-shirt and scarlet shorts that were the uniform of the physical education department. A paper napkin slid unnoticed from his naked thigh.

"If that's all that's worryin' you, it's not worth botherin' about," he said, breaking off a crusty chunk of bread and slathering butter on it. "She's just jealous."

"Aw, c'mon, Mac."

"Waddaya mean, c'mon?" His mouth was full, his words slurred. "You're younger, prettier, probably brighter, and a lot more popular with the kids. How could she *not* feel threatened by you?"

A dusting of bread crumbs fell like snowflakes across his lap. Aggie tore her eyes away from the bulge at his groin.

"Man, it *is* tough coming back to all this chicken shit after a whole, beautiful summer of recess, ain't it, Sadie Mae? We all got a streak o' masochism in us to be here doin' what we do. The best thing about our jobs is that midsummer blowout. I spent six weeks knocking off a list of odd jobs around the house for Sharon and pitchin' the pigskin around the backyard with the boys. Then I packed up the boat with a few cases of imbibables and spent another month whoring my way around the Carribean."

"How does Sharon feel about you taking off with the boys for a month?" asked Aggie. The question she should have asked was if he had any idea how *she* felt about it.

"Sharon's smart enough to keep that to herself," he answered, nonplussed. "That boat comes out of my coaching supplement. I work eleven months of each year supporting my wife and kids. The twelth month is my reward for being a good husband and father the other eleven."

"Does she know about the women?" Her eyes had an accusatory tone she hadn't intended.

"I'm smart enough to keep that to myself," he answered.

She tried to imagine the women Mac made love to. Sharon had just given birth to their third son when Aggie first met him. She hadn't known he was married then. By the time she found out, it was too late.

"She reminded me a lot of you through the chest," he said swallowing another mouthful, "but she was a little broader in the beam."

"What?" she asked, startled.

"Sadie Mae, don't try to tell me that wasn't gonna be your question. Why don't you eat a little a' that starch. You could stand about five pounds on ya. Round out your ass a little!"

She fell into the looking glass of her own wonderland world. She was Botticelli's blond Venus, rising naked on a seashell from some primeval sea. And Vance, wearing an Errol Flynn pirate shirt sailed up and snatched her from her crustacean womb and taught her with just one thrust of his skillful rapier what it means to be a woman.

Gaslights shone a gentle glow from within their beveled glass and copper cages. The air was pungent with brine. Beyond a porthole pounded the waves, concealing their passion. And she and her blond love god clasped in rapturous embrace on satin sheets.

"Imagine that! Sailing to St. Thomas to meet a topless dancer from Miami."

She came out of her reverie. "Is that all you ever think about? Tits and ass?"

"Hell, no! I'm really into shapely legs, full-lipped mouths, and tight, juicy little . . ."

"Mac," said Aggie. "At the table?"

"Or on it or under it. Just say when."

The bulge had swelled, almost imperceptibly. She could feel her pulse beat in her right thigh.

"Met your star linebacker today," she said, changing the subject. "He walked into my third-period class in his practice jersey with a groupie hanging off each arm." She tapped a cigarette out of the pack on the table. "He reminds me of a walking Coke machine."

He interrupted his meal and struck a match. "Boogie Man!" he laughed, leaning closer and cupping the flame with his hands. His teeth gleamed white and even as the smile spread across his face.

She took the light and backed away as if burnt. His

27

breath had been warm on her face. "Boogie Man?" she
asked, exhaling a wreath of smoke that slowly climbed the
sunlight to the open window. "Is that the kid I know as
Benjamin Hooper?"

He shifted his weight in the chair and the bread crumbs
rearranged themselves on his fly. His penis lay clearly outlined against the folds of the bright red fabric.

"Same one," he nodded. "Kid's only seventeen and he's
six-six. Wonder what he'll be when he grows up! High
School All American and I got him his senior year. One
glorious year. That's all I need!"

His leg changed position and stopped, just a breath away
from hers. She could feel his body heat through her clothing. "Two hundred thirty pounds, clumsy but fast," Mac
continued, still eating. "I'm gonna rebuild my whole defense around him. That big mutha is gonna clear our path
straight to the state finals if I can keep his black ass out of
a sling for one more year." He drained a glass of tea and
sucked on an ice cube.

"What do you mean?" She tried to sound interested. Her
finger nails were cutting tracks in her palms and her toes
curled up in her shoes.

"His school records are a disaster. His last school carried him academically so he'd be eligible to play ball. Football's his only way out of this swamp, and he knows it.
And that's all he knows."

Mac's hand brushed absentmindedly at the crumbs on
his lap. He picked up his napkin and covered his crotch.

Aggie found herself wondering if he slept in the nude.
She drew another drag and butted the half-smoked cigarette into an ashtray. Muscles tightened in her neck and
thighs. Through clenched teeth she drew painfully shallow
breaths. She felt light-headed.

Mac continued eating, oblivious. "If that hulk's half as
good as his reputation, he's got a very bright future," he
said, spearing lettuce leaves with a fork and raising them to
his lips.

He turned his eyes to her and she melted. Saliva flooded
her mouth. She swallowed past the lump in her chest. She
couldn't bear to look at him. She couldn't bear not to. Had
he noticed?

"His mama's raising eight kids alone on public assis-

28

tance," said Mac, sitting back and pushing his plate away. Rubbing his hard, flat belly with an open hand, he faced her. "I'm ready for some dessert now." A slow smile spread across his face. "I love sweets. I'd like to roll you in cherry vanilla ice cream and lick you into submission."

Her nipples swelled painfully against the inside of her bra, which felt as though it were made of steel wool. She poised herself, preparing to accommodate the orgasm that was about to claim her body. Cherry vanilla, melting on satin sheets.

"Aggie, are you all right?" Mac put a hand on each of her shoulders and steadied her against him. "Was it something I said?" Genuine concern clouded his voice.

She felt each of his fingers like electrodes on her body. With the laying on of hands, he closed the circuit, pulled the switch and the voltage of a thunderbolt went through her. Her eyes brimmed with the intensity of the seizure and her pent-up breath escaped in an audible, shuddering sigh. She slumped for an instant against his shoulder—then by force of will, drew herself erect.

"I'm fine, Mac. I'm just fine," she answered, composing herself as her passion ebbed into the deep, green garden of Vance MacCarthy's eyes. "Just hot, I guess." She looked around in panic. None of the other people in the faculty dining room had even noticed.

Taking another napkin from a dispenser, he patted perspiration from her temples. "You looked like you were gonna pull a Scarlett O'Hara routine on me and faint dead away." Releasing her, he returned to his meal. "I guess I'll have to settle for a piece"—he raised a forkful of coconut cream mid-air and paused as he eyed her lewdly—"of pie. Listen, before I commit myself," he said thoughtfully, the foamy mound poised at his lips, "you sure you won't reconsider? We could step into my office and wait for the Good Humor man."

Oh, Mac! You dumb, beautiful jock. If only you knew how much I want you . . . Her fertile mind flew on a magic carpet to Arabian Night's flights of fantasy. Mac was a sheik in flowing robes, carrying her to his satin couch in a tent pitched on the shifting sands of a once-upon-a-time that never was.

"You know I don't fuck where I eat!" snapped Aggie,

annoyed by her own vulnerability and his incessant teasing.

He shot her a shocked, surprised look. "Good gracious, Miss Sadie!" Then he smiled that smile again. "If I promise to be real good for the next eleven months, can I put you down for a twelfth-night cruise?"

"Do I look like a one-night stand?" she sparred, giggling nervously.

"Make it a fortnight. How many days in a fortnight? They're yours. And how could you possibly imply that I would think of you as just a one-night stand? I thought you knew me better than that by now, Sadie Mae," he pouted unconvincingly. "Why, you should know I hold you in the highest esteem. I respect the shit out of you, Aggie Hillyer."

He was nearly shouting. Several people looked their way and smiled, strained, knowing smiles.

"Shut up," she hissed in a stage whisper. "What does it take!"

"I thought I'd made myself perfectly clear," he answered.

"There are no happily-ever-afters in sailing into the sunsets with someone else's prince. It goes against all my beliefs. Marriage means fidelity."

"I may be married but I'm not religious, Sadie Mae." He smiled, stuffing another piece of pie in his mouth. A fleck of cream poised deliciously on his lip. "Most of us gave up those old-fashioned ideas of fidelity along with our cherry. You gonna finish that tea?"

She passed him her glass and fumbled for another cigarette. He took the pack from her hand and ignited two, placing one of them on her lips, as a cloud of smoke formed around his face.

"Just one time," he said, engulfing her with a sexy stare. "Just one little taste, to dream on."

She flushed and shifted anxiously, tearing her attention away.

Oh yes Mac, God! Yes.

"No way, Mac," she said. "No fucking way."

"This is gonna cost me another fin for the kitty," he said resignedly, shaking his head.

"What kitty?" asked Aggie, her interest renewed.

"Oh, it's nothin'. Just a funky little game we fellas play

30

when we get rowdy in the locker room. Like the football pool."

"What's that got to do with anything?" she asked, puzzled by his sly smile.

He took a deep breath. "Well, when you got here coupla' years ago, wasn't one of us guys in that locker room that didn't decide to hit on you. As you started turnin' us down, the odds got interesting. We started extracting a five-dollar penalty for each failure to score. Nearly three hundred bucks has accumulated in the pussy kitty in the last two years, and about half of it's mine," he said, shaking his head.

"Three hundred bucks!" she exclaimed in disbelief.

"Yeah! Even Irv Fishbine coughed up a sawbuck when he admitted thinkin' about it more than once."

"That dear little old man in the math department?" she exploded.

"That dirty little old man in the math department," he retorted.

"Pussy kitty!" she said. "I don't believe it! Grown men! See what happens when you spend so much time with kids?"

"Now don't get riled, honey. We didn't mean no harm," he rejoined to appease her.

"You only meant to reinforce your chauvinistic male egos by auctioning off my butt amongst you. Christ! A price on my ass."

"Speaking of ass," said Mac rising.

Henry Lawler, Executive Assistant Principal in charge of covering for Bo Calloway, approached with the voluptuous type of woman men often referred to as "a piece." She was neither young nor pretty, but she had a good body and a magnificent pair.

Bo's really outdone himself this time, thought Aggie cattily. She looks like the type who has a Frederick's of Hollywood charge card.

Hank made introductions: "Aggie and Mac," he began, "I would like to present our new Librarian, Miss Dixie Lee Beaumont. She's gonna work with our cheerleaders this year, coach," he continued, addressing Mac.

"It's a pleasure to know you, ma'am," Mac said, resum-

31

ing his seat. "Do you fool around?" He pulled a five-dollar bill from his wallet and passed it to Hank.

"Ain't you the cutest lil' ol' thing?" gushed Dixie, eyeing Mac appreciatively.

Aggie considered unbuttoning something.

"Struck out again, huh, coach?" Hank pocketed the money, smiling slyly. "I'll deposit this in the safe along with the rest of the Scholarship Fund. By the way, we ought to start another one this season, coach."

Both men's eyes were riveted on the milky moons that shimmered above the low neckline of Dixie Beaumont's blouse.

"I'm so-o-o lookin' forward to workin' with you this year, Coach MacCarthy," drooled Dixie.

"Mac," he corrected.

"I have a few ideas to attract the fans . . ."

"I'll bet you do!" said Mac.

Just another empty-headed blonde, mused Aggie, staring at Mac while he ignored her.

RED ALERT, blared Martha's frightened voice from the intercom.

BIG RED ALERT! ALL MALE STAFF MEMBERS NOT PRESENTLY IN CLASS WILL REPORT TO THE STUDENT CAFETERIA. THIS IS AN EMERGENCY! BIG RED ALERT!

The fire-drill bell clanged loudly.

My God! thought Aggie, it's happened. The catastrophe that they all feared. She tried to remember the procedures outlined on the mimeographed sheet she had perused too hurriedly that morning, but the terror that she felt fogged her recollection. Mac and Hank both spilled their chairs in their hasty exit, and she stood to right them. She looked at Dixie. Tears washed a black mascara smudge down her cheeks. One bright glittering dew drop sparkled like a diamond on the snowy field of her right breast.

"Them niggers gonna kill us all!" screamed Dixie. "They're not gonna be happy till all white folks are dead and buried and they can run the whole show themselves."

"Get a hold of yourself!" Aggie snapped, shaking Dixie impatiently. "You're supposed to be a professional. They may need some help in there and there's nothing as useless as an hysteric."

32

Aggie grabbed her purse and followed Mac and Henry out the door. She ran around a corner and across a nearly deserted court yard, her heart pounding painfully. Why, Lord? Just a few more hours to go. We were halfway home.

She saw E-Z first, on the far side of the enclosure, accompanied by a uniformed security man and four surley, spaghetti-smeared students in torn T-shirts. One of them, the only Anglo, was bleeding from a wound on his cheek that looked like he'd been raked with an Afro pick.

"What happened, E-Z?" she asked.

"Just an impromptu exercise in human relations, honey," he answered. "Nothin' we can't handle, mate," he said, turning to the guard. "Would you mind escorting these gentlemen to my office? I'll be right there."

As soon as the others were out of range, he turned his worried face to her and lowered his voice conspiratorially.

"Christ, I wish this hadn't happened. Not now. I spent most of my summer vacation trying to placate a group of concerned black parents that it is *not* an indication of racial prejudice at Arcadia that three times as many blacks are suspended for disciplinary reasons as whites. Why can't they just be cool and use their heads? What am I 'sposed to tell those concerned citizens I've had parked on my doorstep all summer?"

"Is that reporter in there?" she asked.

"Screaming about his rights under the First Amendment and snapping away. This is going to look a lot worse than it was by the time it hits the six o'clock news," he said. "I gotta go write it up and call their folks."

"Is Mac still in there?"

"Last I saw him," answered E-Z. "But I'd stay clear a' there if I was you."

Like a salmon working her way upstream, she fought the swirling undertow of the crowd streaming across the courtyard from the student cafeteria. She could taste the bitter bile of apprehension on her tongue. How could it possibly be worse than it looked?

Years ago, in grad school, she had read about some doctor who'd allowed rats to overbreed so they were forced to live with constant crowding. The animals became increasingly aggressive as they competed for the available space

33

and sustenance. They turned to cannabalism as the food got scarce, turning on their weakest, often their youngest members first.

Through the open doors of the cavernous room, she saw Hank Lawler standing on a chair shouting instructions through a bull horn to the mob milling around his feet.

"Please report to your classrooms immediately," he yelled, projecting his voice above the crowd. Long strands of hair bristled like the cock's comb of an indignant rooster from his balding head. "All students please report to your fifth-period class."

The mob was still making its disorderly exodus over the debris of overturned tables and chairs in the cafeteria. Broken glasses and cracked crockery made a dangerous obstacle course out of the refuse-strewn floor. The scene resembled the aftermath of war games staged at the city dump. The Arcadia Lion, immortalized in the mural above the steel grating of the bookstore, was covered with coconut cream.

The cops were now in control inside the spaghetti-stained walls of Arcadia High.

The reporter from the TV station's van surveyed the room with a camera pressed to his eye.

Aggie pressed through the crowd, looking for Mac. She spotted him speaking to an officer in the far corner of the room, and struggled to reach him. A white towel covered with red splotches was draped over his head.

"Oh, Mac!" she cried, removing the towel to examine his injuries. The lump of fear in her throat melted into a giggle. Mac's shining helmet of hair was smeared and matted with marinara sauce. She picked a string of spaghetti fastidiously from his soiled amber T-shirt, laughing with relief.

"What the hell happened here?" asked Aggie.

"Just a food fight," answered Mac. "Like dozens of other food fights we've seen in our years of service. Kinda' helps clear the air, get the year off to a healthy start. Rid the resident radicals of all that pent-up aggression. Problem is, the media will probably play it up as a major race riot. That kid with the camera's just been itchin' to get somethin' on us."

The police began to herd the news crew toward the

door, and it was apparent they were not yet ready to take their leave.

"They' been sittin' on our stoop like vultures, just waitin' for somethin' to happen here," said Mac sadly. "This is sure gonna look bad when they get through with it."

"It doesn't look too good from where I'm standing, ei-ther," said Aggie as they picked their way carefully over the shards of dishes and slimmy goo that covered the floor. "I sure feel sorry for the maintenance staff. Ol' Far-ley's gonna split a gut when he sees this mess."

"At least, you're OK."

"Why, Miss Sadie! I'm plumb overwhelmed with your concern," Mac grinned as the mass of bodies pressed them against one another.

"Nice play, coach," said a burly young man jostling them on his way out.

"You're compromising my good name," said Aggie.

She tried to back away, but he held her around her waist with both arms.

"Well, I figure, as long as we've got the name . . ."

"You're like a hound dog baying at the moon," she laughed.

" 'Cause I'm so horny, or 'cause you're as far as the moon from lettin' me have some?"

"Little bit of each," she sighed. "Why don't you go fetch Dixie? I left her dissolving in a puddle of self-pity in the faculty room."

"Ain't she somethin'!" said Mac.

"What she is is a goddamn racist," snapped Aggie. "What's she doing in a place like Arcadia where three quarters of our students are blacks or Latins?"

It was a question without an answer.

"Why, Sadie Mae, I do believe you're jealous," grinned Mac, misunderstanding her irritation over Dixie.

"Bullshit!" snapped Aggie.

The bell rang.

"Jesus Christ," she gasped. "I'm late to class and it's only the first day. Muriel's gonna burn my butt."

"Come down to the locker room and jump in the shower with me if you need help putting out the fire," she heard him call as she ran across the courtyard.

When Aggie entered her classroom, a fist fight was in progress. A cheering section of kids was piled up on the chairs and tables around a makeshift ring.

Standing in the doorway, rage flaring in her eyes, she extinguished the lights for a moment. The room fell into semi-darkness and total silence.

The two boys tussling on the floor froze like statues.

As she flashed the lights back on she was once more on stage.

"How dare you!" she said, keeping her voice under deliberate control, "Come into my class and conduct yourselves in such a fashion."

"Busted!" yelled someone from the back of the room.

"Teacher gonna fry your ass now, nigger!" said one of the two youths getting up from the floor.

"I'm gonna shut your fuckin' mouth for you, redneck," said the other, jumping up.

"Cut it out!" shouted Aggie. "Pick up your chairs and drop your butts in them," she said, lowering her voice as they all hurried to obey.

"My name is Ms. Hillyer," she began as they settled to an uncomfortable hush. "I'm going to be your teacher this year . . .

4

Aggie had managed to survive the first days of classes. Room 112 was alive with the frenetic activity of the season's opening game. While the Hellions silkscreened the last of 1500 game ribbons at one end of the room and embellished the faces of the marching band's bass drums with the Arcadia lion at the other, three dozen students labored with various degrees of devotion on class projects. Others had abandoned their own work, swept up in a riptide of enthusiasm.

Half a dozen game banners—twenty- or thirty-foot lengths of brown wrapping paper illustrated with proclamations of the violence Arcadia's football team planned to commit against the opposition—were spread across the tables and floors and overflowing into the corridor beyond. Students with dripping brushes and brightly hued cans of tempera tumbled over one another, trying with little success to circumvent the traffic in the hall. Each hour, as the passing bell sounded, the banners were lifted, moved, and replaced, still wet and a bit more dog-eared, as a new crew took over each period. It was a tricky maneuver, executed with something less than precision thus far. A forgotten jar of red paint was overturned and the contents walked across by hundreds of oblivious feet, requiring the ministrations of a mop squad hurriedly equipped from old Mr. Farley's custodial closet. Several high-spirited artisans took time to paint one another's faces and hands with laughing abandon, their hostilities toward one another redirected toward an outside foe.

The only conflict smacking of racial overtones that Aggie had to referee all week was whether to play a Frampton disc or Stevie Wonder on the class phonograph. The

38

music throbbed with a primeval beat and escaped, largely unheeded in the pandemonium, through the open door.

Aggie ran alternately between corridor and classroom, simultaneously supervising each project, like a magician pulling rainbow-colored scarfs and live doves from a magic box. She popped into the classroom, appearing suddenly to lean over a shoulder to whisper praise or encouragement, then suddenly materializing in the hall to lend the guiding stroke of a more experienced hand to an uncertain student.

"It's time for another record," shouted someone as the music stopped.

"I don't want to hear any more of that nigger music, man."

"That's soul, honey."

"If you can't make nice and share, there'll be no music," yelled Aggie. "And keep it down. There are people in this place trying to learn something."

She was on all fours on the hall floor with a paint brush in her mouth and another in her hand when Muriel's sensible shoes walked into her line of vision. She looked up at a painful scowl of disapproval.

"I believe Mr. Calloway would like a word with you, Miss Hillyer."

Oh, shit! thought Aggie. What have I done now?

"I believe your conference period is coming up," said Muriel sternly. "He'll see you in his office."

"OK, gang," she said to her class as she reentered the room. "Let's get this place cleaned up."

"Hey, we've got another twenty minutes till the bell. Why're we cleaning up now?" moaned someone from the back.

" 'Cause Goldilocks has got to see Papa Bear next period," answered Aggie.

"Good luck, Hilly!" yelled Pete, bringing up the rear of the last group with one of the game banners.

She straightened her hair, snapped off the lights, and apprehensively prepared to present herself in the office of the principal. The newly embellished bass drums throbbed like a heart beat across the court yard from the gym as she presented herself at Bo Calloway's door.

"What'd I do this time, boss?" she asked with counterfeit confidence.

39

"Aggie, Miss Peterson . . . Muriel," he corrected himself awkwardly, "said you were behaving in an undignified manner, and that you're wearing a garment that people can look . . ." he had difficulty getting it out. He tried again: " . . . that maybe students can see . . ." Bo's hand flew unwittingly to his chest, and embarrassment shaded his plump countenance,

"Muriel did what?" asked Aggie, unsure,

He extended a mimeographed leaf from the faculty handbook. One paragraph specifically forbade certain articles of clothing. The words *T-shirts, tank tops and too tight sweaters* had been underlined in red ink. A big star marked the margin for emphasis.

"What does this mean?" she asked, confused. "I'm not wearing a T-shirt or tank top, nor is my sweater either too low or too tight."

"Well, I think it's fine, Aggie. Very becoming. But there seems to be a difference of opinion."

"Muriel's opinion?" she ventured.

"We've both got to live with her, Aggie. See if you can do it during assembly so we don't have to dock you the time."

"Do what?"

"Go home and change, Aggie. Don't make waves." He masked his embarrassment with anger.

"Why, that prune-faced pedantic shrew!" fumed Aggie as Bo's door closed behind her with a punctuating bang. "That rule-book-touting despotic bitch," she yelled as she slammed the car door.

From behind the wheel of the 'Vette, Aggie spotted a couple of kids making out in an ancient Chevy. They were also seeking escape into the solitude of the parking lot.

It was suddenly exhilarating to be out of school in the middle of the day. She felt like a parakeet who'd suddenly found the cage door open.

She looked in the rearview mirror. Her brow was furrowed with rage, her lips contorted with anger.

Compose yourself, she admonished, *before that she-witch recreates you in her own image. It would serve her right if I didn't come back today.* She pulled a comb from the console and made a few impatient passes through her unrestrained hair. Replacing the comb, she discovered the

40

slightly rumpled, half-smoked joint in the ashtray where she had left it. *Then she'd have to cover my last two classes,* she thought vindictively, childish mischievousness guiding her hand.

Clipping the roach neatly in a hairclip, she sparked it and smiled slyly. She made a mental inventory of the remainder of her day. Friday afternoon classes were a light attendance load, nothing a last-minute substitute couldn't handle. She inhaled deeply, holding the pungent vapor deep down in her lungs.

Sweet scented smoke filled the car. She was quickly consuming the last of her precious stash, pacing herself, hoarding it like a miser till she could cop another lid. With a sigh of anguish and relief, she jammed the little car in gear and rolled out through the fortresslike gates of Arcadia.

Now she felt her head sprout wings, lift, and rise high . . . A love song throbbed from the FM while the clock in the tower above the palms glared in the heat of the midday sun. And suddenly the white 'Vette became a winged charger and she was Jeanne d'Arc with a shield that bore the mark of a seven-fingered leaf. Wielding her rice-paper roll like a lance, she quixotically assailed the clock in the belfry, rising on the wings of the weed to stay the hands of time. And it wasn't homeward to change the offensive red sweater that she guided the car. Aggie dropped her foot on the accelerator and headed for the healing arms of the sea. There she would seek the solace of the sun and shore, and replenish her sulking spirit.

The sun was directly overhead as she pulled to a sudden stop on the macadam parking strip under the causeway.

With a primeval need somewhat like that of a lemming, she ran shoeless into the cool waves that clutched the shore. Spray rose and broke against the seawall, rained down on her hair and shoulders, cooled her head and soaked her clothes. She ran till she was exhausted, feeling the freedom of unstructured time, then threw herself down on the sand, listening to her heart pound as she fought for breath.

Too many cigarettes, she thought. *I've got to give it up.*

She pulled off her panty hose. Soggy and tattered, they were a sudden symbol of her restriction. They were part of the uniform. A requirement of the system.

A small pool had formed in a hollow in the sand where someone had dug a firepit or a castle moat. And there, in the calm of that little pool, was her own image, staring back at her. The wild hair tamed and plastered down with water and sweat. And if the red sweater was ever an innocent article of clothing, it was now riding every ridge and contour of her body. The wet sweater was mocking her as if to heap additional guilt and embarrassment on her.

Why can't I stand up to her? thought Aggie. *Why do I stand there and take it, then run away and crawl into a hole, like a little mouse? She treats me like a child, and I react like one.*

The face staring back from the pool was that of a pouting child, truant from school, wide-eyed and tearful. And magnified by the convexity of the puddle, the red sweater clung, frankly revealing her ripe, full breasts.

By the time she pulled into the reserved space beneath her second-story window, the sun was sinking over the rooftops, splashing Arcadia's red and gold across the sky. She threw herself onto her bed and fell into a deep sleep.

Somewhere in the other world where our other selves wander when we sleep, she ran. She flung open the numbered doors along the narrow corridor, each opened on nothing but a blank wall. She knew it was after her. She feared each door she opened would reveal the face of the monster in pursuit. Each time she saw it, it frightened her anew. The recurrent familiarity lessened the shock not at all. The beast swooped on gigantic bat wings from the belfry above Arcadia's east lawn. His cyclopean eye was the face of the clock with its hands spinning wildly like a windmill, and its deafening voice was the sounding of the passing bell, magnified and amplified to a painful pounding in her head.

She awoke with a start. The bell was still sounding.

"Hello," she gasped, grabbing up the receiver. "Oh, Maddy, I was going to call *you*," she began apologetically.

Madeleine Gordon had been Aggie's first friend and mentor since she'd come South. She taught art in another of the district's high schools. They'd met at a regional humanities conference, and though Maddy was better than

42

twenty years her senior, she and Aggie shared many things in common and had become fast friends.

"How's it going so far?" asked Aggie. "I haven't spoken with you since school started." She struggled to right herself and reached for the cigarette pack on the table as she listened.

"No," gasped Aggie into the phone. "What happened?" She lit the cigarette and inhaled it with her waking breaths.

"No . . . Oh, no. My God, how bad was it? . . . Did they hospitalize her? . . . Listen, dear, take something for your nerves. . . . well, no, then don't take anything else . . . No, Maddy, I don't think so . . . Well, are you planning on going to the game?" A trembling chill shook her whole body and she burrowed into the pillows. "I don't know. I've hardly had time for Bob since school opened. But I'll ask him when he gets here."

"Ask him what?" Bob's rich baritone startled her into awareness. He filled the door, his solid frame resplendent in the uniform of the Avalon County police, a garment bag slung carelessly across his arm.

"Oh, Maddy, he's here. Hold on!" she said burying the earpiece in her hand.

She raised her head for a welcoming kiss.

"Maddy wants us to meet her and some guy at a club on the strip after the game. Can you handle it?"

The look on his dark, handsome face was less than enthusiastic.

"She's very upset, Bob. Don't say no," she pleaded, knowing she could have her way.

He shrugged his acquiescence and dropped the garment bag on the bed.

"Okay, honey . . . Right! Around eleven at the bar of the Carousel Club. Try to get some rest, Maddy. We'll see you later."

"The Carousel Club?" asked Bob, unbuckling the leather holster at his waist. "That's a pretty racy place, sugar. What's a sweet little old lady like Kate doing on the seamy side of town?"

"You mean, what's a nice girl like her?" teased Aggie as she rose to embrace him.

43

"Well, when you get to her age I guess your alternatives begin to diminish," he answered, holding her.

"C'mon, Bob," chided Aggie. "She's lonely. Don't be so hard on her. I guess she just gets tired of drinking alone."

Bob laid the gun on the dresser and started unbuttoning the blue uniform shirt. Aggie, shivering, fell back into her bed.

"You gotta be pretty thirsty to do your drinking at the Carousel Club. The boys on the night shift make that a regular stop on their route. They get raided about twice a week." He paused, eyeing her accusingly. "By the way, there's something I meant to talk to you about." He fished her key ring from his shirt pocket and tossed it into her lap.

"Where'd you get these?" she asked, confused.

"Where you left them—in the door. Don't you think you're taking unnecessary liberties with your well being?"

"I take my life in my hands every time I report for work." She laughed, a defensive, mirthless sound.

Bob stripped off his shirt and kicked off his shoes. "Another rough day at the zoo?"

"Yeah." She watched him undress.

"Want to talk about it?" He settled close beside her.

"Not after you chastised me for leaving my keys in the door. And after Muriel rapped me with another morality lesson."

"What's this about Muriel?"

"She noticed my tits today and sent me home to change," complained Aggie. "Sent me to Bo's office for violating the dress code."

"No kidding! Busted again, huh?" he hooted, enjoying the joke. "Is this the offending garment?" he asked, noticing the red sweater for the first time. It still clung to her. "I've been checking that out. I notice you didn't accommodate her," he added, pulling her against his naked chest. "What'd you do, take a bath in it?"

She felt his strength, and his urgency. But her mind was elsewhere. "No," she answered. "I went to the beach this afternoon."

"Ditched, huh? Did it help?"

"To a point. Till Maddy called to tell me about the

trouble at King today," she answered glumly. "Did you know about that?"

"Yeah!" He tightened his embrace. "But I was hoping you didn't. I'm gonna have to talk to that ol' busybody about upsettin' you," he said, rolling over on top of her.

She exploded out of his arms. "Don't protect me, Bob. I want to hear it. Another teacher was attacked on the job today. Don't think I don't think about things like that. What are the statistics . . . about 150,000 teachers every school year?"

"Well, don't get so serious about it, sugar," he chided, propping himself on an elbow and grinning slyly at her. "I'm about to attack a teacher myself," he said, trying to grab her again.

"It *is* serious," said Aggie. "I've been lucky. I was mad as hell 'cause Muriel sent me home to change my sweater. It isn't the damn sweater. It's *me*. It was humiliating to be told by a superior that you're behaving unprofessionally, that you're out of uniform. And then somebody else gets hit on and I start wondering if I'm a good teacher because I'm a woman."

"An exceptionally well-endowed woman, Aggie. You really should be more careful when I'm not around to defend your virtue," said Bob. "Or better yet, marry me and let me take you away from all this."

She laughed aloud. "I can't marry you because of Muriel."

"Fuck Muriel. She's probably a bull dyke dying to get you in her clutches," he laughed lewdly. "On second thought, forget about Muriel. Fuck me."

"Tell me about the incident at King!" she persisted.

"Well," he acceded, "better that I set you straight than let the rumor mongers panic you. Victim's a white female, age 26, new to the county, I understand. Alleged perpetrator's a black juvenile, age 15, three priors, no convictions—what else do you want to know?"

"What happened?" she prompted impatiently.

"What do you think happened? He held a knife to her throat and fucked the hell out of her," he snapped.

He studied her face, and softened his tone. "A rape is not an act of love. The worst part is, he'll probably get off."

45

"Whaddaya mean, get off?"

"He's underage—and she's a looker. I saw her when she came into the station to fill out the report. They'll probably make a case for her enticement of a helpless, horny kid . . . By the time they get through with her in court, *she'll* think *she* did it . . . and the kid'll be back in school before they file the records." The sharp edge of sarcasm colored his speech.

Aggie sat, stone-faced. "Doesn't seem right!"

"Aw, shug!" wailed Bob, plaintively. "Does this mean I don't get none?"

She laughed in spite of herself, and he took her back down in his arms.

"Damn it, you're wet," he complained.

"Where'd it happen?" she asked timidly.

"It's happenin' right here, shug," he answered, nuzzling her ear.

"No, Bob. At King—where?"

"Parking lot! Can we get off the subject?" His words were muffled in her hair.

Aggie shuddered, and he released her reluctantly.

"OK," he sighed, resigned. "If my charm alone isn't enough to seduce you, I'm going to have to resort to more drastic measures." He stood and fumbled in his trouser pocket and withdrew a plastic sandwich bag rolled neatly around about four fingers of a crisp, brown herb.

"Bob! Son of a . . . gun!" She smiled, clearly overjoyed. "You sure know how to please a lady."

Opening the drawer of her bedside table, she withdrew a packet of Jobs and began cleaning a pinch of the pungent weed. Amused, he watched her roll, then, rose to remove his socks and pants. He wore no shorts.

"Why don't you let me help you off with those soggy clothes first?"

Solid and swarthy, Bob appeared younger than his forty years. The smattering of silver at his temples appeared like a phrase out of context. His dark eyes brooded from beneath low-slung brows.

"That's so-o-o-o fine!" she exclaimed. A veil of purple haze lifted round her face as she spoke and she nestled comfortably against him, passing the joint.

"And I thought you loved me for my body," he teased, taking a drag and holding it.

"Wrong!" she answered as they smoked. "You know what I love about you?" Her arms encircled his neck. "I love you for your strength and your gentleness . . . and because you make me feel comfortable, and safe, and because . . ."

His mouth descended on hers, explored her lips tentatively.

"And because you always give more than you get."

Compliments embarrassed Bob. "Just like I said," he wisecracked. "You love me for my dope."

"I love you in spite of the fact that you *are* a dope," she chided, connecting with his mouth to stifle speech.

"But it ain't bad," she gasped, breaking for breath.

"The kiss?" he murmured, still clinging to her lips.

"That neither," breathed Aggie. "Where'd it come from?"

"Straight from the heart." His voice was muffled, his breath warm on her ear and throat.

"Not the kiss . . . the dope." Her hands travelled over his chest. "Did you get it from the evidence room?"

"Of course not!" His wiry mustache settled like a caterpillar on a rose bud as his mouth found the nipple of her left breast. The red sweater had left a pink stain on the soggy white bra he tossed to the floor.

"My buddy got it from the evidence room. I traded for it." His hands explored and undressed her. "For an imported .38 I took off a nigger a couple a months ago." He dropped her white panties along side the bra.

"How'd you get the gun?" Her fingers found his groin, and found him ready.

"Arresting officer gets first crack at it if a weapon isn't claimed in sixty days." His preoccupied response was muffled against her skin, still cool and damp against the warmth of him. "They usually hock 'em in the pawn shops down off Eastern Avenue." He shifted his position and pressed his rigid penis against her palm. "It got me a few bags of posies for my lady," he smiled. "My baby's favorite flowers."

"There's more?" she laughed. He lay heavy on her chest, his weight restricting her breathing.

47

"Couple a' more lids in the car . . . but you're gonna have to work for 'em."

"Don't mind a bit," she sighed as his body descended to cover her.

"Don't I know it, shug!" he breathed. "I don't think I've ever known a woman who likes it s'much as you. I haven't felt this way about any one since Gail died."

"Hush," she cautioned, not wanting him to be unhappy in her arms.

A warm quiver rose from her groin and her thighs fell apart.

"You taste salty," said Bob, embracing her. He entered Aggie abruptly, in a single stroke.

"I haven't taken a bath yet," she protested. Then she raised herself up to welcome him and dissolved in an eddy of desire. Wrapping her limbs around his full-muscled girth, she rode out the storm as the bed springs sounded a squeaky accompaniment in the twilight of her darkening room. The dope and the orgasm hit at precisely the same time. Like a nova exploding, she trembled spasmodically . . . then let go.

The liquid warmth that bathed their bodies made a smacking sound like a kiss when they finally fell apart, silent and spent, gasping for breath in the dark. "Probably just as well. You'd have had to do it all again any way . . . now," he whispered.

5

"That big ol' buck got some nice moves," said Bob, stuffing a cigarette in his mouth. "That is the largest kid I've ever seen." The first game of the season was over, and the Arcadia parking lot was full of boisterous youngsters waving red and amber streamers.

"Boogie Man," smiled Aggie.

"Yeah," grinned Bob. "Boogie Man. How come I've never seen him before? He didn't play last year." He maneuvered his car deftly through the traffic. "Too bad we missed most of the game."

"The Boogie Man came to us from out of state. Alabama, I think. He's a high school All-American." She stared at the students swarming by in their decorated cars, tooting and waving. "Yeah," she continued, "I think Vance said he came from Alabama."

"Vance?" repeated Bob, quizzically.

"Our coach," she answered flatly.

"Friend of yours?" asked Bob.

"I do a lot of work for the athletic department," answered Aggie. "Are you interrogating me?"

"I'm too clever to be that direct," he evaded. There was another pause. She hummed with Simon and Garfunkel, harmonizing with the FM.

"I see those kids out there, I think of Bobby . . ." began Bob, changing the subject. "His grandma's good to him, but she can't get out and toss a ball around with him."

She knew where his conversation was headed, and closed her eyes to avoid a reply.

"You'll love Bobby, shug," he ventured, looking for a reaction from the corner of his eye. "You're so good with

50

kids. You should be married, Aggie. Settle down and raise a family of your own."

"Is this another proposal?" she asked listlessly. "Let me tell you a contemporary fable. Back when I was in school, I dated a guy that was studying to be a scientist. A bunch of us were up in the woods one weekend, camping out, getting in touch with nature. Tony and I were messing around on a blanket by a lovely little stream. Suddenly he jumped up and tossed a sweater down on the ground and pounced on it. He captured two tiny little orange lizards, still locked together in a mating position. I'm not overly fond of reptiles, and probably no less perturbed over the interruption of my own mating ritual than the lizards were. But Tony stuck them into an empty olive jar and took them back to the city. He said he wanted to study their habits. He set up an aquarium to simulate their natural environment, fed them live insects, but they never did anything after that. The whole time Tony had them under observation, they never came near one another. Eventually, they both died."

"How does that apply to you and me?" asked Bob patiently.

"Things that come naturally in one situation don't necessarily translate well to another. I've never had a kid of my own. I've been too busy raising other people's kids. Teaching is a commitment," she said, "not just a job."

"I'm not asking you to give up teaching, Aggie. Just make room in your life for me," he pleaded. "We both need someone."

There was a silence begging to be broken. The disc jockey on the radio stepped into the void. She fished in her bag for a cigarette.

"What happened to Tony? Did he stop screwing around too?"

"Not immediately." She didn't want to be led into this reminiscence. It was becoming painful.

"You've never mentioned Tony," said Bob. "Was he your first love?"

"Yeah," she answered. "We were engaged."

"What happened?"

"I went off to art school, Tony enlisted in the Marine Corps."

51

"I can see where that was headed. The hawk and the dove. It's natural you grew apart ideologically."

"No it wasn't anything like that. I wasn't very militant when I first got to college. I was very young. I had more romance in my soul than ideology in my head. Tony was an athelete, with an athlete's perfect body. A Greek statue caste in bronze. I used to sit and draw him while he slept or watched TV or worked out. He was training for the Olympic gymnastic team. A lot of people thought he had a pretty good shot at it. The only ambition I had in those days was to marry Tony and have his babies. My future was all tied up to his."

"And he got cold feet?" asked Bob, aware he was treading on fragile ground.

"No. They sent him to Vietnam . . . He died there."

"Aggie, honey . . . I'm sorry. You never said . . ."

"No need. It was a long time ago." She reached for the cigarette lighter and lit up. There was an uncomfortable silence.

"Is that why you're so afraid, shug? Are you afraid I'll up and die on you?"

"It's crossed my mind. I see you tuck a pistol in your belt every time you walk out the door, it's hard *not* to think about it. It would hurt to lose you, regardless, Bob. It's just that I need more time. I'm just not ready for marriage."

Another pause.

"You know I love you. I'll be good to you, Aggie. You won't regret it, baby, I promise. I'll always be there for you."

She didn't answer.

"Is there someone else, Aggie?" he questioned, cautiously, as if afraid of her answer. "That blond coach . . . the big guy . . . Vance?"

She closed her eyes again for an instant. Vance's face floated to the surface of her consciousness. "No, Bob," she said, "there's no one else. Can't we talk about something else?"

His dark eyes were somber in the glare of oncoming headlights. The knit shirt that hugged his torso bulged at the waist where he stashed his weapon.

"This is a rowdy neighborhood, honey," he said testing the ice. "Sure you're up to it?"

An alien nightscape unravelled itself beyond the window. Streets grew narrow and the lighting dim in a shadowy collage of garbage cans and ill-kept storefronts. The headlights unfurled a ribbon of light along the road as they made their way slowly through the unfamiliar streets.

"It really is a nasty part of town," said Aggie. "Can you imagine having to live down here?"

"Yeah, babe," said Bob. "I grew up in a neighborhood very much like this."

She was about to ask him about it, but never got the chance.

Two shapes shot suddenly from the dark, hurling themselves into the glare of the car's headlights. They heard a woman scream. Bob braked to a screeching stop and flung open the car door. "Stay there!" he ordered her sternly. "Hold it," he yelled from behind the car door, the revolver poised and ready.

She froze at the authority in his voice.

So did the two figures in the glare of the headlights.

A lean young Negro with his hands held high turned slowly and eyed them arrogantly.

As sudden recognition overtook her, Aggie sprang from the car and hurried to Bob's side.

"Stay back!" he shouted again.

"Wait, Bob!" she yelled, catching up with him. "I know him. He's one of my kids."

Bob's face registered shock.

"Ernie, isn't it?" she directed her question at the student who stood frozen, "Ernie Nesbitt," she repeated. Bob searched him perfunctorily for weapons, and relieved him of an 18-inch stiletto.

Ernie didn't answer.

"Art 1, period three," she explained. "He's one of mine."

"Not out here," said Bob. "Out here, he's mine. That your name, son? You know that knife could put you in jail?"

Ernie answered with sullen silence.

"I asked you your name, boy!" repeated Bob. This time it was not a question.

"Pride," he spat defiantly. "They call me Pride." A red

53

silk shirt was tucked into custom-tailored trousers, cut to a merciless fit. Gold chains gleamed at his throat and wrists.

"Pride, huh? smiled Bob sardonically. "Well, what's happenin' here, Pride?"

"Private business," he snarled.

He couldn't have been more than sixteen.

A sob escaped from Ernie's female companion cowering with her head in her hands.

Aggie rushed to her side and raised her to her feet. Her honey skin shone in the halflight, and her straight, black hair framed her face and shoulders like a dark veil. Her taut young body was covered by a short shift that barely skimmed her stocking tops. Her purse had spilled on the pavement. Gathering up her possessions, she stood uncertainly on her platform sandals and stared silently through tear-stained almond eyes.

"Sheila! gasped Aggie, amazed.

Sheila Morrow's right eye was swelling. Her nose dripped trickles of blood.

"This a sample of your business?" asked Bob sarcastically.

"Leave him be," sulked Sheila finding her voice. "He didn't do nothin'! I fell, that's all."

"You're kidding," laughed Bob incredulously. "You're just gonna let him get away with it?"

She turned away without a word.

"You gonna read me my rights or can I go on about my business?" hissed Pride.

"I know him, Bob," pleaded Aggie into the silence, anxious to bring the sordid scenario to a quick conclusion.

Ernest Nesbitt's heavy-lidded eyes followed her.

Bob slipped the pistol back in his belt and Aggie heard his breath escape, bespeaking both frustration and relief. "You lucked out tonight, fancy man," he said. "But if I catch you beatin' on one of your girls again, I'm gonna take you on myself. Just for the fun of it."

Pride turned to go when Bob stopped him with a final admonition.

"You owe this lady," he said, indicating Aggie, "for the *character reference*."

Pride scowled, then with deliberate slowness ambled off into the night.

Sheila bolted for the alley. Bob flung himself at the retreating girl and held her as she struggled in his grasp.

"Hold on girl," he panted as she squirmed. "You just settle down. No one's gonna hurt you."

She became submissive, and he released her cautiously.

"Leastways," he concluded, "not tonight."

"You takin' me in?" Her dark eyes searched his fearfully.

"For what?" asked Bob. "Being stupid? Go home. You need some attention."

"How'm I supposed to get home? Pride left me!" She started to cry.

"Oh, Sheila, honey," said Aggie, laying her arm on the young girl's shoulders.

"I don't need no pity from no honky teacher and her loverman cop," snapped Sheila. "If you through with me, I got to get back to work."

"You're through for tonight, for sure," said Bob. "Get in the car."

"Come on," said Aggie gently. "We'll take you home."

Sheila got in reluctantly, then gave instructions brusquely, guiding them through a maze of unfamiliar back streets. Seated between them, clutching her purse nervously on her lap, she remained silent.

They turned a final corner past a liquor store where a wino was rummaging through garbage cans. Sheila pointed out a door among a row of similar doors in a project house. Back yards grew ragged lines of sooty laundry and rusting refuse instead of rose bushes and trees.

Well, this is it!" said Sheila defiantly.

"Do you want us to come in with you?" asked Aggie, hoping insincerity didn't show in her voice.

Sheila laughed. "This ain't the kind of place that folks like you gen'lly come to call." Her body indicated she was ready to leave them, but Aggie made no move to let her go.

"Sheila," she began hesitantly, "Why?"

Sheila laughed. "The world's oldes' question about the world's oldes' profession. Well, who the hell do you think I am? Do you have any idea what it's like behind those doors? I live in that hole, with four other people: my mother, my kid sister, and both their bastard sons. Ain't never known no daddy, and my mother's spending her life drinkin' herself to death. She put me and my sister on the street soon's we got the curse, so's we wouldn't starve while she drunk up the welfare checks. And my ten year ol' brother learnin' how to be a thief."

Aggie sat, mute.

"The only thing I ever learned, that I ever needed to know, was how to survive."

"Sheila, I'm trying to understand."

"They no way you unnerstan' till you been hungry 'nuff to sell yo' ass, teachuh!" she snapped. "Man, tomorra I got to answer to Pride. I ain't made my quota."

"You think we shoulda' cruised on by and let him beat you senseless!" exclaimed Aggie angrily.

"No . . . She seemed uncertain. "I guess I owe you, too. For gettin' me off easy with Pride tonight. He was so pissed, he mighta kilt me."

"How can you worry about that animal after what he's done to you?" asked Aggie, insistently.

Sheila smiled, as an indulgent adult would smile on a guileless child. "Girl on the street needs a man to protect her, show her. Pride, see . . . he my man."

Bob came around to open Sheila's door. Balancing herself on his arm, Sheila slid out of the car. The lilac-flowered hem of her skirt skimmed her crotch, exposing a patch of crisp black hair.

"See anything you like?" she vamped as Bob pulled her out. "Well," she turned to Aggie, "see ya in school, teach! Pretend you don't know me, OK?"

And swinging her ass up the walk, she disappeared behind the anonymous door. Bob resumed his place behind the wheel.

"You still want a drink?" he asked, lifting his hand to look at his watch. "It's after midnight."

She heard her voice as from a great distance. "No. I'll speak to Maddy tomorrow. She'll understand."

Bob turned the car onto Highway 41 and the projects vanished. The moon was a brilliant crescent in a star-studded sky.

"She's right, you know," he ventured.

"What?" she asked, shaking off exhaustion.

"I said, you'll both be better off if you don't get involved."

She felt naked, as if he'd read her thoughts. A half-formed plan had taken shape—a plan for Sheila and the Hellions and Pete.

"You can't fulfill a frustrated maternal instinct by picking up every underage stray you meet," said Bob.

"She's a bright girl," said Aggie, "and she's so beautiful. She needs to succeed at something."

"She's earning more than the two of us combined," he said. "Did you see that little cunt flash me? Stop pretending you're dealing with Pollyanna. She's a two-bit prostitute."

"There's a bit of whore in every one of us. That's why there're so many of us."

"Would that make more sense if we were high?" he laughed.

She rifled her purse for a joint. There was a diner coming up ahead.

"You want some coffee?" he asked.

"I'll make you some at my place. I want to go home." She paused, and he looked at her as though waiting for the other shoe to fall. Her hand found his lean, hard thigh in the dark.

"I'll make a pot a' coffee, and you can tell me again about Sheila."

"What for?" he laughed. It was too dark to see his expression.

"So I can make the most of a terrific hard-on," smiled Aggie, confirming with anxious fingers what the darkness concealed.

6

DING DONG BELL
THE SCHOOL DAY'S GOING WELL
THE BOYS AND GIRLS ALL GATHERED 'ROUND
AND NOBODY BURNT THE SCHOOLHOUSE
  DOWN . . .

"Don't take out your work, class, please," said Aggie, standing hall duty as her students streamed in the door. "I have something special planned for you today."

"No shit," said a voice from the crowd. "You mean we don't have to do any work today?"

"You don't do any work *most* days," said someone else knowingly.

"Hey, Ms. Hillyer, what're we doing?" said another, nearly tardy, taking his seat.

"As soon as you settle down I'll tell you," she said as the bell rang. On cue, she took her place at the head of the class.

"I've borrowed a slide presentation from a friend at the university," said Aggie. "How many of you have heard Don McLean's song called 'Vincent'?" she asked.

A few hands shot up.

"We got to listen to that honky music?" somebody complained aloud. "I've got a good album I wanted to play."

"You're gonna love this," said Aggie enthusiastically. "I promise. Settle down now so we can get started."

"I'll get the lights!" said one, jumping up.

"I need the audio-visual monitor to run the slide projector," interjected Aggie. "George, please pull down the movie screen."

"The subject of this presentation is a man named Vincent Van Gogh," she began, but was interrupted by a barrage of comments.

"Are you going to lecture all period?"

"How long does the movie take?"

"It's not a movie, turkey!"

"Hey, look," said the AV monitor. "There's a tape recorder comes with it."

"Although Van Gogh was Dutch, he lived most of his life in France," continued Aggie. "He was born in 1853, but didn't begin to paint till late in life."

"Are we supposed to be taking notes, teacher?"

"Ms. Hillyer, we got to remember when he was born?"

"The goal of the study of great artists and their work," answered Aggie patiently, "is to try to arrive at an understanding. Far more important than remembering when he was born or the date of completion of his last major work is to understand what he had to say about the world as he saw it. It necessitates a knowledge of history, psychology, aesthetics, sociology . . ."

"Does that mean we don't have to remember when he was born?"

"Shut up and let the teacher talk."

"Yeah, some of us are tryin' to learn somethin'."

"OK," smiled Aggie with a sigh. "Let's take a look at it. Then we'll discuss Van Gogh."

The lights went out, the sound came on. The screen was brilliantly aglow with the gold fields and azure skies of a pastoral landscape that faded out and panned back on a bowl of sunflowers.

Impressionistic images of light and shadow danced across the screen, reflected from the eyes of an audience mesmerized with wonder.

"Hey, this ain't bad!" said a voice in the dark.

"Shut up! I can't hear the words!" yelled another.

A portrait of the artist filled the screen.

"Hey, what was this guy on?"

"Looks like he was doin' acid."

"Or dust," said someone else. "Isn't this the guy who cut off his ear?"

The passing bell sounded.

"Summarize your reactions to this presentation and submit a single-page critique tomorrow," said Aggie as they stampeded for the door.

"Oh, Linda," called Aggie to a homely girl struggling to gather her books. "I'm glad I caught you before you left." She snatched up her grade book and crossed the room to sit beside her student. "It's about the days you've missed, Linda. Art class is a work shop, and it's difficult to catch up when you miss the work . . ."

The small face blanched beneath the freckles. "I know I'm behind, Ms. Hillyer, but I'll catch up. This is about the only class I care about. You're not gonna drop me?" she asked, her apprehension apparent in her voice.

Aggie smiled and shook her head reassuringly.

"See, it's my mom. She's real sick," offered Linda, fear and pain coloring her face. "When the county doesn't send someone to stay with her, I gotta be there."

Aggie's mind flooded with compassion and only key phrases jarred her comprehension:

Cancer, . . . tube in her throat . . . can't talk or swallow . . . can't hardly breathe . . .

"Linda, if there's anything I can do . . ." Aggie offered lamely.

Poor Linda, she thought as she closed her attendance register. There were things no book could cover. "There are forms," she said to the girl. "I'll help you fill them out. We'll appeal your excessive absences. Be sure to check with me next week," said Aggie, handing her a late pass. Aggie's eyes misted over as Linda left. "Shit! What a bummer!" she exclaimed, impotently venting her frustration.

She retreated to the Cave to fix her face while period three began to drift into the room. How would she handle this with the girls' dean? she wondered. The rules specified that more than fifteen absences in a semester justified withdrawal from a course without a grade, or the computer would simply register an automatic failure. Well, she thought, I'll take the problem to E-Z. He'll know what to do.

She took her place at the head of the class and prepared to begin again.

DING DONG BELL
THE KIDS ARE RAISING HELL.

61

"Quiet down, quickly!" she ordered. "Roach," she called across the room to a boy who was provoking a classmate to an audible wail. "Come sit up here where I can keep my eye on you!"

He reluctantly obeyed, seating himself sullenly at her feet. In the corner, by the sink, Pride languished in the rapt attention of buck-toothed Cocoa on one side and almond-eyed Sheila, who was filing his nails, on the other.

"Sheila . . . Cocoa . . . your attention, please," said Aggie.

"Miz Hillyer, Roach is looking up your skirt."

She pushed his chair away with her foot.

Aggie put her fingers to her lips and emitted an ear-splitting whistle. "Now hear this!" she glared into the sudden silence. "I have prepared a surprise today"—she paused for dramatic effect—"a special slide presentation I've borrowed from a friend at the university. Ernie, please sit up and pay attention."

Ernie smiled slyly. "I'm right on, teach. Just do your thing."

"All right," she said, rapping her fist on the desk. "Knock it off and settle down." She launched into her introduction. "In order to understand art, one must understand about the artist and his time."

"Bull crap," hissed Ernie under his breath.

"I beg your pardon." Aggie looked up, reluctant to give him the attention he craved but unable to overlook his rudeness.

Ernie smirked. Producing a magazine, he began thumbing the pages indolently.

"I'm unwilling to waste any more class time on this, Ernie. Why don't you stay and see me after class? We'll discuss it then."

"Sure, teach!" grinned Ernie. "I don't mind a private conference with a good-lookin' broad like you."

"I'm going to ask you to leave my class now," said Aggie, determinedly cool. "Report to the office immediately."

He stood slowly and never took his eyes off her as he sauntered out of the room. "See ya' later, teach," said Ernie. Sheila and Cocoa both stood to follow him out.

No, thought Aggie. *Not Sheila. Please, Lord, make her*

stay. Let her have the guts to stay. She caught her eye and stopped.

"Sheila!" snapped Ernie from the door.

The class sat in stony silence, observing the melodrama that was being played out.

"You go on, Ernie. I'll ketch up wit' ya later," she said as she resumed her seat.

Thank you, prayed Aggie with a sigh of relief.

She cleared her throat and began again.

"Vincent Van Gogh was born in 1853 . . ."

DING, DONG, WHAT THE HELL.
HANG ONTO YOUR HALO UNTIL THE BELL.

"Shelia, stop and speak with me a minute before you leave, please," said Aggie.

"Whatever you think I done, I'm not the one you oughta be yellin' at. I didn't do nuthin'," she said defensively. The swelling in her eye was almost gone.

"I'm not about to yell at you," Aggie smiled, hoping she sounded reassuring. She pulled a sheaf of papers out of the drawer and extended them across the desk.

"What's that?" asked Shelia, reaching tentatively.

"Application forms . . . for the court of the Homecoming Queen," said Aggie. "I've already spoken to Pete Santini—he's president of the art squad—and he thought it was a great idea. The art squad will sponsor you and pay the entry fee."

"Well, you shoulda spoke to me first," snarled Shelia dropping the papers as if they were hot. "I think it stinks!"

"Why?" said Aggie. "You're a beautiful girl, and I've checked your grade point average. With a little tutoring in math . . . well, who knows? Why not?"

"Why not?" gasped Shelia. "What you tryin' to do, teach-ah—get me kilt? Don't you know nothin'?"

"I know one thing you don't know," said Aggie, stunned by Sheila's outburst. "I know a bright, beautiful girl who's throwing her life away on a bunch of punks, pimps, and no-good low-life. Is that all you can see in your own future, girl? Is what you got going for you worth that? Are you content with staring at your battered face in the mirror for the rest of your life, without ever once reaching for some-

63

thing more? There's an open scholarship in it for the winner," she concluded, almost as an afterthought.

"Don't think I got one chance in hell a' makin' it!" she answered.

"You're right," said Aggie. "You probably don't have what it takes, anyway."

"You never seen what happens to people who step over," said Sheila fearfully. "You think what you seen Ernie do to me befo' was bad . . . You ain't seen nothin'. You just don't understand." But she slipped the application into her notebook before she left.

Ominous clouds darkened the midday landscape beyond the oversized windows as Aggie straightened up and prepared to leave the room. Thunder sounded on the far horizon, and most of the cars streaming down Eastern Avenue already had their headlights on. She reminded herself to write up a couple of discipline referrals on Roach and Ernie, but she'd already used half her lunch hour. She'd take care of it later, she thought as she snapped off the room lights and opened the door.

"Ernie!" she said, startled. "I thought you'd gone. Come in." She stood aside to allow him access to the darkened room.

He leaned languidly against the door frame, a toothpick dangling from his lips. "I came to tell you somethin' you need to know." His eyes gleamed in the darkness, but his body blocked her access to the light switch. "You keep messin' wit' me, and a division of cops ain't gonna help you."

She backed away from him, just a few paces, but he followed her. "Ernest," she began, unwilling to let him terrorize her, "I'm tired of sparring with you in front of my class. I'm tired of your disruptions and your rudeness . . ."

He laughed without amusement. "Stuff it, teach!" he exploded with the suddenness of a lightning bolt. "Keep your mouth shut and your do-good mitts off my girls. Stop fillin' their dumb heads full o' shit before you get in over yo' head."

"Are you threatening me?" she scowled, anger overtaking apprehension.

"Not yet," he said coldly, his voice deliberate and cutting as a razor. "This is just a little warning."

Then he was gone.

"Hey, Hilly, what's up?" Pete Santini poked his cheerful cherub face in the door, munching the last of a chili dog. "What you sittin' here in the dark for? Are you OK?"

"Yeah, I'm fine," she answered. How long had she been sitting there?

"Cafeteria's serving chili dogs. Want me to get you one?"

"No, thanks. I'll go get something."

"Well, then, mind if I get an early start?" he asked. "Got some stuff to finish for the game tonight."

He snapped on the lights.

"Sure," she said leaving. "Don't let anyone in till the bell. I'll be right back."

Another peal of thunder ripped the bleakness beyond the window.

"You're goin' tonight, aren't you?" he yelled. But the door slammed shut behind her, sparing her a decision.

It was an away game on the new field of King High, and Aggie looked forward to seeing Kate even though she would be in the cheering section of the opposition. Maybe they'll call the game for the rain and make up my mind for me, she thought.

"Aggie!" came Betty's shrill squawk resounding down the empty corridor. The last person I needed to see right now, thought Aggie. "What's up?" she asked as her plump friend caught up with her.

"Haven't you heard?" puffed Betty breathlessly. Her overstuffed frame fairly trembled with the news. "The board's standing firm on their initial offer. The ATA demands they submit to arbitration within the week or we all walk."

"Oh, Betty, not now," said Aggie, annoyed.

"Whaddya mean, not now!" sputtered Betty. She was not getting the response she sought. "They're gonna call a strike," she wheezed, nearly shouting.

"It'll never happen," retorted Aggie. "Not here. Up North, where I come from, maybe, but after what happened last time they tried it, never! This faculty is far too meek."

"Don't count on it this time," warned Betty, stamping her foot for emphasis. She waddled away down the hall.

Aggie made her way toward the open courtyard and the

65

faculty dining room. The rain had begun, and the palms in the patio were being drenched with torrential force. She wished for the umbrella she'd left in the trunk of the car. She'd almost decided the sandwich wasn't worth the trip when she heard a sound like a baby. From where? she wondered, looking down the empty corridor. Then again, softly, like a sound of weeping . . . from the girls room?

She cautiously pushed open the swinging metal door. The bleak interior was a surrealistic study in filth and debris. The contents of the metal garbage can, which was lying on its side, had been strewn across the sodden, smelly floor. One of the toilets sounded an uninterrupted rush of running water. Rain pelted the fly-streaked, steel-meshed windows, but no smoke rose from the stalls, no one vied for space at the small, cracked mirror above the sink. The place was empty. She turned to go, then she heard it again, a whimper above the storm that howled outside.

She inched her way inside, fearful, remembering the threat in Ernie's eyes. Then she saw it. Red . . . in the puddle at her feet.

"Blood?" she gasped.

A freckle-faced cherub with a baby's sleeping face, lay semi-nude and semi-conscious on the floor of the last stall. What appeared to be her dress was stuffed in the toilet, fetid water soaking her face, which bled profusely from an open wound across her cheek. The cups of her bra had been cut away, exposing her small breasts through two gaping holes.

"Oh my dear God!" she gasped. "Help, somebody . . . E-Z . . . Oh, God!" she shrieked, running with a clatter of high heels on the slippery, granite floors.

DING DONG BELL
SOME OF US LIVE IN HELL
THE BOYS AND GIRLS ARE GATHERED 'ROUND
MAYBE THEY'LL BURN THE SCHOOLHOUSE DOWN.
THE BLOOD OF THEIR VICTIM WATERS THE GROUND . . .

Red fingers of light pierced the window from the ambulance backed up to the east gate of the school yard.

"Brian, pull the shade please!" Aggie called in a voice devoid of feeling. "Judy, come away from the window." Drop the curtain, turn your head, thought Aggie. Maybe they're right. Pretend it didn't happen and it'll all fade away and we can go on with the show.

"Who is it, Ms. Hillyer?" someone asked as the slicker-garbed attendants hoisted the stretcher into the vehicle idling on the rain-soaked lawn.

"Anybody get her name?" asked someone else as the shade came down to shut out the grizzly view. The red light pried its way past the ragged edges of the blind like blood seeping from a wound.

"What does it matter!" said another. "She was just white trash."

"Didn't know enough to stay where she belonged! Dumb-ass cunt messin' with a blood. Maybe now them honkies'll get the message and stay up north where they belong!"

"Black boy's whore," said a white student.

"Stop it!" she yelled, unable to absorb anymore on her battered senses. "I've prepared something special for our class today," she began, her voice flat and numb. She focused on their faces; they all looked unfamiliar.

She swallowed and tried again.

"Just let me take roll, and we'll get started . . ." There was an awful hurting in her throat. The monster with the thirty heads sat silent. She suddenly found herself in a roomful of strangers. She struggled to remember the familiar words. "A friend of mine at the university has put together this slide show . . ."

"Aren't we gonna work today?"

"I gotta finish a project."

"About Vincent Van Gogh . . ."

"Whatever happened to good ol' Vincent?" yelled a voice from the back.

"He killed himself," she said.

DING DONG BELL
IT'S FRIDAY, AIN'T THAT SWELL?
IT'S 3:00 P.M. AND SCHOOL IS OUT,
LET'S ALL RAISE HELL!

"How do you live with it every day?" she asked Bob. "How do you swallow all that senseless violence?"

"We peace officers are trained to handle these situations, ma'am," he said drily.

She laughed, then worrying it again like a terrier, she persisted. "Do you think it's true, Bob? That violence feeds violence?"

"Sure," he cracked. "But only among the bad guys. The good guys kiss a horse, jump a dame, and ride off into the sunset."

"Can't you get serious?" she pouted.

"I'm working on a very serious hard-on," he teased, embracing her impatiently. The rain drummed a steady beat on the glass wall that spanned her second-story balcony. Soft shadows played across the ceiling from the candle that flickered on the glass cocktail table. He rolled her in his arms to the edge of the sofa to retrieve his half-filled wine glass, offering it to her lips before he drank.

"Sure is tough trying to score with a woman with 150 kids!" he complained.

She laughed and stretched her body close to him against the length of the sofa. "No more kids!" she said pressing her cheek to the crisp, dark tendrils on his naked chest. "The kids are gone for the night." She embraced him tenderly. Her trimly tailored robe slid open, exposing an enticing expanse of naked thigh. "The kids are at a football game 'cross town, battering each other muddy and bloody in the rain." She nibbled his ear invitingly. "And Mama Bear and Papa Bear can stay and play house."

Bob's free hand disappeared under the soft wool of the bathrobe, and he turned his head to sip the kisses she delivered to his lips.

"Alone at last," he murmured, devouring her mouth.

"The phone," she said, his tongue blocking her words.

"Hum-m-m?" he asked, without interest.

"It's my phone," she repeated, forming the words deliberately against his teeth.

"Don't answer it" he suggested, still holding her.

"Don't turn a page," she said, rising, the wool robe gaping wide. "I don't want to lose my place."

"Hurry up!" he called as she raised the receiver to her ear. "The condition I'm in, I won't last long!"

68

"Oh, Pete . . . hi," he heard her say.

Bob groaned from the sofa. She shot him an impatient look, then her face changed.

"What?" . . . Where are you? How? . . . Who?"

"You sound like a hoot owl," hooted Bob from the sofa, refilling his glass. "Hurry on home to papa, shug," he teased, extending his open arms toward her.

"Yeah, Pete! Thanks for calling."

She hung up the phone and came toward him, slowly.

"That was Pete Santini from school," she said.

"I had that figured out. Jesus Christ, Aggie! I'm trying to make out."

Her face registered fear and shock and horror and pain.

"What happened?" he asked, suddenly serious.

"Another accident. Hank Lawler, our assistant principal. You know him—the dirty old man who drinks too much." She sat down beside him. "You know, just the other day some of us were having lunch together in the faculty dining room . . ."

He wrapped her shoulder protectively with his arm.

"We all got to talkin' about the union negotiations, and our benefits, and retirement, and Hank made a crack about how he didn't much care 'cause he'd never live to collect his."

"Yeah?" he urged, sensing her need to talk.

"He's dead, Bob. Hank Lawler's dead."

"Holy shit!" he exclaimed, rising. "What happened?"

"Someone shot him at the football game," she whimpered. "Pete said he was shot by a—nigger!" she choked on the word. "Bob," she said timidly, in her small-girl voice.

"Yeah, shug. What is it?"

"How do you know when you've reached a point of emotional overload?"

He pulled her protectively into his arms. "Honey, the baby's cryin' an' I think it's my turn to go," he said. By the time she followed him into her bedroom he was dressed in his uniform, strapping his leather holster to his hip. She didn't have to ask where he was going.

"Call the station, tell them I've gone over to the high school on the south side to lend a hand before all hell breaks loose. They'll put some extra cruisers on the street.

69

I'm off to school, shug!" he kissed her hurriedly as she ushered him out into the dark and the rain.

She stood mute while tears traced shining paths across her shell-shocked face.

7

Monday. It was not yet noon by the clock overhead when the dismissal bell sounded, bringing to an abrupt close her last class of the day.

"Joyce, Charlene, I want you girls to wash those brushes. Alan, please remember to wipe that desk. Don't anybody leave till you put your chairs up so Mr. Farley's crew can clean these floors."

Aggie stood watching from the window as they rushed to board the buses lined up in front of Arcadia's main gates.

The flag that flew from the pole at the center of the cement island on the east lawn was drawn down to half staff, an ignominious symbol of the tragedy that had befallen them, but the students hurling themselves into the buses paid it no attention at all. The joy generated by an unexpected afternoon off was far more relevant and real than the lamentable event for which it was granted.

Dark clouds were gathering on the far horizon as Aggie raised the pole hook to close the transom. Rolling up her sleeves, she turned her attention to the task of cleaning up the wreckage of her last class. The tables still weren't very tidy, there were still paint cans and brushes piled up in the sink. She made a mental note to tighten up on her class monitors. She'd been spending too much time on janitorial duties. Thank heaven for good ol' Farley, who always managed to slip her some extra towels and cleanser.

The room was unnaturally quiet, as it always was when the kids were gone.

She was standing on a counter top stapling students' work to the large, burlap-covered bulletin board on the back wall when a sudden peel of thunder racked like a gun shot, shaking the room. She felt the wall tremble beneath her hands and found herself leaning into it as if by force of will she'd hold the building up.

"Even surrounded by the works of your prodigies, you are a work of art, Aggie." Gomez's face appeared in the door.

"Nandy. C'mon in."

He lifted a hand to help her down. "How about a hot cup of coffee?" she asked as he followed her into the Cave.

"I came to ask you to share a Taco Bell burrito on the grass, my darling, but the gods have not favored us," he said in his heavy accent.

"The gods have not favored us very much lately. It's as bad a day for a picnic as for a funeral," answered Aggie, setting out two plastic cups of coffee on a packing crate. "A little girl gets gang-raped by a pack of alley cats because she dated across the color line, a vice principal shows up late for a game without his gate pass and gets killed for it . . . Jesus Christ. I get this scary feeling that it's all a part of an escalating pattern of violence."

"Hank was drunk. He was nasty when he was drunk," said Gomez.

"I don't doubt it. He probably baited that man. I was in the faculty lounge one day when E-Z nearly took a swing at him, and E-Z's the patron saint of patience. He kept referring to E-Z and his entire race as 'you boys'."

"He didn't like Latinos very much, either. Every time I see him in the hall, he say, 'Hey, señor, how's our gay caballero?' You know, in that big loud voice of his."

They both laughed.

"The little girl, she was in your class?" he asked, sipping his coffee.

"Till last Friday. I got a memo this morning from Rita in guidance. Her father's a big-shot liberal lawyer who's launched himself into the community political arena."

"His beliefs led her to offer her innocence to a black lover?" His oddly worded observation presented a perspective she hadn't considered. Gomez was more apt to see the inherent danger of choosing the wrong lover.

"If they did, the situation didn't present a moral dilemma of a magnitude to keep him from suing. Paternal outrage obviously has a price."

"The child will recover?"

"They'll stitch and bandage her, but I don't think her wounds will ever really heal. Christ, Nandy, you had to have seen it to believe that these children can be so vicious. Left her sitting in the toilet stall propped in a puddle of her own blood. Norma said those shears were the ones ripped off from the Home Ec. room."

"She was a victim of the war."

"You mean a civil war? A race war?" she asked. An unusual chill prevaded the room as the sound of the rain rattled the windows.

"A revolution. I am no philosopher, Aggie, but I think the world is in a state of constant evolution. And this evolution takes place as a series of small revolutions, just as the earth rotates, and each in its time like the seasons of the moon. Each turn of the earth sees yet another revolution—nation to nation, state to state, school to school, and finally, man to man.

"When war came to my country, it began in the universities. It is the students, the youth with their brains and genitals aflame that spur us toward our destiny."

"Not if they all commit Hara-Kiri," said Aggie. "If we have any influence on their inflamed brains we ought to be smart enough to keep them from hurting each other."

"This is a difficult time, a critical time. A young man comes of age and there is no rite of passage that will prove his manhood. If you bring strangers of another color to their territory, you give them a way. The oldest way—that of the warrior, the hero who vanquishes the enemy and rapes and plunders and enjoys the spoils of war."

"What are we supposed to do, Nandy? Sit and watch it happen?"

"We do what we must. We do all that we can. Because, my darling, somebody must. And when our hearts become too heavy with sorrow we must turn away our eyes and go on . . ."

"Nandy," interrupted Aggie, breathless. "I've been getting this nightmare—it's always the same. I'm running through the hallways of the school, flinging open doors numbered consecutively in descending order. Each of the doors leads nowhere. Finally I run out of doors. I have this unholy apprehension that we're running out of time."

"Each of us runs from our own demons, Aggie. My

shrink says I run from my nightmares in the refrigerator, where there is always a light, day or night, and food which comforts me like my mother's milk. This very expensive doctor says I am so fat because I build a wall of flesh around me to hide in, because I am ashamed of what I am. And because I hate my mother, and so deny her grandchildren."

"That's ridiculous," said Aggie. "I know from the things you've told me how much you love your mother."

"That's right! It is because I also love to eat, I am so fat," he said, chuckling.

Another bone-jarring flash of thunder and lightning touched down close enough to make the lights flicker off for an instant. A heavy downpour hammered like a drumroll on the windows.

"I know Hank went to heaven, even so. He spent all his life loading up so he could piss on us at his funeral. You want to go with me?" he queried. "I'll drive. That little skate you roll around in will be up to its flip-top in this flood."

"I'm not going," answered Aggie. "I hate funerals, and I'm sick to death of this whole Hank Lawler thing. Bob spent all weekend on the case. The papers were full of it Sunday. I'd feel like a hypocrite sitting there listening to them eulogize him. Besides, I could use the time to ctach up on a lot of paper work—grades, a supply order, another week's worth of lesson plans for the Beast of Arcadia."

"She's making you do lesson plans? Since when?"

"Since that day she sent me home to change my sweater and I cut out on her. Nobody knew what to do with my kids. They all work on contracts. Well, not all of them. Just the ones I feel can be trusted to work with a minimum of supervision. But that's still a lot of activity going on. No wonder I always feel like I'm living in an amusement park."

"If it was always amusing, eh? Why must your man work all weekend? They have the man who killed Hank."

"The guard's gun, Nan. They never found the gun. Bob was there when one of my kids called about it. He was one of the first officers on the scene. He said the guard had time to stash it, if he didn't take it too far. Guard claims he dropped it on the ground, but the police and sheriffs deputies spent all weekend scouring the building and grounds and haven't turned it. All the witnesses came on the scene after the fact. No one actually saw the shooting."

Gomez went gray. "I seen it," he said. "I was witness to the shooting. I been fighting the closet wars with Randy. I have enough, I walk away, I go to the game. I am unhappy. The rain starts and I leave, in the middle of the first quarter. As I approach the gate, Hank is facing me and shouting and swearing and waving his umbrella." Gomez demonstrated visually, gesturing as though about to swing a baseball bat.

"Then the black man turn and go to his car. He take something from inside, and Hank is, how you say, crashing the gates."

He stopped for breath; she nodded compliance, urging him on.

"Then I see the guard, looking for something in his car. And just in the moment when Hank walk by him, the black man pull the trigger. Blam! In an instant. Done. And I am standing alone in the parking lot looking into the eyes of a man who is holding a gun. Hank is lying very still on the ground. I run like a rabbit. I run and do not stop to look behind me. I read in the paper that it is an accident. Aggie, the witnesses could not have seen the gun go off by accident. He killed Hank in cold blood, and when the shot was fired, I think this is wrong. Who is this man to me? Would this black man say justice was done because I call him a murderer? Or would he hate all of my people because his family go on welfare when he go to jail? I go tell what I see that night, they ask me how I sleep the other nights, I don't want anyone looking in my bedroom. I could loose my job, my life. And this racist gringo, he would have stood up for me? He would defend his 'gay caballero'? I do not lie to my priest or to my friends. I am a scholar, not a hero. When I find out, in Havana, they come to arrest me because I am teaching subversive ideas to my students, I leave my old mother alone, I run to America . . . I am not a brave man."

Another blinding light so strong it left an after image on the retina flashed briefly on the darkened sky, and took the power out with it for a second time. They were suddenly sitting in almost total darkness.

"Hold my lighter for a minute, Nandy," she said, groping on their makeshift table top. "I've got some candles in one of these cabinets." The cold remains of her coffee spilled over her hand as she found the lighter and extended it toward him in the dark.

"Here I am, alone with a beautiful woman . . . Ah, Aggie," he sighed. "If I was any kind of a man I would throw you to the floor and ravish you."

She found the candles and extended one toward the lighter he held. As the candlelight showed her his mournful face, she reached to squeeze his hand.

"A real man doesn't have to prove himself by assaulting a woman," said Aggie.

The lights came on with such a start they both jumped.

"Ah, good! Now I do not leave you alone in the dark. I leave you, to do the last thing anyone can do for Hank: Pay my respects and put him in the ground."

8

With her short skirt askew and her long, lovely legs gracefully arranged across the bench at the bus stop, Sheila Morrow focused her burnt almond eyes on the page of the blue-ruled notebook in her lap.

A big blue Buick cruised by, and a middle-aged man in a business suit leaned across the passenger seat to call out.

"You lookin' for a ride, sister?"

Without breaking the intensity of her concentration, Sheila sat posed as breathlessly beautiful as a Gauguin canvas.

"I ain't lookin' to go no place wit' you, mother fuck!" she yelled. The drawing taking form under her intense absorption could have been a self-portrait. It was a rendering of an ebony-skinned goddess in a white gown patterned on the style of a Grecian toga.

"C'mon, you little cunt," shouted the man in the Buick. "Don't flash that snatch in the middle of the street an' say it ain't for sale. How much?"

"More than you got, sucker," yelled Sheila.

"Cunt!" shrieked the man as he gunned the Buick.

She looked up in time to read the bumper sticker on the back of the car. It said 'Have you hugged your kid today?'

"Bastid!" she spat as the car sped away and realized for the first time there was someone behind her.

"Pride," she smiled, shoving the notebook into her oversized purse. "I been waitin' for ya, honey."

"Ya ain't been waitin' long enough, girl. You jes' turned down a trick."

"I was afraid I'd miss you, honey," said Sheila, leaping to her feet. " 'Sides, I already got your money fo' you."

She offered him a roll of bills and a dazzling smile.

79

"Either you holdin' out on me, girl, or you ain't workin' hard enough."

"I needed some things, Pride. A girl's gotta look good to get the good dates. A girl's gotta have clothes."

"You gotta buncha balls, girl, turnin' down tricks an' askin' fo' mo' bread," said Pride, pocketing the bills.

"Hey, listen, baby," squeaked Sheila. "I'm lookin' out for you. You don't want folks on the strip sayin' Pride don' take care a' his wimmin."

Was he buyin' it? She was about to hit him for an advance. If she didn't score some speed she'd never get up for school tomorrow.

"Listen, honey," she began to explain about the pills. "I need another three hundred—"

"You jus' blew it on clothes, girl. They ain't no more cash in yo' account this week."

"I'm the one been humpin' ugly old pricks for that dough! You can spare a few hunnert ev'ry now and then and never miss it. Jes' stick a little less of it up your nose."

"You would deny yo' man a little snow to cool his hot head, girl?" asked Pride as Sheila fingered the fourteen-karot coke spoon twinkling almost inconspicuously among the gold that circled his smooth brown neck.

"Don't I buy you pretty things?" cooed Sheila. "Don't I treat you right?"

"When I keep on ya', Sheila girl," sneered Pride. "I shouldn't have to watch you all the time. I like to know my ladies are loyal."

"I am, baby," she lied. "But I am also the one who lays my body down for all them potbellied ol' honkies with bad breath and veins showin' all ovah! And that's worth a lot mo' than I'm gettin'."

"You gonna get exac'ly what you deserve, bitch!" snarled Pride, delivering a deflating blow with his fist to Shelia's groin that doubled her over and made her sob. "OK, goddammit. Get your act together and get back to work."

"I'm gonna go on home," cried Sheila. "I got homework . . ."

"School's out, girl. Out here you take care a' business. You get straightened out and you take Pride," he beamed, pulling her into his arms and raising her face to look into her streaming dark eyes. "And Pride gonna love you and look after you."

Yeah, she thought. Take care of me my ass, you mother-fuckin' cocksuck'! I seen how you take care a' me. Clutching her belly, she doubled over on her knees on the sidewalk and vomited once, then again. She raised herself to her feet and watched Pride pull his ancient Olds away from the no parking zone in the bus stop. Sheila Morrow walked painfully home to the projects with blood trickling from her womb.

9

Under Bob's loving hand "The Officer's Lady" leapt across the water almost airborn.

With her sleek black nose high out of the water and her 455 Olds engine wailing a siren's song, she assaulted each advancing wave like a filly jumping fences. At about twenty knots the choppy surface of the river was as hard as cement. The impact of each white cap lifted the boat like a bucking bronc, threatening to throw Aggie from her seat astride Bob's shoulders. Aggie wound her legs more securely against his armpits and felt Bob's biceps tighten reassuringly. His coarse dark hair rubbed against the insides of her thighs; her breasts heaved with the craft's each rise and fall, straining the brief strip of spandex of her bikini. They whooped and waved to the bathers along the shore as Bob aimed the twenty-foot black bullet like a gunsight along the length of the Arcadia to the basin where the river spilled into the sea.

Aggie drew a cool, foamy sip from the beer can she was holding and bent forward to offer him a belt.

"Oh, shit," she shrieked against his ear, pressing the beer can into his hand. "I've got to dismount."

"Not now," Bob yelled, straining to be heard above the motor and the wind. "What's the matter?" He set the beer can snugly between his legs and guided the boat effortlessly under the causeway overpass, following the marker bouys along the channel.

"That last bump broke my strap," answered Aggie.

She felt his body shake with laughter, trembling against her thighs with the boat's vibration. Her skin was slick with perspiration and her sunglasses kept sliding down her nose.

"Take it off," he shouted, his words whipping away in the wind. "We're nearly there."

She glanced back over her shoulder to where Mitzi and Joe were necking on the bench seat in the stern. Mitzi was on her back, spread out vividly against a big green beach towel, her green-lidded eyes shut tight against the sun. But Joe looked up in time to see Aggie's bra drop uselessly to her waist while she clutched to cover herself with one hand and pressed the back of Bob's head against her pelvis with the other.

Bob slowed the motor and eased the boat carefully through the shallows of a small sandy reef that rose no more than five feet out of the water at its highest point.

She slid off his shoulders as the engine died and fell across his lap.

"Grab me a towel, will you?" asked Aggie. "I've got a problem."

"The only problem you got is me, shug," answered Bob. "I can't keep my hands off ya."

"Joe's watching us," she whispered, struggling to release herself.

"Joe's been my partner and my best friend for the last five years, I can't remember ever doin' anything Joe hasn't seen me do at one time or another."

"Well, he hasn't seen *me* in this condition," whispered Aggie, wriggling unconvincingly in his arms.

"He can look all he wants," he murmured, his lips close against her ear. "But friend or no"—he caught her earlobe in his teeth—"I'll break the arm of any other man who lays a hand on you." Then in a single, startling gesture, he flung her out of his arms and set her on her feet. Standing bare-chested and embarrassed for an excruciatingly long moment, Aggie dove for a pile of clothing lying behind the seat and rummaged for something to cover herself. The first feasible thing she found was Bob's t-shirt.

"Great galloping Gazangas," yelled Joe, picking his head up. "I died and went to heaven. I'm surrounded by boobs."

"What's the matter?" whined Mitzie, trying to roll Joe's weight off her chest and sit up.

"Aggie's bra didn't make the voyage," laughed Bob as she pulled his shirt over her head. "You wanna give me a hand with that line, ol' buddy?"

Joe pulled himself together and jumped the side into the shallows.

"Don't be embarrassed, honey. I'll take my top off too if it bothers you," said Mitzi in her nasal voice. "Actually, you've got very nice titties for a teacher."

"I beg your pardon," said Aggie, dumbfounded.

"Well, when Joe told me you were a teacher, well, I mean, you're not exactly what you expect a teacher to look like, if you know what I mean."

"No," answered Aggie, more amused than annoyed. "You mean you thought I wouldn't have tits 'cause I'm a teacher?"

"Well, maybe not such nice ones," said Mitzi. "Are they your own?"

"Are they what?" Aggie was incredulous.

"I had mine *augmented*," proclaimed Mitzi proudly. She untied her hot pink bra top and exposed her "augmented" breasts for Aggie's approval. "Kids in school used to tease me," she explained. "They used to say 'itzy bitsi titsi Mitzi'." She recited the sing-song phrase. "I used to get so mad, well, I'd just cry all the time . . . but no more." She cupped them lovingly with each hand. About the size of cantalopes with saucer-sized tits, Mitzi's breasts stood at proud attention, defying gravity.

"What was it you said you did?" asked Aggie, not certain she'd ever been told.

"Oh," giggled Mitzie, untying a black bandana to unfurl a shock of bright red, perm-curled hair. "I'm a dancer. I dance down at the Pussycat. You know, that big place on the strip where all the waitresses wear those cute little ears?"

Joe cut loose with an appreciative whistle, and Bob just stared as they finished securing the boat.

"I'm a featured dancer," boasted Mitzi as Joe came around to lift her out. "I bet you could get a job there."

"I doubt it," answered Aggie drily.

"Aw, don't be modest," said Mitzi. "I could put a word in with Conrad, the owner. I bet it pays a lot more than teachin'."

"What was that all about?" asked Bob as Aggie handed him a duffel bag of gear over the side.

"Nothin' at all."

"Wait here while I stow this stuff ashore. I'll be right back for you."

"Bullshit," answered Aggie, swinging her bare legs over the side. "I can get there on my own two feet." He offered his free arm to steady her.

"There *is* something to be said for femininity," he chided. 'Why don't you let me *do* for you, more."

"You mean act like a helpless simp so you can feel like a hero?"

"Something like that," he answered, slinging down the duffel bag.

"We're both above that sort of thing." Aggie pulled a blanket from the duffel and he helped her spread it on the sand.

"Don't be so sure. *I'm not*," said Bob. She looked up to see him looming above her. She kept forgetting what a great-looking guy Bob was. Crisp, dark body, hair peppered his barrel chest and full, muscled legs. A swath of white swimsuit encircled his well-rounded butt and tight belly; the fly was rising with the beginning of an erection.

"You're beautiful when you're mad," she teased.

"God, it's hell being a sex object," he winked, picking up the cue. He rolled onto the blanket beside her. Grabbing up her hand, he pressed it to his white-sheathed shaft and said, "Why don't you come here and take care of this for me?"

"That's a big negatory, good buddy," she answered, pulling away. She unpacked a radio and another six-pack from the duffel bag. "It was Mitzi's tits got you hot and bothered," teased Aggie. "Go get her to come finish the job."

"Her type a' woman doesn't do a thing for me," he said, staring into her agate eyes.

"That's a bunch a meadow muffins," she chirped, chuckling. "Remember when Sheila flashed you? That was one of your best nights in a whole string a' winners. The whole time we were makin' it *I* was grateful to *Sheila*."

He pulled her into his arms with an appreciative smile. "Sheila," he remembered. "Wasn't she the little black whore we picked up that night?"

"You watch yo' mouth, boy," said Aggie. "You're talkin' about Arcadia's next homecomin' queen."

"You're jivin' me! I've seen you pull off some shit, Aggie

86

Hillyer, but I don't believe you're running a professional prostitute for Arcadia's homecoming queen."

"The hell I'm not! My club's sponsoring her."

"Christ, she is without a doubt the most beautiful piece a' black ass I ever set eyes on, I'll give ya' that! But homecoming queen? Honey, even you can't pull *that* off."

"Why not? You just said she was beautiful."

"Because homecoming queens are supposed to be more than just pretty, shug."

"Her grades qualify her, Bob. She meets all the stated requirements. She wasn't gonna do it at first. I don't know why she changed her mind, but—"

"Aggie, let me explain this to you again. There are two types of women, in the broadest sense—" He chuckled, discovering the pun. "Homecoming queens are supposed to be imbued with those virtuous qualities of the girl next door. Sheila is a knockout, granted, but—"

"Why, you male chauvinist pig," sputtered Aggie. "What do you mean, two kinds of women? You mean those that screw and those who don't?"

"No, shug, now, calm down. There are women who are cunts. Nothin' else, just cunts. And then there's women like you who got a head on their shoulders and somethin' more to offer a man," he smiled, sweetly sincere.

"And you feel a woman's worth is measurable in terms of what she's got to offer a man?"

"You're gettin' this all screwed up, shug."

"No, you're all screwed, Bob. You're a fantastic fuck, but your head is all screwed up. That's what it's all about with Sheila. If just once in her short miserable life I can get her to think of herself as something more than just a cunt, she'd have a chance. But that child has been taught since she was just a baby that her entire value and her sole worth was just being a cunt."

"Goddammit, Aggie, you get so wound up in those kids of yours, I feel like I'm datin' the ol' woman in the shoe. Look, a man isn't a man without a woman to love. And a woman doesn't become a woman till she gives herself to a man. That's the way it is," said Bob, opening his arms to her.

She resisted the temptation, knowing she had not yet made her point.

87

"Come on, shug. I don't want Joe and Mitzi to hear us fightin'. We're supposed to be here to have some fun."

She came to him, resigned. She had not yet found the way to make him understand, but she would accept his abundant devotion.

"I wonder where they went?"

"Who?" asked Bob, fondling her under his shirt.

"Joe and Mitzi, who else?" asked Aggie.

"They're over the next dune, makin' out," he answered.

"Do you know that woman has built a career on her synthetic boobs?" smiled Aggie ironically.

"See there?" he exhalted. "That's what I meant. Mitzi doesn't have much sense and not a lotta education. So she makes a livin' off her ass, and parties down spreadeagled on her back. I got me a certified intellectual with a body that won't quit, and I'm sittin' here havin' this discussion about women's liberation."

"That's right," she yelled, glowing red in the reflection of Bob's back-up lights. "No, no, not right. Left, take it a little to the left."

"Make up your mind, dammit," yelled Bob. "I gotta have the time to turn the wheel the other way." He eased the boat and trailer into the slip he rented in the lot behind his apartment house.

"OK," she shouted. "That's about got it."

Alighting from behind the wheel of the wine-colored Chevy, Bob unhitched the trailer, then parked the car in the reserved space near his door.

She didn't know what time it was, but she knew it was late when they dropped off Joe and Mitzi. By the time they'd hosed down the boat and put it away, another couple of hours had passed.

"Good God, it must be late," she muttered. "You may have Monday off, but I've got to be at work at 8:05 tomorrow."

"You brought another outfit, didn't you?" asked Bob as they unloaded their junk.

"One I hope will pass," she sighed, grabbing a cooler and a stack of wet towels from his arms. "But I really ought to go on home and get some sleep."

"You'd get a bit more sleep if you pass up the trip and

88

bed down here," he answered, tucking a couple of bundles under each arm and leading her to his door.

"I never get any sleep in your bed," she laughed. "You're such an animal."

His apartment was unimaginatively furnished in browns and naugahyde. A stereo system and a large color TV dominated the living room and a king-sized waterbed with a mirrored backdrop, the bedroom.

"What do you mean, animal?" said Bob, defensively. "After not seeing you for nearly two weeks I spend the whole day with you, hump you one time, and I'm an animal? Joe and Mitzi just met and they hardly came up for air."

He dropped the garbage he was carrying in the middle of the floor and, sweeping her easily into his arms, he carried her to the waterbed.

"What if I oversleep?" she worried.

"It'll be one of the toughest things I've ever had to do," he answered, searching for her lips in the cool dark of his bedroom. "But I promise to kick you out of my bed by six-forty-five. That'll get you there in plenty of time."

"The 'Vette's giving me a problem turning over in the morning. I'm gonna' have to get up early to start the car," she protested, returning his kiss. Their mouths were salty and their bodies grainy as he pulled her against him in the rolling lap of the waterbed.

"I'll jump you now and jump-start your car in the morning," he whispered, groping for her in the darkness. "All the more reason to stay with me. I can take care of ya."

"If I wasn't so stoned, I wouldn't let you talk me into this," sighed Aggie with mounting passion as he peeled away the last of her gritty clothing.

By the time she laid her heavy head against his shoulder and closed her weary eyes, the clock face on Bob's nightstand read a quarter after four.

10

One of the most punishing ordeals ever endured by the body human is to roll out of the warm arms of an indulgent lover into the cold, gray reality of one's job. It would be interesting to know just what percentage of the nation's work force reports on any given Monday hung over and burnt out.

Her eyes red-rimmed and her temples throbbing, Aggie worked the combination lock on her mailbox. Balancing an unwieldy sheaf of intraschool junk mail, she bounded into the crowd of kids in the corridor, and dashed like a demon for her door.

It was already open.

She was still fifty yards away when the tardy bell rang and Martha's voice crackled across the PA with the daily ritual.

I PLEDGE ALLEGIANCE . . .

She could hear it being recited from every classroom door as she rushed apprehensively down the hall.

Had Muriel had to start her class? Had anyone else? In which case it might as well have been Muriel, for she would surely hear of Aggie's tardiness. Christ, what a way to go into Monday. She wouldn't even get a chance to plug in the coffee pot.

TO THE FLAG . . .

The door of her room stood open. She could hear her class sing-songing the familiar words. How the hell did they get in?

She'd been busted for sure. The only other key to her room was in the office. Was it Muriel standing now before her class?

She slipped noiselessly into her room.

91

OF THE UNITED STATES OF AMERICA . . .

Unobtrusively dropping her things onto the paper clutter on her desk, she surveyed the room.

Two boys were only now rising to their feet, having noted her presence.

Several other students, seeing her, suddenly came to attention.

But to her relief and unending gratitude, Aggie discerned there was not an adult in attendance.

AND TO THE REPUBLIC . . .

Everything had begun exactly as it should.

As Martha's voice faded on the intercom, Pete Santini poked his head out of the Cave and, seeing Aggie, disappeared behind the Dutch doors to emerge in an instant with a steaming mug of coffee.

"Hey, Hilly," smiled Pete, handing her the mug. "Why don't you go in the Cave and drink this while I read the morning bulletin?"

"I'll take the roll, Ms. Hillyer," said a girl named Sandy.

She took the coffee gratefully from Pete's hand and headed for the Cave.

It was a beautiful thing for a teacher to discover her class had almost unanimously attained a level of respect and responsibility sufficient to start the day without her. She was proud . . . of them and of herself. She was also grateful they'd covered for her.

At the passing bell, the students filed out in noisy profusion. Pete appeared at the door, his bright face a singular smile.

"Hey, Hilly, it must a' been a hard day's night. You look like shit," said Pete, noticing her red-rimmed eyes.

"The first thing I want to do is thank you," said Aggie.

Pete grinned, feigning modesty.

"The second thing is," she continued, "I want to know how the hell you got in here."

"There ain't a lock I can't open," he grinned smugly. "I'm known as 'the finger', remember?"

"Pete, this time you bailed me out, and I don't want you to think I don't appreciate it, but one of these days . . ."

"One of these days, we'll all be gone from here, and it won't matter," he answered. "You have a fight with your boyfriend or something?" he asked. "You look like you been cryin' . . . or smokin' dope."

"Watch it now," she warned. Along with a tendency to take charge, Pete had a way of overstepping his bounds.

"Hey, Hilly," he said, "I'm sorry. I can see you're in a bitchy mood. I was just tryin' to help."

"And *please* stop calling me Hilly before it catches on," she pleaded, rolling her bloodshot eyes toward the ceiling.

"Man, you really are in a snit," he grinned, undaunted.

"I'm sorry," she sighed. "I've got a headache."

"Hey," he piped. "I've got a great cure for headaches."

He came up behind her and began to rub the back of her neck. "What are you doing?" she protested.

"Just relax and let me show you," answered Pete. "If you don't relax, it won't work." Leaning her head back in one hand and placing the other firmly under her upturned chin, he suddenly snapped her head almost imperceptably toward her right shoulder. She heard her neck pop in several places.

"Hey, what are you do—" she began, but he held her firmly against his groin. Another quick twist to the right, another series of cricks, and the haze of pain lifted a few inches from behind her eyes.

"Did that help?"

"It really did, a little. Where'd you learn that?"

"Man, I can do about anything with my hands," he answered matter-of-factly.

"I know. You're incredible," smiled Aggie. "Sometimes I just don't believe you."

"That good, huh?" said Pete, smugly. "Hey, listen, Hilly. I wrote myself a pass for this period. I gotta split to hand out posters for Sheila. I want the last thing anybody sees before he heads into that auditorium to be Sheila Morrow's face."

He began gathering up a stack of elegant posters printed in black on silvery mylar with a photoserigraph of Sheila's face.

"Hold it," said Aggie as Pete was about to rush out the door. "Where'd you get the passes?"

"In your desk," answered Pete.

"You broke into my desk?"

"I didn't want to bother you," he replied.

"Pete, you can't go through the building breaking into rooms and desks, forging hall passes," sputtered Aggie.

"Why not?" he asked, as though the notion had never occurred to him.

Her class was filling the room beyond the Dutch door.

"Pete," sighed Aggie, wishing she had the time to explain, "we're gonna have to have a talk real soon." She took out a pad of passes to make out a new one for him. "There's a breach, Pete, that exists between us that is as high as my desk top and as wide as a blackboard. I am your teacher, and you are my student. You must not encroach on that arrangement or take advantage of my fondness for you."

His downcast eyes heaped guilt on her.

"Where did you say you were going?" she asked. "I want to make sure you don't get busted for being out of class with a forged pass."

"All over. I gotta get these up all over. Just sign a blank pass and I'll change the place in pencil when I move."

"Pete," she warned, "I'm trying to keep us both out of trouble."

"Hell, Hilly, I got three more hours till the assembly. Do you want us to get Sheila up there? There are about seventy girls runnin' and they're only gonna pick seven that get a shot at it!"

"Don't strongarm me, Pete," she said calmly, conceding the hall pass. "Or so help me, just to prove who's boss I'll have to slap you down."

"But would you still love me?" he grinned, sheepishly, looking for reassurance.

"Like a mother her wayward child," she answered.

"Yeah. So long, mama," he chirped as he left.

Mr. Feeney was playing with the microphone on stage. He was wearing a mustard-gold leisure suit and a red and yellow polka-dot tie.

It was tradition to wear the school colors the day of a game. It was also customary to suspend the afternoon classes so that students could attend a pep rally in the auditorium—in two shifts, since the pupil population was roughly three times the capacity of Arcadia's ancient auditorium.

It was an unsatisfactory arrangement, since about a third of the students that should have been in assembly for each shift were not going to show up. They would disperse to the porn shop across the street to watch the quarter peep show, or split for McDonald's crammed into all available transportation, or else just hang out in the smoking area until someone caught them smoking home-rolled.

The ones that did make it to the auditorium were expected to scream themselves hoarse at the expert urging of twelve cheerleaders in scarlet skirts and gold-braided tunics, eight baton twirlers in red and gold sequins, and a uniformed brass band.

They stood, en masse, as the band played the national anthem.

E-Z Jordon, whose father had been a Baptist minister, led them in a convocation, his throaty baritone rising over the murmur of the less than reverent crowd.

Then he turned the microphone over to Bo Calloway, who was making one of his rare appearances before the student body for a few opening remarks.

E-Z came down the center aisle to where Aggie stood taking a visual head count of her class. Since attendance was mandatory, it was necessary that teachers take roll and report to the deans the names of those who ditched.

Aggie was standing in the aisle taking roll when E-Z descended the stage and joined her.

"It's almost impossible to get an accurate head count in this place," she complained, entering what she hoped were the names of her truants for her report.

E-Z grunted his agreement while his eyes darted nervously around the enormous room. "Kinda' like tryin' to stick a finger in the dyke to stem the tide, huh?" he sympathized.

Bo looked uneasy in the face of the student's high-spirited restlessness, and soon relinquished center stage to the real star of the show.

They greeted Coach MacCarthy's ascent to the stage with a tremendous ovation. The band broke into a few bars of Arcadia's fight song.

"Thank you, Mr. Calloway . . ." Vance's amplified

voice floated unchallenged above the crowd. "Ladies and gentlemen . . . loyal Lions of Arcadia . . ." He addressed them solemnly, as though calling them to worship. "I want to thank you all for turning out today and expressing your appreciation of our athletes."

They applauded themselves.

"And I'm here to tell you, on behalf of my boys, that we have rewarded your faith with our ultimate effort. We come, unbeaten, to our final game of the scheduled season."

They cheered tumultuously while the cheerleaders worked the aisles shaking their red and gold pompoms.

"He sure puts on a show, doesn't he?" smiled Aggie proudly.

E-Z didn't answer. He stood, stonefaced, his dark, troubled eyes searching the crowd.

"And I mean to tell you," blared Mac's voice from the oversized speakers, "that tomorrow we're gonna' do it again. We're gonna show the Jefferson Chargers who's the best team in the county."

Their cheers set the rafters ringing in the great vaulted chamber, while the bass drum that the Hellions had embellished with a golden lion thundered resonantly against the ceiling.

"E-Z," said Aggie, concerned. "What is it? Is there something wrong?"

"There's a whole lot wrong, honey. Something's so wrong I spent the whole morning trying to talk our beloved principal into calling the game."

She noticed the veins knotting in his neck and temples.

"Calling the—Jesus, E-Z, you can't cancel the homecoming game."

"So I've been told," he snapped. He must have been upset to be so surly and she was suddenly scared. Vance was introducing the finalists who would vie for the title of homecoming queen. Would all their work on behalf of Sheila Morrow pay off? she wondered.

"Why, E-Z?" she pleaded. "Why do you want to cancel the game?"

Vance was calling the candidates to the stage alphabetically.

"Amy Antonelli."

Amy's supporters whistled and cheered as the petite brunette mounted the stairs of the stage.

"Please, E-Z," said Aggie, grabbing his arm.

The stage was filling with the prettiest and most popular of Arcadia's coeds. Vance was up to the M's and there were only two more candidates to be named.

"Elena Martinez," called Vance amidst yet another chorus of squeals and applause.

Aggie had her fingers crossed.

"And our final candidate," said Mac, signaling for silence, "is Miss Sheila Morrow."

The ovation was overwhelming. Sheila Morrow ascended the platform smiling through her tears, the only black candidate in a school where blacks were an ethnic majority.

"Oh, Christ!" exclaimed Aggie, unable to suppress her excitement. "E-Z, she made it. She's got a shot at it. Oh, E-Z, look! They're lovin' it."

Vance was having a hard time being heard. He raised a hand and recaptured their attention as easily as if he'd turned down the volume on the TV set.

"Now that you've met the beauties, friends," continued Mac, "it's time to meet the beasts. You know these guys . . . you've all turned out faithfully every week through all sorts of adversity . . . through the grief we've shared over the loss of our beloved assistant principal, Mr. Henry Lawler . . . through the injuries and hardships our team has sustained . . . you've all been enthusiastic and devoted fans. Now, we aim to take this team, and the name of our school, to the state championships for ya this year."

The students went wild again.

"And these are the boys who're gonna do it for ya," said Vance, preparing to produce his unbeatable football team.

"Shelia's the candidate my art squad is sponsoring," Aggie said to E-Z.

Her happiness had drowned her apprehension momentarily. Suddenly E-Z turned and began striding forcefully up the aisle toward the rear exit. She hurried after him. "Dammit, E-Z, tell me what's going on. You can't just drop a bomb like trying to call off homecoming without telling me why. Me and my kids have been working our butts off for this."

"OK," he acceded as she followed him into his office. "We busted a couple a' kids who'd been dealin' drugs around school this afternoon. As I was interrogating one of them, he started bragging about all the big deals he's set up. Last Monday night he traded half a pound a' Jamacian pot for a .38. We're pretty sure it's the weapon that wasted Hank."

"How the hell did the other guy get hold of it?" gasped Aggie.

"Indirectly, from the guy who first found it at the site. The security guard who shot Hank has claimed all along that he dropped his gun at the scene. The cops have never been able to turn up that weapon."

"I know," she nodded. "Bob was one of the first officers on the scene. They assigned him to the case. I gotta tell him."

"No," snapped E-Z. "I already suggested that to Bo. He don't want no more cops on the campus, and I can't say I blame him, what with the trouble we've had already. They'd have to conduct a locker-by-locker search . . . and I don't think it's in the building."

"You mean you didn't get the gun?" she asked with something akin to terror. "Where is it?"

"Our young entrepreneur traded it for a quarter ounce of cocaine. Who the hell knows where it is by now?" he hissed.

"E-Z," she queried carefully, "who's one of the biggest dealers in the school?"

"I know," said E-Z. "Ernie Nesbitt. He hasn't been in school for the past three days and his mother says she hasn't seen him since last Thursday."

"You think it's Ernie?" asked Aggie.

"I hope not," said E-Z. "That's a very mean dude. But at the current cost of coke, I can't think of too many kids around here who can afford that kinda bread."

By the time Aggie finished cleaning up and closing up her room for the long weekend, she could feel the pain mounting, creeping up the muscles of her neck. She looked forward to the quiet solitude of her own apartment . . . a couple of aspirin, a joint or two, and bed.

Cutting across the courtyard, she saw a familiar figure

sitting, or rather sprawling, spreadeagled on the stone steps, puffing on a Marlboro.

"Cocoa!" exclaimed Aggie, approaching. "What are you doing here? Did you miss your bus?"

The girl had been crying. Red-rimmed eyes glared angrily from the plump, sweat-polished black face.

"I din wanna go on no bus!"

"Well, everyone's gone. How're you planning on getting home?" asked Aggie, concerned.

"I make it," said Cocoa flatly. "When I'm ready."

"Come on, I'll take you home," sighed Aggie dreading the drive through the projects.

She started toward the parking lot but Cocoa made no move to follow. She just sat there, stonefaced, smoking, her books and belongings scattered about her.

"Well, come on," called Aggie. "I'm not gonna offer again."

Cocoa snuffed the cigarette against the sidewalk and gathered up her things.

"Want to tell me about it?" asked Aggie casually as they breezed along in the open car. Huge muddy clouds rolled over the brown, sun-baked landscape.

Cocoa didn't answer, but a tear escaped her left eye as Aggie watched her immobile profile.

"Want to tell me what you're so upset about?" Aggie tried again. Still no response. She rummaged her purse for her cigarettes with her free hand, and shaking one out of the pack, offered it to Cocoa.

"It's Sheila!" said Cocoa, lighting up. "Since she been involved in all this homecommin' stuff . . . she was my bes' friend once." Cocoa blew smoke through a bucktoothed grimace.

"Why should that make a difference?" asked Aggie. "Sheila has a lot on her mind now. You're her friend . . . you should understand . . ."

"I understan'," snapped Cocoa. "I understan' Sheila Morrow think her shit don't stink. I understan' she don't give the time a' day to her ol' frien's no mo'. She all into goin' down for nothin' fo' her football jock, now. Turn raht, here," she ordered.

"What?" said Aggie, executing a right turn deftly.

"You heard me. You done raht!" said Cocoa, confused.

99

"No, about Sheila," pressed Aggie, trying to suppress a smile. "Who's Sheila going with?"

"That big-deal, mighty-ass, oversize back on the football team," snarled Cocoa.

Aggie exulted silently. If anyone could wrench Sheila away from Ernie, Ben Hooper could.

"But she'll get hers too!" said Cocoa, glowering.

"What do you mean, get hers?" Aggie became alarmed.

"Nothin'," snapped Cocoa. "I din't mean nothin'. Turn left theah at that laht!"

"What did you mean, get hers?" repeated Aggie aggressively. "Is Ernie planning something?"

"She'll get hers, is all," spat the girl, looking guilty as hell.

"Is Ernie planning to hurt Sheila?"

Silence. She was no longer crying, but streaming sweat down her face and neck.

"Answer me!" snapped Aggie. "You ditched the end of my class last Friday when that little girl got cut up . . . you usually hang out in that bathroom, Cocoa. Did you see that happen? Were you there?" Aggie's voice was cold as stone.

Cocoa boiled over. "Yeah, I seen it!" she hissed. "I seen it an' I was in on it. An' I'd do it again if I had to! But Pride'll handle it! Sheila belong to Pride, like I do. She be back. He set her straight and she be back where she b'long."

"What is it with you? Why is it you can't stand to see anyone get up on their feet? Your best friend is trying to make something of her life, so instead of following her example and trying to raise yourself up, you try to pull her down again."

"Turn raht again at the corner!" commanded Cocoa.

"Does that make any sense?" yelled Aggie into the wind as she took the corner, the 'Vette's wheels shrieking. "Why don't you take a shot at being somebody?"

"Stop up there! That's it."

Aggie braked the car to a sudden halt. The project apartment looked exactly like Sheila Morrow's place.

"You and Sheila are neighbors, huh?" she asked in a softer voice, no longer competing with the wind.

"We were both born heah," Cocoa answered flatly. "So were my daughters," she added solemnly.

"I didn't know you had kids," smiled Aggie, sensing a crack in the girl's shellacked exterior.

"Twin daughters, two years old," she grinned, her buck teeth flashing for just an instant.

Juat a baby herself, dragging up two kids of her own in a sweltering slum. "Don't you think you owe it to them—to yourself—to try to be somebody?" asked Aggie as Cocoa let herself out of the car. There wasn't time for tact.

"I know who I am," she answered. "I'm not pretty and smart like Sheila. An' she ain't got a coupla kids to support . . . an' a habit!" Cocoa pushed up the sleeve of her sweater. Angry purple welts and blisters were festering on the tracks on her arm.

"Oh my God!" flinched Aggie, repulsed. "What have you done?"

"I'm a junky, teach!" said the girl without apology. "I ain't goin' no place but down. There ain't no way to get out of this shit hole fo' me. Ah'm gonna die here."

"There's places you can go, people who can help you," stammered Aggie.

"Don't go messin' in my life," said Cocoa. "I got enough trouble wit'out you. Thanks for the ride," she yelled over her shoulder as she went up the walk.

Aggie couldn't overcome her squeamishness. Stunned, she pulled out and headed back to her own safe world. Cocoa was among the walking dead, another victim of the poverty and pain of the ghetto. But Sheila and Ben, thought Aggie, maneuvering her way uncertainly through the unfamiliar streets. That couldn't have worked out better if I'd planned it myself.

The ominous threat implicit in Cocoa's conversation rode all the way home with her, and sat heavy on her soul the whole of a long and restless night.

101

11

Thanksgiving Day descended on Avalon, not with the crisp cool of falling leaves and impending snowfall, but with the mind-melting heat of a subtropical swamp.

"Don't you wonder where they get all that energy in this heat?" yelled Aggie to be heard above the din of the crowd.

"Don't ask me, I'm just a kid myself," answered Bob, cradling her protectively with his arm as they climbed the bleachers. The stands were rife with fans garbed in red and gold. The chain-link fence that separated the stands from the playing field was hung with banners in praise of both teams. This was a far-reaching rivalry and the fans had turned out in full force. The best seats were gone, early.

As an ROTC color guard carried Old Glory onto the field, the crowd rose for the national anthem.

Arcadia's cheerleaders, in new costumes, strutted their stuff on the sidelines.

In the press box above the stands, a local celebrity sportscaster was preparing to broadcast the biggest event of the season. The local papers had sent their top sportswriters to cover the game.

On each side of the stadium, the spectators attempted to outdo one another in creating a state of mass hysteria as their champions took their places on the field of battle. Far below her, on the field, Aggie watched Coach McCarthy pace tensely with a walkie talkie pressed to his ear.

The whistle blew and the figures on the field, poised in frozen tableau, suddenly came alive.

The opening kickoff drove the ball deep to the twenty yard line. The Chargers ran it back to the thirty-five, then lost a yard in three downs.

"Man, they're gettin' no place with a runnin' game," said Bob with a ring of admiration for Arcadia's defense.

"Bob, look! Over there, about three rows down in the red and yellow blouse." His eyes found the girl in the blouse, who had her back to them and was obliviously engrossed in an intimate huddle with a curly-haired, bald-faced boy.

"Do I know the kid?" asked Bob.

"Probably not," giggled Aggie incredulously. "But I do. He's a semiliterate greaser named Wayne Ellis. He's in my sophomore homeroom," she explained. "He's only fifteen. Is that vulgar?"

"What's vulgar about being fifteen?" asked Bob as the Charger quarterback faded back to pass.

"I don't mean it's vulgar to be fifteen," explained Aggie. "Just look at what's going on down there."

"Yeah, I know," said Bob. "They're on the Arcadia eight-yard line and it's been uphill all the way. You've sure got to admire those kids . . ."

"No, no, not the game," she scoffed. "I mean what's going on down there in the bleachers."

Wayne embraced the red and yellow blouse, planting lingering kisses on his willing partner as they watched. They never left off long enough to allow her to turn her face to the crowd, but Aggie recognized the profile.

"So?" questioned Bob, unmoved. "So he's a horny teenager scorin' a few points with his girl at a game. So what's so vulgar about that?"

"So his girl is our new librarian," said Aggie, outraged. "That's Dixie, the South shall rise again, Beaumont. She's older than I am. What's she doin' makin' out with a sophomore in public?"

"You mean that's the one you were so jealous of?" he teased.

"Who's jealous?" she answered defiantly.

Suddenly a cry of despair went up around them as the crowd rose to its feet. On the far side of the field, the joy of the opposition wafted across the field.

"Hey, you made me miss the play," complained Bob. "Jefferson just scored."

The clock ran out on the first quarter with an early lead for the Chargers, 7-0.

Neither team made much progress in the second quarter.

As doggedly as bull terriers, the Chargers gained a few yards with an intricate series of passes, but each time they tried to run the ball, they ran into Arcadia's concrete defense. It was becoming apparent that the Boogie Man was stalking the Charger quarterback. It seemed each time he got his hands on the ball, there was Ben Hooper, looming like a bad dream.

"Boy, that poor quarterback is taking a beating," said Bob. "I thought they were gonna have to carry him off the field that time."

As the time ran out on the second quarter the Chargers were still ahead, 7-0.

"You want a drink?" asked Bob as the Chargers gray-garbed band marched onto the playing field.

"Yeah," answered Aggie, "but I'll go for it. The candidates for homecoming queen are getting ready in the girls' locker room. I want to go wish Sheila good luck."

He handed her a bill and she began to work her way down the steps of the bleachers.

Great dark clouds rolled over the azure sky, coloring the halftime landscape in the somber gray of the Jefferson band. Then it was the red and gold of Arcadia that covered the field. The band marched smartly in formation, striking up a crisp fanfare as the officials prepared to announce the winner of the race for homecoming queen.

Wouldn't it be wonderful, Aggie thought, if stories all had happy endings? Wouldn't it be wonderful if Sheila won? Well, she mused, she's won enough to have come this far. She's already found a new man . . . maybe she'll find a new life. This was more than she had dared hope for.

Bo Calloway squirmed under the collective attention from the stands. The speaker system blared, amplifying his discomfort.

Six lovely young girls, all in white dresses, were lined up, nervously patting their hair and their gowns into final perfection.

The seventh was conspicuously absent.

"Where's Sheila?" asked Aggie.

"She the black girl?" asked a cute little blonde. "She's still inside, I think."

With a jolt of apprehension, Aggie ran for the locker room. Following the sound of voices, she made her way to the far end of the large room through a maze of metal lockers to the white-tiled shower room beyond.

There was Sheila, regal and beautiful in a white crepe evening dress that cut a diagonal swath across one shoulder. A narrow gold bracelet worn high on her naked arm gleamed against her coffee and cream skin, and her glossy black hair was piled high on her head like a crown.

But she was not alone. Like a chicken hawk with a sparrow in its talons, Pride's arm was clasped hard around her throat.

"Sheila!" shrieked Aggie, breaking into a run.

"No, Ms. Hillyer!" cried Sheila. "He's got a gun."

Aggie stopped dead in her tracks.

"Now, Ernie," she began, with as much calm as could filter through the terror. "You don't want to do anything you'll be sorry for. That gun has already caused one tragedy."

She inched forward slowly.

"Get outta here and mind your own business," rasped Pride. "This time it *is* a warning, and it's the only one you're gonna' get!"

The thunder of the crowd in the stands rumbled remotely from the field.

"They're probably calling her right now, Ernie," said Aggie, struggling to maintain her composure. "You're never gonna get away with this . . ."

She took another step forward.

Pride raised his hand and a shot rang out, reverberating against the white tile ceiling like an echo chamber.

Sheila screamed. Aggie stood her ground, frozen with fear. Had anyone heard the shot? Please, God, send help.

"OK, teach, move it," said Pride. "We're all gettin' outta here."

Her feet refused to obey. Sheila was sobbing as Ernie began to drag her toward the door.

"I said move, bitch," Pride snarled.

Aggie pushed open the swinging door and headed back toward the maze of lockers beyond, with Pride and his hostage close behind.

"Drop it, bastard," said a familiar voice as the door swung shut behind them.

Pride's weapon clattered to the floor as she and Sheila turned to see Bob, grim-faced and armed, take their tormentor into custody.

"I warned you, boy," said Bob. "You're gonna do some time for this caper." He shoved Pride at a uniformed policeman who pushed through the open door. The crowd that had gathered behind him parted soundlessly as the young cop recited the boy's rights in monotonous liturgy. The only other sound was Sheila's weeping, reverberating against the sterile walls of the empty locker room, and Aggie cooing consolation as to an infant awakened by a nightmare.

"Is it all over?" sobbed Sheila.

"It's all over," murmured Aggie, cradling her protectively on the cold tile floor.

"I lost, didn't I?"

"No, baby," answered Aggie, with an edge of victory in her voice. "You won. You've won more than you'll know, now and for a long time."

"How can you calmly sit there eating a hot dog after what just happened," she asked, rejoining Bob in the bleachers.

"I'm hungry," he quipped. "How's the kid?"

"She'll be okay. I don't know what I'd have done if you hadn't followed me down there," said Aggie with relief as they climbed back up the bleachers. "How'd you know?"

"I didn't," he answered. "But when you didn't come back with my soft drink, I thought you'd run off with my sawbuck."

"Oh, shit!" she whispered, removing the money from her cleavage. "I never got your soda."

He removed a can from each of his jacket pockets and offered her one. "Gimme back my dough," he said with mock seriousness.

"When did we score?" she asked, surprised, as she resumed her seat. The stadium scoreboard recorded the third quarter score seven all.

"We scored when we found that gun," he smiled. "I pre-

107

dict it will figure prominently in the DA's case against the guard that snuffed your venerable Mr. Lawler."

A sudden rush of guilt overtook her. Could she have prevented this if she'd told him what she knew about the gun?

"Too bad about Sheila," he said. "You almost pulled it off, shug."

"She's all right. What's gonna' happen to Ernie?" she asked.

"You and Sheila are gonna' sign complaints and they'll put him away for awhile," he answered. "At least long enough for her to graduate."

"You learn to be grateful for each small reward," she sighed.

Down on the field, the Chargers were kicking off the fourth quarter as the Arcadia team tensed for their final push.

Then the sky opened up. The first drop that hit her face was as large as a quarter, and they came in rapid succession from the sooty sky.

"Christ, it's gonna pour. What else can happen?" asked Aggie of no one in particular.

In an attempt to protect their quarterback, the Chargers were double-teaming Ben Hooper. As the field got wetter, the level of competitive hostility mounted.

The Chargers lined up on Arcadia's 18—fourth down and seven. The Arcadia fans moaned in agony as the ball split the uprights and the clock showed the end of the third quarter.

Arcadia received the Chargers' fourth-quarter kickoff on the thirty-five yard line and ran it back for ten yards. But the next three grimy plays produced a gain of only five yards.

"You want to leave?" Aggie shouted, huddling in her yellow windbreaker.

"Not on your life," Bob answered as Arcadia punted.

The rain rumbled down as the figures on the field churned up the muddy turf beneath their cleats. It was beginning to be difficult to distinguish the numbers on their filthy jerseys.

Not a soul left the stands as the storm gained momentum.

Chain lightning broke open the sky on the far horizon. The thunder that followed rumbled like a locomotive over the open stadium.

With little more than a minute left on the clock, the Charger quarterback rolled out for a play-action pass. Then number 57 broke through the line. Like the Loch Ness monster rising from the depths, Ben Hooper emitted a roar of pure rage and, leveling two backs and a Charger guard, flung himself like a live projectile at the quarterback.

The collision of living flesh and bone cracked across the rain drenched field like a lightning bolt as the fans howled their approval.

For an agonizing moment, the ball rose, spinning like a giant mud pie, suspended over their heads, and came to rest with the accuracy of a bullfrog alighting on a lily pad in the capable hands of Ben Hooper.

"Boogie down, Boogie Man!" came the hysterical command from the stands.

"Yea, yea, all the way," yelled the cheerleaders, their sequins melting in the rain.

And in the end zone, Ben stood with his arms raised victoriously over his head, like Samson in the temple of the Philistines, his torn jersey hanging in shreds from his massive muddy frame.

Arcadia picked up their final point on the kick as the clock ran out and the scoreboard recorded a fourteen-ten win for Arcadia.

The band was playing and the rain still pelting the flooded field as the team raised their coach to their shoulders for the ritual run to the shower room.

And Aggie, proud and overjoyed, watched till they carried him from sight.

12

Steam rose from the wheels of the last car as the Long Island Railroad chugged out of the station.

There was a determination, a quickened pace evident in the crowds that descended the platform, bundled up against the chill wind that moaned across the winter sky.

Aggie wrapped the oversized coat protectively around her and hurried to the parking lot to reclaim her mother's car.

Her breath rose in a misty cloud around her face as she struggled to insert the key into the ignition with frozen fingers. The engine gave a cough of complaint before it caught. She let it run for a moment before she pulled out into the traffic lane and headed for the expressway where the late afternoon traffic was already building toward the rush hour.

She flashed a reminiscent thought to the white 'Vette she'd entrusted to Bob's competent care. Was he, this very moment, free-wheeling it down an open, sunny, Southern highway? It occured to Aggie as she inched the sensible little Pinto through the heavy traffic that perhaps she was homesick for Florida.

But it was the sights and sounds and smells of home that brought her winging northward to the bosom of her family for the holidays. It was good sometimes to touch base with one's heritage, to renew the nostalgic ties that were the root of one's being.

She guided the little car carefully down the very street she'd first ridden on a bike without training wheels . . . danced lightly up the wooden steps of the porch where she received her first kiss from a boy one moonlit autumn night . . . and burst joyfully through the front door of the neat frame house enveloped by the warm, pungent smells of turkey in the oven and hot apple pie.

"Lord, it smells so good in here, it makes your mouth want to come," said Aggie, planting a kiss on her mother's cheek, still girlishly smooth for its years.

But for their coloring, the two women were like a mirror image of one another. But for her mother's close-cropped, silver hair, and porcelain-pale complexion, Aggie was a golden-tressed, sun-bronzed replica of the woman bent over the kitchen table rolling out pie dough.

"Now mind your mouth," chided her mother gently, smiling the sweet, indulgent smile of a concerned and loving parent. "Where've you been all day?"

"To town," answered Aggie, shedding layers of outer wear. "The museum's got a new exhibit of Impressionists. The Gauguins are magnificent."

"You spent the whole day looking at paintings?"

"Not the whole day, Ma," answered Aggie. "I watched the skaters in the park, I rode the subway, I bought pretzels from a vendor on the street . . . admired the holiday decorations."

"You went alone?" asked Mrs. Hillyer.

"Sure, alone," answered Aggie. "With whom would I go?"

"I was hoping you'd returned Tom's call. I'm sure he would have been happy to . . ."

"Aw, Ma," wailed Aggie. "Don't start that again. There's no sense leading him on. That was all over long before he ever married. I only have a few days. I'm not about to spend my precious time listening to a play-by-play of Tom's pending divorce. It's depressing."

"It's not safe, a young girl running around alone in the city these days," sighed Mrs. Hillyer. "I worry about you, Aggie."

"I know, Ma," answered Aggie, contrite. "But honestly, I can take care of myself."

"You're past thirty and I still don't see a sign you're ready to settle down. That's not taking care of yourself!" said her mother adamantly. "You know, Tom's father left him a lot of real estate when he died last year."

"Thanks for letting me borrow your car and your coat,"

said Aggie. Taking up a bowl of bright red apples and a paring knife, she seated herself on a chrome-legged kitchen chair to peel them.

"Wash your hands before you touch food," said her mother. "You know, Bloomingdale's is having a sale on coats. You should take my card and go try some on. It'll be a present . . ."

"Thanks anyway, Ma," answered Aggie, sloshing her hands under the kitchen tap and resuming her seat at the table. "What would I do with a winter coat in Florida?"

"I guess I keep hoping you'll come to your senses and come home. You know what Jeff bought Samantha for Christmas? A full-length mink. He already gave it to her because it's been so cold this year. It's beautiful, Aggie. Pale gold, like your hair."

"I'm sure it's just what she always wanted," answered Aggie drily as they worked.

"Don't be jealous of your sister, Aggie. You were always the clever one, the pretty one. You could have all that and more. Your own house, a family . . . you had no dirth of eligible young men calling at your door . . . I'm going to have to wait for that turkey to finish browning before I put another pie in the oven."

"The only thing Samantha ever had that I envied," answered Aggie, "was her name. I look more like a 'Sam' than she does."

"You wouldn't look bad in that coat, either. I was always certain you would marry first. You were so popular in school. And you could do about anything with your hands. The gifts you made me! Bouquets of wild flowers arranged in ceramic bowls you'd made in school, the paintings on the walls, the pretty pictures. You're gifted, Aggie. That's probably why you were always such a daydreamer, always pining for faraway places."

"There's a lot of world out there to see, Mama," smiled Aggie.

"You just took a trip on your last vacation," said Mrs. Hillyer, trying to understand.

"Mama, a two-week cruise to St. Thomas is not exactly high adventure. I want to see the Michelangelo's on the Sistine ceiling. I want to see the Mona Lisa and the Parthenon. I want to see a Pacific sunset . . . and the northern lights . . . and the dark-skinned exotics that Gauguin painted in Tahiti."

"What would you do in Tahiti?" laughed Mrs. Hillyer.

"I'd paint. You know how long its been since I've had a chance to paint?"

"A gift should be exercised, or it will wither like an unused muscle."

"I know. But by the time you finish teaching five classes every day, it's like taking a busman's holiday."

"Well, it's a profession that leaves you plenty of time to travel, if that's what you want."

Aggie sliced the crisp white fruit into neat wedges, contemplating her mother's words. What *did* she want? She once thought she knew. She wanted to paint, to find the font within her where her visions were born and transpose them to canvas for the world to see.

Was she any closer to her destiny in the balmy tropics of her new-found home?

"I'll say one thing for sure," said Mrs. Hillyer. "The climate down there certainly agrees with you. I've never seen such a lovely tan . . . if you're through with those apples you can dump them in that pot on the stove and start setting the table. Jeff and Samantha and the kids should be here any minute."

"Are these all off the backyard tree?" asked Aggie.

"Your tree," nodded her mother, reminiscing. "Remember how you used to sit up in that tree with your books or your sketch pad?"

Yes. She remembered the gnarled old apple tree in the backyard. She would climb into its ancient arms, dream her dreams amidst the changing of the seasons. Spring was her favorite time, when the tree was in flower, heavy with the scent of apple blossoms. The first cologne she'd ever worn had been the scent of apple blossoms.

"We had a good crop of apples this year. I've made an extra pie for Sam to take home for the kids," said Mrs. Hillyer. "I used to wonder how you spent so many hours up in that tree, alone in your own little world."

She remembered the last time she sat up in her apple tree. It was the day she received word Tony had died. She spent most of the night crying up there. By the time she was ready to climb down, she felt she'd somehow passed

114

into instant adulthood. That night, Aggie had left a piece of her childhood hung on the weathered trunk of an apple tree.

"Your dad used to say it was his fault you spent so much time up a tree," said her mother. "He thought it was because he'd harbored a secret hope his first-born would be a boy. But no one was prouder when you went off to college. I think that's when everything all fell apart, honey. That business with the protest marches and the . . ."

Aggie stopped, poised with the silver flatware in her hand, to look at her mother.

"Well, honey, it's not easy even now to tell you." She straightened, wiping her flour dusted hands on a dish towel. "It's still hard for us to understand how you got mixed up with all those unwashed hippy types, and the drugs . . . oh, Aggie, you don't know how glad I am you're over all that. How many sleepless nights I've spent worrying about you."

Aggie, wordless, was awash with guilt.

"Well, at least you're a teacher instead of a starving artist in some East Village garret. Thank God you've got yourself a nice, safe profession."

Aggie laughed as she took a stack of dinner plates down from the cupboard.

"What's so funny?" asked Mrs. Hillyer.

"I'm probably in less danger wandering the streets of New York than in my own classroom. We've already had one of our administrators murdered . . . an adolescent pimp was holding me at gunpoint the day before I got on the plane."

"Aggie, you frighten me when you speak this way. Honey, you don't have to prove anything to anyone. What is it you're running from? What is it you're looking for?"

"I don't know, Ma. I'll just have to have faith enough to know when I find it."

"Aggie, baby. It's possible that what you're looking for has been right under your nose all along. Look at Samantha. She's found her fulfillment in her husband and family."

"Samantha got knocked up at nineteen and she's been making the poor bastard pay for it ever since," snapped Aggie.

115

"I don't think that's fair, Agnes," said Mrs. Hillyer, bristling. "Your sister chose to be a wife and mother. She just got her timing a little confused."

"Oh, Ma, I'm sorry. Lord! One of the reasons I came up here was to get away from that kind of pressure. Bob's been on me with all the same arguments you're offering."

"Your young man in Florida?"

"Yeah," said Aggie. "My young man in Florida."

"The one who's proposed?" asked her mother.

"Yes," answered Aggie, laying out the stemware on the counter. "I think these need rinsing."

"What's the problem with Bob?" she asked.

"Nothings wrong with Bob, Ma," answered Aggie. "It's my problem. Bob is marvelous. I'd die if I lost him. He's a strong, sensitive, sexy man. We have so much fun together. But he resents sharing me with my kids, and I know I'm going to resent sharing him with his."

"If your relationship with Bob is based on good times now, how will that change with marriage?" asked Mrs. Hillyer. "Dad and I have been happy for 35 years."

"Bob's son comes to live with us as soon as the ink on the license is dry. I inherit an instant family."

"I see," said her mother. "It's the same story, Aggie. You haven't let anyone close enough to touch you since Tony died. You can't go on hiding in the apple tree Aggie. Sooner or later, sweetheart, you've got to grow up."

13

The first person to greet her after the holidays was Sheila Morrow. She was waiting for her when she approached her room, standing surreptitiously on her stoop like a foundling.

"Why Sheila," said Aggie, surprised. "What are you doing here so early?"

"I wanted to talk to you, in private," said Sheila.

"I never had a chance to congratulate you," said Aggie leading the way to the Cave. "You want some coffee?"

"Yeah," said Sheila as Aggie dumped dark crystal granules into styrofoam cups.

"I didn't win," she said apologetically.

"Yeah, you did," said Aggie.

"Yeah," she smiled. "I made the court." Her skirt nearly covered her knees and her burnt-almond eyes were innocent of makeup.

"I knew it all along," smiled Aggie.

"Ain't a lotta people ever done nothin' for me," said Sheila, "so I ain't had much practice sayin' thanks, but I wanted to thank ya' for all ya' done." She sounded shy, the hard, brassy edge gone from her voice.

"I didn't do it, honey," answered Aggie. "You did."

"And Pete, and the art squad, and Ben . . ."

"Ben?" asked Aggie.

"Yeah. I know you told me I got to make it on my own, but I figured he was the only one who could get Pride off a' my back. See, it wasn't like I jus' used him or nothin'. Sheila always pays her debts. I gave that boy a lotta love . . ."

She stopped, suddenly self-conscious. "Well, he be goin'

118

off to play ball, and me, well, ya know, I thought maybe if I went out of town, I could get a new start."

"That sounds like a good idea. Can you handle it financially?"

"Oh, yeah," answered the girl with the exotic eyes. "I been holdin' back on Pride fo' a long time. I got some money saved. What's gonna happen to him?"

"If you work it right, you can get your diploma and be long gone by the time he gets out," answered Aggie.

Sheila set her coffee cup down and retrieved her oversized handbag from where it lay on the floor.

"We all got these trophies wit' our names, and these here little crowns," she said, extending her arm to offer the items for Aggie's perusal.

Aggie took the trophy from Sheila's hand to read her name inscribed on the silver plaque.

"You know what else we got 'sides all this junk from local stores? We got this complimentary introduction to this heah charm school. They train you to be a model, you know?"

Aggie nodded, clenching her teeth against the tightness in her throat.

"I'll probably go," said Sheila. "I figure, why not give it a shot?"

"Why not?" said Aggie, trying to sound casual.

Sheila, still holding the rhinestone tiara stepped forward to place it on Aggie's head. "I wanted to give you that," said Sheila. "I wanted to give you somethin' I didn't rip off or turn a trick to buy. Well, thanks for the coffee," said the girl, heading out the door. As the room filled with kids, Aggie swallowed her tears and prepared to meet her class.

Vance had been away, too. She'd seen his face grinning off the sports page of the local paper. He was a hometown hero in a town starved for celebrities.

He'd sail into home port like a pirate to deposit his last cup of captured gold, and the trophies displayed in Arcadia's main foyer just kept mounting.

Where was he now? she wondered. Downing creamed chicken and peas with the Rotarians? Fielding passes from the press at an All-County High School Sports Conference?

Or drilling his team for the state high school championship?

It wasn't with an excess of hope that Aggie made her way across campus to the Phys Ed office. If she did find him there, she was certain he'd forgotten to eat. At the very least, she could offer to bring them sandwiches. If I'm lucky enough to find him in, she thought.

She turned the handle of the door without knocking. Had it been locked, she would have assumed he was elsewhere, and gone her way a bit lonely and sad.

But the door gave way without a sound and she saw him, seated on the edge of his desk, his red shorts draped around his ankles. And seated on his creaky wooden swivel chair, Dixie Beaumont had her face pressed against his groin.

It was a moment before his eyes rolled up in ecstacy, which turned to terror as he spotted Aggie, her hand frozen on the door knob.

"Aggie!" he gasped as she slammed shut the door and fled the scene, devastated.

Her eyes red-rimmed and swollen, Aggie sat staring at a portion of an inert grayish matter covered over with a lumpy sauce.

"Pardon me, is this seat taken?" asked a familiar voice above her. Dixie stood with a loaded lunch tray.

"Yes," snapped Aggie. The faculty dining room was nearly empty, and the chair Dixie was indicating was one of three, unoccupied, at Aggie's table.

"Then I'll sit here," said Dixie, placing her tray at a second vacant seat.

"Dixie, I really haven't a thing to say to you," said Aggie, curtly.

"Well, I've got a few things to say," said Dixie, tucking the corner of a napkin into her cleavage.

"There's nothing you've got to say I want to hear," answered Aggie.

Dixie chopped off a chunk of what might have been meat loaf and, loading it into her mouth, she continued speaking around it. "So you're pissed off 'cause you caught me sippin' his stem. So what? Anyone who can get it up

120

around here is stickin' it to someone. But it don't mean no more than sharin' a drink or a dance."

"You were neither drinking nor dancing," snarled Aggie, rising to collect her tray. "Christ, why am I arguing about this with you?"

" 'Cause you want reassurance I'm not easing you out of the picture with your hunky coach."

"He's not *my* coach," sneered Aggie, disdainfully. "I don't care who you mess with. You can screw your way through the entire male faculty and the student body for all I care. I just think you might be a little more discreet about where you do it. The gym office, the bleachers, you don't care *where*."

"Sit down," said Dixie calmly. "You're attracting attention."

Aggie hesitated. Dixie reached for her arm and pulled her into the chair. She sat tensely on the edge of her seat. "What if it had been a kid that walked in on you? But, of course, I'd forgotten. After the show you put on in the bleachers during the homecoming game, it's obvious you don't care who sees you." Aggie wondered how Dixie could just sit there and calmly stuff meat loaf into her mouth right after . . . right after Vance.

"Why don't you relax and finish your lunch?" asked Dixie.

"I'm finished," said Aggie, rising.

"I'm not," said Dixie, placing her hand on Aggie's arm to restrain her. She swallowed before she continued. "Listen! What goes on in this building has nothing to do with reality, you know? I mean, it's like play period. A fringe benefit. So if you've already got the coach staked out, well, you were here first. I'll back off and let you take care of him."

"There's nothing like that going on between Coach McCarthy and myself," was Aggie's righteous reply.

"Then you are a damn fool," said Dixie, " 'cause everyone *thinks* there is."

"I don't care what people think," said Aggie.

"Then get off my ass about Wayne," said Dixie deliberately, stuffing her mouth again.

"Wayne is a student. He's only fifteen years old," answered Aggie. "Don't you feel any responsibility as an adult? As an educator?"

"Yeah, I'll admit it was a problem at first," said Dixie. "I'm still sorta fightin' it, about Wayne's age. That's how come, I guess, I'm still lookin' over the field. But, I'll tell you one thing. What that boy lacks in experience, he sure makes up for in enthusiasm. He's every bit as hung, and twice as horny as any guy I ever met, including yours."

"No guy of mine would get that close to you," said Aggie. "And I'm not certain I want to get too close either. People's reputations are built on the company they keep."

"Well, then, you've shot your reputation moonin' around the coach," she sneered. "Come on, honey," Dixie's voice dripped sarcasm. "I've seen you two sittin' in here. Maybe you've never actually spread your legs for him, but the way I seen you look at him, I know you would in a minute, given half a chance."

"You're so crude," said Aggie, wondering if her embarrassment showed. "I won't sit still for any more of this."

Dixie continued over a mouthful of the unidentified substance on their plates: "It's OK, honey, everyone of us has got our little indiscretions." She mispronounced the word. It sounded like something you do in the toilet.

"Not all of us are quite so open about our sexuality . . ."

"You mean honest, don't you," said Dixie. "I'm just a little more honest about it, is all. Some women are CT's, you know?" Aggie bristled. Dixie had hit a sensitive nerve. "I just act on my feelin's, is all. If I like someone, I don't see any harm in lettin' him know it. The world would be a better place if we all spread a little more love around."

"Are you trying to tell me all these casual encounters are love matches?"

"I already told you," answered Dixie. "The coach don't mean a thing."

"You mean you're saving the serious stuff for the students," said Aggie, aware it was a cheap shot. She was still hurt and angry, the more so because neither she nor Dixie could lay claim to the coach . . . and her visible anger embarassed her. She wanted to strike out at Dixie, to humiliate her.

"Yeah," said Dixie. "You know, of all the men I been

122

with, Wayne's the all-time champ. That pistol never runs out a' ammunition. Long as I been lookin' I never expected to find it in a younger man."

"You mean kid," answered Aggie. "Wayne's a kid . . . a fifteen-year-old kid."

"He'll be sixteen in another two months."

"And you're still gonna have a good twenty years on him."

"And he's still gonna have a good eight inches on me," laughed Dixie.

"How much sustenance are you going to derive twenty years from now from a guy who carries all his assets under his fly?" asked Aggie.

"Hell, in twenty years, who cares? I have enough trouble worryin' about tomorrow night. God damn, Aggie. I thought you'd understand. You're a foxy-lookin' lady, but you're not a spring chicken either, you know? Haven't you ever been afraid of bein' *alone* for the rest of your life? Didn't you ever lay awake hungerin' for a man so bad you'd like to die? Someone to hold ya' when you're scared of the dark?"

"I've never been desperate enough to crawl into the sack with a student," said Aggie, rising to leave.

"Don't knock it till you've tried it," hooted Dixie as Aggie walked away.

By the time the passing bell rang, Aggie was already across the courtyard and approaching her door.

"OK," she called, pushing open the swinging door of the girl's toilet near her room. "Everybody out. Get to class, right now!"

A reluctant group of girls filed past her and dispersed to their respective classes, grumbling.

She'd made a point of checking that bathroom ever since . . . ever since that little girl, Nancy, what was her last name?

A crowd followed her in as she unlocked her door and flipped on the lights.

"Everybody get your work out and settle down so I can take roll," instructed Aggie.

"Miz Hillyer, can I go to the bathroom?"

123

"Michele, I just saw you come out of the bathroom," answered Aggie. "What are you doing, majoring in rest-room?"

"Didn't work this time, Michele," teased one of the boys.

"Fuck off!" yelled Michele across the room.

"That's enough of that," said Aggie. "I told you all to take out your work and take your seats. You should all be working on your final projects now. If I haven't approved your project yet, bring it up to me this period."

"Miz Hillyer," said a voice behind her.

"Cocoa, I asked you to take your seat."

"I got to talk to ya', *now*!"

"It can wait till I take roll."

She was clutching at her gut, really laying it on.

"It can't wait! I need to go."

"What makes you think I'm gonna write you a lav pass when I just said no to Michele?" asked Aggie sternly.

" 'Cause I feel sick," explained the girl.

"You've made it this far," said Aggie, defeated, offering a compromise. "You can wait till I take roll."

"Jes' mark me here," said Cocoa. "I'll be right back." And she bolted for the door and disappeared. "Cocoa!" yelled Aggie down the deserted corridor. But the exit door banged at the far end of the hall and Cocoa was gone.

Outside in the balmy sunshine, Cocoa wrapped her long-sleeved cardigan around her trembling body. Sweat broke out on her glistening face, her buck-toothed mouth was drawn up in a grotesque mask of fear and pain.

The cramp in her belly was making it hard to stand up-right. Each step wrenched another stitch under her ribs. She was nearly doubled over by the time she reached the phone booth. Dropping a dime in the slot, she waited im-patiently as she listened to the repeated ring.

"Answer, fucker! Answer the phone," she swore under her breath.

"Yeah?" said a voice on the other end.

"Where you been, you mothah fuck?" spat Cocoa into the instrument. "You 'sposed to bring me a package las' night."

"Listen," said the voice on the phone. "I got hung up."

"I'm gonna hang you up by yo' balls nex' time I see you," said Cocoa, " 'less you get me my stuff."

"Keep your pants on, junkie. I got you your shit!"

"Pride nevah strung me out like this," said Cocoa. "Pride wouldn't like you not takin' care a' his ladies. How'm I gonna work this way, you dumb prick? How you 'spec' me to work?"

"Be cool, baby. I'll get it to you tonight."

"Tonight's too late, sucker. I'm crashing now!" screamed Cocoa.

"You got the money?"

"I got it. Jus' get me a fix. I'm really sick, man. Jus get over here now!"

"Where are you?"

"I'm on Eastern Avenue, in a phone booth near the school."

"Well, I ain't bringin' it by no school. Too many cops near schools."

"I cain't walk," wailed Cocoa. "Please, I cain't walk. I'm hurtin' too bad." The trembling turned into deep, retching spasms. She stuck her head out the phone booth to vomit.

"OK. But just this once. Next time you need your needle, girl, you gotta come get it like everyone else. You caught me in a generous mood," said the pusher. "I'll do you a favor!"

"Aggie, I got to tell you, straight," said E-Z. "I hope we got enough respect for one another so we don't need to be sensitive to this color thing that's going down around here. I've got this parents' committee on my ass about the high ratio of black kids that get discipline demerits or suspensions here. So either you're gonna have to start clippin' your own kind or you're gonna have to let a few things slide."

"E-Z, you know I don't have a discipline problem," said Aggie. "This girl that cut my class is unstable. She's a heroin addict. She was sick when she sprang, and I hassled her about a lav pass."

"Well, if she's already left the premises, Aggie, it's too late to keep her after school. And we ain't got the time to worry about it. We got a faculty meeting in five, and you know it takes special dispensation from Tallahassee or a death in the family to get out of a faculty meeting around here."

She was seated in her usual isolated spot under the balcony overhang when she spotted Betty rolling down the aisle.

Oh, Christ, thought Aggie. Every time I see her she traps me with another high-pressure sales pitch for the Association.

"How've you been, Betty?" asked Aggie sweetly as Betty stopped expectantly beside her. Betty sat down, clucking like a laying hen, and pulled a package of Twinkies from her purse.

"Aggie, I know you've heard all this before, but I definitely think you ought to make a resolution to join up before the New Year," began Betty as a prelude to her usual monologue.

A repository of current statistics, Betty recited through squirrel-cheeked mouthfuls the constipated state of the group's contract battle with the school board.

"You can't buy a Cadillac for what they pay your average teacher a year," she said.

"You see a Cadillac in this neighborhood, you're looking at a pimp or a pusher," said Aggie. "What would you want with a Cadillac?"

"It's just the idea that because you chose this profession," complained Betty, "you have to resign yourself to the fact that you'll never be able to afford the nicer things in life. Jesus Christ, in my house a pot roast is an exotic delicacy and when I can afford to pop for it, it's for canape-sized portions."

"You don't look like you're starving," smiled Aggie. "How can you consume so many sweets? No wonder you're so hyped."

"Don't be critical, Aggie. We're all addicted to something. Mine's food. Is that illegal?"

Betty's barb came too close to chipping the glass house she lived in and Aggie fell silent.

"May I join you lovely ladies?" smiled Gomez from the aisle.

Betty rolled her eyes in an agonized expression as he

126

carefully guided his girth into the seat on the other side of Aggie.

"Will you be here for rehearsal tomorrow morning?" asked Gomez.

They were rehearsing an entertainment for the faculty party.

"Tomorrow's Saturday," said Aggie.

"Mr. Farley will let us in to use the stage," answered Gomez.

"I'm doing an aria," Betty offered. "Maybe Wagner, or Puccini."

"What's that got to do with a South Seas theme?" asked Aggie. "The party's supposed to be a luau."

"We all contribute according to our own abilities," said Betty, vocalizing a few shrill soprano notes. Other teachers turned to stare.

"A preview of our exciting revue, folks," quipped Betty. "Catch the rest of the show at the Christmas party."

Accustomed to her eccentricities, they soon lost interest.

"I hope Bob hasn't made any plans for that Saturday," said Aggie. "He so rarely gets a weekend off."

"If you can't make it, call me tomorrow," said Gomez. "We get together after school next week."

Betty took a soda from her purse and popped the top.

"What are you doing this Saturday night?" he asked Aggie.

"I really don't know what Bob had planned, Nandy. Why?"

"Want a slug?" asked Betty timidly. Aggie took a hit and passed it to Gomez.

"Gracias, señora," said Gomez, returning the can to Betty. "I am receiving an award for the work I did for the youth center. I am being honored this Saturday evening and I want my friends to share my joy."

"Congratulations, Nandy, my sweet," smiled Aggie. "I will certainly bring Bob to help you celebrate."

She was going to have to handcuff and horsewhip Bob to get him to a civic award presentation.

Betty was wiping the lip of the soda can.

"Why did you hand it to him?" whispered Betty in Aggie's ear as Bo took the mike on stage. "Who knows where his mouth has been?"

127

Aggie's inner eye suddenly swept back to the scene she'd stumbled on in Vance's office.

"What are you saying?" asked Aggie, turning toward her. Betty had her head back with the pop can pressed to her lips.

Gomez was becoming curious. She turned her attention his way to throw him off the track. She cared too much for Nandy to cause him to be hurt by her tacit acceptance of Betty's bigotry.

"You certainly deserve some recognition for the time you devote to the kids of this community," said Aggie.

"I wouldn't want him around *my* kids," rasped Betty, almost inaudibly. With the cola can propped firmly between her plump thighs, Betty began to unwrap an Almond Joy.

"Can I get you a saucer of milk to wash that down with?" quipped Aggie with a forced smile.

"*I* didn't get invited," said Betty. Aggie was glad that Bo finally stepped forward to the mike to begin his salutation to his staff. The applause, though less than overwhelming, was enough to mask Betty's tactless remarks.

"It's not something you can catch, you know," she replied. Lord! She'd sat back here to be alone.

Chastised, Betty offered her half an Almond Joy by way of an apology. Aggie snatched it out of its wrapper and passed it to Gomez, still blissfully unaware of Betty's hostility. If the sweet were a peace offering, it should go to the offended party, she thought as he accepted it with negligible resistance.

"Si, gracias," said Gomez savoring it appreciatively. To the smack of finger lickin' sound effects in stereo, her two fat companions finished the candy . . . but Betty was grousing over the outcome of her generous gesture.

Bo was not alone on stage.

There was a man at his side with a receding hairline and the start of a middle-aged paunch protruding almost imperceptibly from beneath the vest of his smartly tailored suit, but he had the same general physical appearance of the type of ex-athlete Bo favored among his male staff.

"Well, bless my soul," sighed Betty. "What have we here?" For a brief time she was sufficiently distracted to stop stuffing her mouth.

"I'd like to start right off by introducing the newest member of our staff," said Bo.

"Mr. James Joseph Wingate the Third," he began, launching into a recitation of the stranger's academic and athletic credits.

"Another mental giant," sneered Gomez facetiously. "We got another joke on the staff."

"I think you mean jock," whispered Aggie.

"That's what I said," answered Gomez. "That's not right?"

"Yeah, you're absolutely right," she smiled. The newcomer was certainly attractive on a purely physical level. But there was something disturbing about his eyes . . . something stealthy and surreptitious.

"Well, he's prettier than our last vice principal," said Betty, sucking coconut from between her teeth.

"And poor Henry hardly cold in his grave," sighed Gomez, shaking his head sadly. "Where is he from?"

"Weren't you listening to his credits?" asked Aggie. "Georgia State, sixty-nine."

"Is that his graduation date or his sexual preference?" kidded Gomez. Betty overheard and winced.

"He looks to me like the sort of man we need around here," commented Betty in defense of the new vice principal. "Maybe he can kick some life into this ho-hum place."

"Only if it was shaped like a football, I'll bet," said Aggie. "There's no way that he is going to change anything single-handed."

"I keep telling you how important it is for all of us to hang together," Betty began her predictable pitch by rote.

"Not now, Betty," snapped Aggie, feeling suddenly trapped. There was no inconspicuous way to pry her way out past the padded laps of the persons on either side. She couldn't sit through another soliloquy on the merits of the ATA.

"I want to mention what a fine job you've all done with a touchy situation so far this year," said Bo, winding up the meeting. "You've all displayed an admirable amount of team spirit. I know that we in the administration can count on the continued support of the finest faculty in the county."

The audience applauded, but it was unclear whether the ovation was for Bo or for themselves as a group.

"Just a few more announcements before we adjourn to the faculty room for some punch and cookies and a chance for all of you to meet Mr. Wingate in person in an informal atmosphere. I know not a single one of you want to miss that."

"I don't think that's an optional invitation," said Gomez.

"Sounds mostly mandatory to me," agreed Aggie.

"I've been asked to do a few less agreeable things around here," said Betty. "The best thing our food service produces is their desserts."

Aggie relieved Betty of her empty soft drink can and lit a cigarette. "How can you still be hungry?" she asked.

"These meetings make *me* hungry," interjected Gomez.

"Everything makes me hungry this time of day," confessed Betty.

"You two ought to get to know each other better," grinned Aggie. "You have so much in common."

"What are you wearing to the faculty party?" ventured Betty, leaning over Aggie to talk to Gomez for the first time since he'd joined them. Aggie sighed—she hadn't meant her facetious suggestion to be taken seriously.

"It's a big surprise," he smiled mysteriously.

Vance MacCarthy ascended the stage. "I just have one quick thing to say," he said, "and then we can all run into the faculty room and spike the punch. I'm sure you're all aware by now that we're playing for the state championship next week."

The enthusiastic response of her peers reminded Aggie of a student assembly. The faculty rarely showed such enthusiasm as a group.

"I want to thank you for the support you've given our boys in their fund raising efforts . . . without the participation of their teachers and their classmates, my boys wouldn't be enjoying this unprecedented success. I'm happy to report that we've managed to raise all the money we needed to send the team to Lauderdale for the play-offs, and we've got enough for a few extra seats on the busses for our loyal boosters on a first-come, first-serve basis."

"The scenery sure got good around here," sighed Betty, staring raptly at the handsome coach.

I wish I'd never seen him today, the lech, thought Aggie, her anger returning. I wish that perverted bastard was nowhere near Avalon today.

She contemplated cutting out of the social hour after the meeting in order to avoid having to face him, but her worries were unfounded. Vance would be on the field drilling his prize-winning football team. He'd been granted a dispensation of the highest priority. He was grooming the team for their final victory, and hadn't the time for punch and cookies.

They adjourned to the faculty room and found a table for four. Gomez was just setting three plastic cups of punch down when Dixie joined them.

Not again, thought Aggie, as she saw the redhead approach.

"You all have a seat for sale over heah?" asked Dixie in her most kittenish drawl.

Who's she trying to seduce at this table? Aggie wondered irritably.

"I'll go for another cup and some more cookies," offered Gomez, politely holding the chair as Dixie sat down.

"What do you gals think of the new man?" asked Dixie conversationally.

"He's a man, all right!" answered Aggie, unable to resist another shot at someone whom she still saw as a rival. "I guess that makes him fair game, huh?"

"You know, Aggie, I really am trying to make friends with you."

"Please don't put yourself out on my account," answered Aggie without a trace of graciousness.

Betty, sensing an interesting bit of intrigue in the hostile exchange, was taking it all in with unabashed delight as she washed the last of her sugar cookies down with an artificially colored, oversweetened pink punch.

Gomez deposited another plate of sweets on the table and tasted his drink.

"This could be improved with a good stiff shot of rum," he said.

"Look what's coming this way," said Betty, nervous as a virgin on a waterbed.

131

"Bo and Jimmy Jo," observed Aggie. "They sound like an act you'd catch at the Grand Ol' Opry.

"Ladies," began Bo. "And gentleman," acknowledging Gomez almost as an afterthought.

"May I present your new vice principal, Mr. James Wingate . . ."

Georgia State, sixty-nine, recited Aggie in her head.

"Jimmy Jo," corrected the stranger extending his hand to each of them in turn.

"Welcome to Arcadia," said Gomez, rising.

"Delighted," said Dixie, looking like she meant it.

"Likewise," said Betty, releasing his hand reluctantly.

"And our lovely art teacher, Aggie Hillyer," concluded Bo.

She offered her hand and he held it. The way he riveted his piercing gaze on her body and avoided her eyes made Aggie uncomfortable.

"My pleasure, Miss Hillyer," he smiled, emphasing the "Miss."

"Ms. Hillyer," she said, snatching back her misappropriated right hand.

"I need a few suggestions for redecoratin' my new office," said Jimmy Jo. "S'pose I drop by sometime soon so's we can talk about it? They tell me you're a whiz at things like that."

Everyone at her table stared at her, and Aggie was mortified by his boldness.

"Can't understand anyone wanting to tell you things like that about me," she kidded. She couldn't bring herself to smile at him.

"Well, you certainly didn't waste any charm on him," sniped Betty after Jimmy Jo and Bo went on to the next table.

"There's something about him I just don't like," said Aggie.

"Well, at least he's better lookin' than the last one," said Dixie. "Lord, don't it make you think that trial's gonna go on forever? Whyn't they jes' hang that nig—" She stopped herself. "Well, it's time they do somethin' to protect decent folks," she finished lamely when she caught the look on Aggie's face.

"Hank wasn't everyone's idea of decent!" said Betty, still

132

staring at Jimmy Jo's backside from afar. "Some folks think he brought it on himself, bullyin' people the way he had a habit of doin'."

"They're just trying to make a case for desegregation out of it," said Dixie. "It's probably a federal plot."

"That Negro security guard has six kids. If they lock him up for murder, who'll feed those children?" asked Betty with maternal concern.

"He should of thought about that before he shot Hank Lawler," said Dixie.

"Well, Hank could've remembered to pick up a gate pass," said Betty. "Some of these guys that get their own offices act like the rules they make are just for others."

"It's been my experience you can get away with most anything if you go about it right," said Dixie.

"Well, you'd be the one to know that," sniped Aggie, arising.

"Where you going, darling?" asked Gomez, about to dissuade her.

"I've put in an appearance," answered Aggie. "It's after five. I'm goin' home."

The sun was setting, bright and round on the western horizon as she headed the 'Vette out of the school yard.

In the alley behind the porn shop, a young girl retched and shivered in the late afternoon shadows. The setting sun was still warm and bright on the earth, but its comforting fingers failed to penetrate the darkness of her hiding place. She didn't know how long she'd been waiting, but she did remember how much it hurt the whole time. The sun was blood red, and big as a balloon. Not just a balloon, thought Cocoa. Those big suckers she bought for the girls at Disney World. She'd take them there when they were old enough. She'd for sure take 'em there. Where the fuck was that sonofabitch? She'd kill him when he came.

But by the time the score was made, she would have sold her babies for a fix. She gave him the money without an accounting, without reservation. It didn't matter that he'd short-weighed her. She forgave the hours he'd kept her waiting with her pain. She fell on the packet voraciously and began to wrap the strap of her handbag around her left thigh.

133

She remembered that the sun was red . . . round and red like a kid's balloon. And that's the very last thing she remembered.

Her body was discovered sometime after midnight by a wino rumaging the alley for salvage . . . and when the cops came they saw the syringe still imbedded in her infected vein. They shook their heads knowingly and turned the body over to the coroner. "There's nothing more anyone can do for her now," said an attendant loading the anonymous remains into the ambulance. "She's been dead since sometime after five P.M.

"What's she doin' here?" snarled Ernie of the armed guard who accompanied him into the austere visiting room of the Boy's Correctional facility.

Aggie didn't recognize him until he spoke. He was wearing baggy Levis and a denim workshirt, and his neck was naked of the gold chains that had been his signature in another life. His luxurient Afro had been cropped close to his head.

But the voice was the same, arrogant and angry and unrepentant.

"What the fuck's she doin' here?" he roared.

The guard stepped forward, but Aggie waved him away.

"What'd you come here for, you fuckin' cunt . . . to gloat?"

"I didn't drive for three hours to get here to gloat," said Aggie.

"You're the one who put me here, you cock-suckin' cunt," he screamed. The veins in his neck and temples were bulging with rage.

"I don't think this is workin' out, ma'am," said the guard gently as Ernie raved. "I'm gonna' have to take him back to his dorm. He's just not ready for visitors."

"Yeah," yelled Ernie. "Get me out of here before I kill 'er."

"Please," Aggie pleaded. "I've come so far to see him."

"Well, you shouldn't a' bothered," said Ernie.

"This is the first visitor you've had up here, son," the guard said. "I mean, besides the lawyer the court appointed. When are you gonna get it through your head that these folks are tryin' to help you?"

134

"This broad got me busted!" shrieked Ernie, approaching the fringes of hysteria.

"You got yourself busted, you oversized crybaby," retorted Aggie. "Why don't you quit wailing the nobody-understands-me blues. You're a brat . . . a spoiled, self-indulgent, pull-the-wings-off-a-butterfly kind of brat . . . and so wrapped up in self-pity you can't muster a normal measure of curiosity about my visit."

"I know why you came," said the surly young man.

"That was one of your most debilitating handicaps," said Aggie. "You think you already know it all, and that there's nothing left to learn."

"Lady," said the youngester with the ancient eyes. "If I was you I'd git my fancy wheels and split . . . I'd get a good head start, teachah," he growled, " 'Cause when I get out of here, I'm comin' after you."

"That's it for sure, boy," said the guard, grabbing him firmly by the arm. His tone was no longer gentle nor paternal.

"Wait, please," asked Aggie. "I've brought you something . . ."

"A token of your honky, middle-class guilt?" asked Ernie.

"It's a book," she answered. "I thought you'd get the time to read . . ."

"You already got me the time, teach. Don't try to tell me how to spend it. Why didn't you bring me a couple a' cartons 'a Marlboro's? Or a lid a' 'lumbo. Or, if you can find it, stick a hacksaw blade up your snatch," he sneered. "Bring me somethin' I can use."

The guard was ready to usher him out the door.

"Ernie, wait a minute," called Aggie. He turned his sullen face to her again.

"Ernie, something's happened . . . to a friend of yours, she stammered. "I didn't think it was the kind of thing you ought to just hear about in a letter. The loss of a friend is always a shock . . ."

If Ernie's sensibilities were shocked, or his vulnerability broached, the emotion failed to register on his polished ebony face.

135

"Cocoa's dead," said Aggie gently. "She died of an over-dose."

"What I care about that dumb-ass, pin-cushion pussy?" he sneered as the guard led him away.

14

"Where's Pete?" asked Aggie of the group assembling in the great vaulted foyer inside Arcadia's main entrance.

"He said he'd be in later to tell you why he couldn't come," came the reply.

"It'll take him that long to think of an excuse he hasn't used yet!" said another.

"I want to thank you all for giving up your lunch hour to help with the decorations," she said, distributing cartons of balls, bells, and tinsel.

An ersatz evergreen stood forlornly in the alcove beneath the spiral staircase. In the velvet-swathed glass trophy case gleamed the golden spoils of five decades of combat on the fields of competition. There, too, stood the latest, greatest tribute to the team . . . and to Coach McCarthy, the man who'd led them to glory—the two-foot championship trophy just presented to Arcadia.

Aggie wondered what was keeping Mac occupied now that the season was over. "Eugene, be careful," she said to the boy perched precariously atop a fifteen-foot ladder. "Somebody hold onto Eugene before he breaks his neck. Tom-Tom, go back to my room and get another roll of masking tape." She dispatched him with her keys.

They attacked their task with competence and vigor. Soon, red and gold garlands graced the trophy case and glittered from the carved oak talons of the gargoyles glaring from the ceiling above. Every door along the corridor now sported life-sized likenesses of Afro-coiffed magi, dark madonnas, and a red-robed Santa urging his reindeer-drawn sleigh over snowy clouds of cotton.

"That's fine, can you hold it there?" asked Aggie of the

kid suspending nylon filament across the ceiling to hang snowflakes on. Tommy returned with the tape. "How about giving Sarah a hand with the tree?" suggested Aggie.

"I'm doing fine," answered Sarah stoically. "I don't need no dumb boy to mess it up."

"Who you calling boy?" asked Tommy, insulted by the unintended racial slur.

"Tommy, what are you doing?" asked Aggie irritably.

He stood, applauding malevolently. "Givin' her the only hand she's gonna git from me," said the boy called Tom-Tom.

"Come on," urged Aggie. "Let's see a little brotherly love blossoming among the mistletoe and holly."

"Ain't none of these turkeys no brutha of mine," snapped Sarah uncharitably, climbing down from the chair. She stepped back to admire her handiwork. "Man, that's bad!" she said, lavishing her highest praise on their production.

"Bitchin," agreed Eugene, descending the ladder to take in the view.

The tree thrust its star-capped apogee heavenward, its overloaded branches dripping rainbow bright ornaments. The bannister bore an aritstic arrangement of green pine boughs festooned with red and gold ribbons that wended their way upward. Tall tapers of paper maché radiated an incandescent glow, reflecting softly off the glass wall of the trophy case.

"It's beautiful," breathed Aggie. She tore herself away. "Eugene, you and Tommy get that ladder back to Mr. Farley. The rest of you, please help me get this stuff back into the room before we get stampeded. The bell's about to ring."

"Miz Hillyer, are you gonna curve the grades?"

"Give me a break, Allen. I haven't given the test yet!"

"Miz Hillyer, my desk is dirty. I can't take a test on this desk."

"Go get a sponge, Julia," Aggie answered. "You know where we keep them."

"How come I gotta clean up someone else's mess?"

"Whoever sits there next period cleans up after you at

139

times, I'm sure," she said. "And I clean up after *all* of you sometime or other. Stop complaining . . . it's not gonna kill you."

"Miz Hillyer, I don't have a pencil."

"How come we gotta take a test in art?" came the query from the back of the room.

"School policy states that 25 percent of your semester grade will be determined by a written midterm exam," answered Aggie. "Wouldn't you rather get it over with now than have it to come back to after Christmas?"

"That means you want to grade 'em over Christmas, huh?" someone asked.

"Right," said Aggie. "Correcting exams is my favorite thing to do over Christmas."

"Then don't give it," suggested several of them.

"And deny myself all that fun?" asked Aggie sarcastically. "Let's just settle down and get it over with."

"Can I take roll, Ms. Hillyer?" asked a girl named Angela.

"No thanks," she replied. "But you can pass out the test while I do it." She ran hurriedly through her class list.

"Where's Roach?" she asked. "Has he been ill?"

"You might say he become a shut-in," someone laughed.

"He done got busted for shopliftin'." The speaker wore a small gold hoop through his left earlobe.

"He's gone spend Chris'mas at the County Home," said someone else.

"Linda Carpenter," she continued. "*Linda Carpenter*," she repeated.

"Is that the mousy little chick that sits over here when she comes?" asked one of the girls. Linda's attendance had been so sporadic her classmates couldn't place her. Now she'd miss the midterm, and if she didn't appeal her excess absences to the review committee, she would be subject to automatic failure. Aggie resolved to give her a call. If she was staying home to be with her invalid mother, she may not be aware of her disastrous academic situation.

"OK. Let's get started! Last name first on your Blue Book, please. Let's go over the exam so I can answer any questions beforehand. What is it, Elton?" she asked acknowledging his raised hand.

"I got a question," said Elton.

"Well?" She suspected it was another tactical delay.

"Can I be excused to go to the bathroom?"

"Define the following terms for a total of twenty-five points," she began, ignoring him.

It was the fourth time she'd read it aloud that day. By the next period, the last, she'd have it memorized.

"And if you have the time, I'd like you to tell me in a few words on the last page of your exam, what you've derived from your participation in this class."

"What does derived mean?" came the question.

"What you got out of it," explained Aggie "Something you feel you can take away with you, after it's over."

When they were all settled to the task at hand, Aggie began her assault on the exams that she'd given that morning. She was appalled by the low level of literacy that their written work displayed.

WHAT I DRIVE FROM ART IS THE JOY OF ART AS A HOLD, wrote David. I MUST SAY THAT I LERN A LOT OF THANGS THAT I NEVER KNOW. ART IS NOW A BIG JOYABLE PART OF ME. THANGS YOU.

She skimmed the stack of uncorrected exams on the desk before her.

SOME OF THE PEOPLE IN CLASS WAS FRIENDLY AND THERE WAS SOME NOT BECAUSE THEY JUST HARD HEAD, wrote Manuel, mistaking her request for an invitation to comment on the fragile state of social relationships in the class.

I FEEL I CAN TAKE SOMETHING OF ART AWAY WITH ME, was Valerie's comment. AND I DON'T MEEN SOME OF THE ART SUPPLIES THAT GET RIPPED OFF.

Who the hell is Valerie, thought Aggie, trying to remember. Is she that quiet girl with the long straight hair that would only draw horses? A good teacher knew her kids by name before the close of the first quarter. By the time they took their midterms, a truly devoted and observant instructor could look at an exam and know which student produced it, but the name on the paper failed to register. Hey, here's one that's not only legible, but articulate.

I REALLY ENJOYED SILKSCREENING MY OWN CHRISTMAS CARDS, AND I NOW HAVE MY OWN LITTLE BUSINESS AMONG MY FRIENDS REPRO-

DUCING THE JEWELRY I LEARNED TO MAKE IN YOUR CLASS.

The paper was unsigned. Someone always forgot to sign their paper. Who was that girl who got hung up on jewelry? She'd go through her grade book and identify the anonymous author through the process of elimination. The next one was refreshingly familiar, and particularly fulfilling.

I'VE FOUND OUT A LITTLE OF THE BULL AND HARDSHIPS AND FUN THAT TEACHERS GO THRU DAILY, wrote Sheila Morrow. ONE OF THE BEST THINGS ABOUT THIS CLASS WAS THAT THROUGH IT I HAVE GOTTEN TO KNOW YOU, NOT JUST AS A TEACHER BUT AS A FRIEND.

Win some, lose some! she thought. They got Cocoa, but at least there was Sheila to even the score for the good guys.

"Hey, teach!" came the greeting from the door.

"Hey, stude," she replied.

"You mean, like in student?" asked Pete Santini.

"Shhh," she whispered. "They're taking a test. I also mean like stewed as in scrambled. Where were you when I needed you to help decorate?"

"I got hung up." It was simply an explanation, not an apology. "It looks like you managed to do it without me. It's looking good out there."

"No thanks to you!" Aggie was steamed. "I got you excused from another class to help me, not go trotting around the building. You knew we had to get that stuff up for the chorale's concert tonight—what else was that important?"

"Well, I'm trying to tell you," said Pete. "It's this girl . . ."

"You mean you got her in trouble?" asked Aggie.

"Hell, no! Nothin' like that," he protested. "But trust me, Hilly. It's heavy shit just the same. I need a favor."

"What is it, Pete?"

"Well, see, this girl, she's in Miss Peterson's fourth period. She doesn't get along real well with ol' pruneface. She's really a good artist, but she's failing Art. You'd like her, Hilly. She's good people."

"There's nothing I can do for her in Miss Peterson's

142

class, Pete," answered Aggie apologetically. She had no desire to mess with Muriel.

"You could get her transferred in here," said Pete matter-of-factly.

"No way," answered Aggie. She had no way of justifying a transfer request, and certainly she didn't need an extra pupil.

"Hilly," moaned Pete. "How can you say no after all I've done for you?"

Oh Jesus! thought Aggie. He's playing this one downright dirty.

"Pete, I can't just ask Miss Peterson to send me one of her students."

"Yeah, you can," he insisted. "If she gives you a bad time for asking, I promise I won't bug you again."

"By then it could be too late," answered Aggie.

"You know I wouldn't ask if it wasn't important," he badgered.

"How important?" she asked. "Is this the reason you've been cutting out on me lately?"

She thought she saw guilt color his complexion before he dropped his eyes. Well, maybe Muriel would consider dumping a slow student . . . and she owed Pete for the miracle he'd helped perform with Sheila.

"Pick up some transfer forms from Guidance," she said. "I'll see what I can do."

"Right here and all filled out," he grinned, withdrawing a rumpled sheaf of papers from his pocket.

"Did it ever occur to you that I might turn you down?" asked Aggie.

"Not for a minute," he answered, flashing his most disarming smile. "I knew I could count on you, Hilly."

It was after the last passing bell and almost as an afterthought that Aggie grabbed up the class card that was imprinted with the address and phone of Linda Carpenter. Preoccupied with her own plans, she was anxious to get home. Bob would be by to collect her this evening so they could go to meet Bobby's plane. What would she wear? Jeans, perhaps, in order to avoid looking too like a teacher. But wait . . . where would Bob take them to eat? Would jeans be appropriate for anything less casual than their favorite beer and pizza joint? This meeting was an auspicious and long-awaited occasion. What would she say? What would he think of her? That she was trying to step into his mother's shoes? Could she keep her cool, and win him over?

Pushing open the door of the faculty lounge, she found it deserted.

Poor kid, thought Aggie as she punched out Linda's number, remembering how concerned she'd been over the prospect of impending failure.

"Why, Miss Hillyer, what a pleasant surprise," said the man who came in the door, smiling broadly.

"Mr. Wingate, good afternoon," she acknowledged curtly, listening to the phone ringing on the other end.

"I didn't think I'd be fortunate enough to run into you again so soon."

"If it's about the art work for your office, next week sometime would be better. I'm really quite busy." The unanswered phone kept ringing.

"Oh no, no," he answered, seating himself near her. "That can wait till I'm a little more settled. I think it would be wise to familiarize myself with my new environment, and get to know my staff."

The unheeded ringing reverberated against her eardrum in the silence that ensued.

Jimmy Jo wore that penetrating stare that had made her so uncomfortable before.

Linda's mother was incapable of being left alone. Why didn't somebody answer? She hung up, irritable, and stood to leave.

"Since we're both through for the day, why don't you let me buy you a cup of coffee—or a drink, and we can talk some shop . . ."

"No. Thank you, just the same," she said.

"Just a quick drink with the new boy in town," he pleaded. "Surely you can spare an hour, Aggie." He confronted her, barring the exit.

"I already have a date this evening, Mr. Wingate," she said coolly.

"I hate to drink alone," he insisted. "An hour . . ."

"Perhaps some other time," she said unconvincingly. Anxious to be on her way, she shifted her hand bag uneasily and stared him down defiantly. "Good afternoon, Mr. Wingate," she said.

He didn't move. He just stood, staring for what seemed like an interminable interval, blocking the exit with his body.

Her initial aversion intensified.

"Some other time," he finally repeated, holding the door to usher her out.

Aggie felt his eyes following her down the hall. She caught herself wishing for Hank Lawler's reincarnation from the grave. Hank had only been obnoxious when he was drunk.

The address on Linda's class card was only a few blocks from school. She'd just drive by . . . she had a gnawing apprehension about the unattended phone. Aggie contrived a dozen reasons why no one had answered her call, but none of them sufficed to suppress her dread.

The address was a cul de sac that dead-ended against the raised embankment of the new extension of northbound 41.

The house was a decaying cottage set way back from the street in an overgrown thicket of scruffy date palms and thorny weeds. Uncollected mail, mostly addressed to occupant, bristled from the mailbox. The shades were up, but the house was dark as she looked in the windows and leaned on the bell.

Nothing. No lights, no noise. Something was wrong. Frustrated and frightened, she rapped repeatedly on the windows, grabbed the doorknob and rattled the door. It swung open in her hand. The first sensation that assailed her from the darkened interior was the smell. An incredibly rank odor emanated from inside.

"Linda?" she called, venturing in cautiously. "Is anybody here?"

She found a light switch, illuminating an incredibly cluttered room, furnished with a mismatched excess of overstuffed furniture and the dishes and debris of a month's worth of junk-food dinners. Gigantic cockroaches crawled for cover on the coffee table.

"Linda!" yelled Aggie, wondering if she should phone somebody. She wondered if Bob could help her explain what she was doing rummaging around a stranger's house if anyone should ever ask.

Somewhere as from a distance, a fawcett dripped, rather like a distant heartbeat. It was the only sound to be heard in the stillness of the room.

"Linda, please! Where are you?" she shouted tapping on another closed door. It opened.

A picture of Jesus hung on the wall above the bed, and an assemblage of medical apparatus was rigged on either side. The figure in the bed lay very still. The odor overwhelmed her.

"Mrs. Carpenter?" Aggie approached the bed. The skull of the cadaver was bloodlessly colorless, the wasted, twisted hands were cold and rigid to the touch. A bug as big as a rodent disappeared into the tube inserted in the throat.

Her every sense convulsed with revulsion, Aggie Hillyer screamed.

"Linda! Linda!" She searched the house in a frantic delirium. Aggie found her in a back bedroom staring soundlessly into space.

"Linda, get up!" she commanded, pulling the girl to her feet.

Linda had wet herself, and she stunk of urine.

"Linda!" Aggie shook her, hard. "Linda, we've got to get you out of here." She dropped her back onto the narrow soiled bed and began to pull clothing from the closet.

Linda watched with dull, unblinking eyes as Aggie stuffed a pillow case.

"Dear God, who to call, what to do? Linda, can you hear me?"

"Ms. Hillyer?" A small flicker in the empty eyes. "I didn't know what to do. Tell me what to do."

It was the last thing she would say . . . for a very long time.

"We'll take care of it, Linda. We'll take care of it together. You're not alone, anymore," cried Aggie, bundling her into a soiled blanket from the bed.

"Are you a relative?" asked the young cop.

"No, this is her daughter," answered Aggie. "I'm just her teacher."

Linda held her tightly, buried her tearless face against Aggie's shoulder, and whimpered.

"Do you know of any relatives in town?" he questioned.

Aggie watched them lift the body bag into the hearse. Linda was still trembling on her shoulder as they sat on the steps in the chilly air. The temperature dropped fast as the sun went down.

"No, no I don't," answered Aggie. "Can we get her some kind of help? I think she's in shock," she said, indicating Linda.

"There's an ambulance on the way," said the policeman.

It struck Aggie as odd, somehow, that the hearse arrived before the ambulance. She wished she'd worn a jacket. It was getting cold.

"Well, she can't stay in there tonight," he said. "That body's been decomposing for at least a week. It'll take six months to fumigate the place. They'll probably take her to County General and keep her under observation for a while."

"Then what?" asked Aggie.

"Then if they can't track down any of her family, they'll have to place her in a foster care facility."

Linda continued staring catatonically into space. Where had she gone? Released from the enslavement of her mother's illness, where had Linda's mind retracted? Would she ever return?

"I don't think there's anyone," said Aggie. "They were county wards. Couldn't she just come home with me tonight?"

"Ma'am, that's not up to me," he replied. "But there's no tellin' how she'll act when the shock wears off. I wouldn't take the responsibility if I were you."

Aggie drove Linda to County General in her own car and turned her over to a motherly, middle-aged nurse. "That child's not gonna sleep that sedative off till tomorrow. Why don't you go home, miss?" urged the white-clad angel of mercy.

It wasn't till she retraced her steps through the hospital lobby and spotted the clock on the wall that panic overtook her. Bob . . . and Bobby . . . and the plane . . . Christ, he would have been there hours ago. What must he think? She raced homeward.

Bob's car was sitting in front of her apartment house. The door was open on the driver's side, and he was lounging over the wheel as she pulled up beside him. A Christmas carol drifted melodically from the car radio, and a young boy occupied the passenger seat.

She hurried to embrace Bob, anxious to explain.

He backed away and held her at arm's length. "Where the hell you been, Aggie? You know how important tonight was to me," he accused. "I barely made it to the airport in time."

"Bob, you don't understand," she began. She had never seen him so angry. "See, it started with a simple call . . . to a student . . . I didn't mean to get involved, but it was the kind of a situation . . ."

"I knew it had something to do with one of your kids. It's always *your kids*."

"Bob, let me explain," she said.

"Hey, Dad," yelled Bobby from the car. "When are we gonna eat?"

"Soon son," he answered.

"Look, Bob," she offered, shivering in her inadequate clothing. She was rumpled and reeking with the lingering stench of urine and death. "Why don't we all go upstairs, and I'll fix you both something to drink? I bought some pop for Bobby . . . give me ten minutes to shower and change . . ."

"Dad, I'm hungry," wailed Bobby persistently.

"We're goin' right now, son," he shot back sharply.

"If you let me explain," she begged, needing his forgiveness and his strength. "I know you'll understand."

"I understand, Aggie. I understand as long as I live, if I love you, I'll have to settle for second-hand scraps. Your heart belongs first, last, and always to your students. You haven't enough left over for anybody else . . . including me."

"If you'll let me get a word in," she replied, "I'll tell you the reason . . ."

"I'm sure you have a terrific reason for all but standing me up, shug. Call me when you're not so busy. I'm entertaining an out-of-town guest."

The trembling that had been a symptom of the chill

night air increased to a tremor of fear and loneliness as she watched him drive away.

Feeling very alone and full of grief, she climbed the stairs by sheer force of will, placing each leaden foot heavily before the other.

Her head still reeling with the impact of the day's events, she wandered, distracted, through her empty rooms.

The oppressive isolation deepened her despondency. She resolved to call Maddy. She dialed the number and heard it ring. Maddy would offer the compassion she craved, Maddy would be there for her. The phone rang a second time and then a third. Maddy would soothe her sore psyche and her ragged nerves. Maddy understood what it was to be alone.

"Oh, Maddy," gasped Aggie with relief as her friend answered. "I know it's late, but I just had to speak to someone."

"What is it, young 'un?" asked Maddy in that lovingly maternal way she had.

"Maddy, I blew it with Bob for sure tonight," said Aggie, then recounted the ordeal she'd just endured.

"Now, I'm sure he'll come around when he cools off. Why don't you just get some rest and call him in the morning."

"Maddy, I've got to see you," she began.

"I'll be right there," she heard Maddy yell to someone at the other end. "What was that, Aggie dear?" asked Maddy.

"I'm sorry," said Aggie. "I won't keep you. I didn't realize you had company."

"Why don't you pour yourself a nice stiff drink and get some sleep," suggested Maddy kindly. "I'll check in on you later."

"Yeah, later," agreed Aggie, laying the receiver into its cradle.

Fumbling in her bedside drawer, she dropped two Valium from a prescription vial and lit a joint. She wanted to scream, to relieve the tightness in her throat. She wanted to yell to someone how unfair it was, how unjustified Bob's anger, how misunderstood she felt. And how lonely. Bob was probably even now beginning to realize his mistake. She'd get a chance to tell him, and he'd understand.

She headed for the bathroom and turned on the shower. Smoke and steam wreathed her tear-stained face. Pain and loneliness reflected from her bloodshot eyes. She smoked the joint down to a burnt stub before she dropped the roach into an ash tray. Shredding her rumpled clothes, she stepped into the tub, then turned the knob to transfer the rush of luxuriant spray from the spigot to a hand-held shower head. Liquid warmth engulfed her face and breasts. Visions from her altered consciousness danced before her in the rising steam.

But it wasn't Bob she summoned from the well of her own emptiness. The cozy, curtained enclosure cuddled her in a watery womb. The shower jets tingled as their tiny fingers probed her naked skin. Somewhere on the earth there slept a man whose wife's embrace denied her his touch. Her inner eye conceived him from a dream. His smiling face took form against the bathroom wall.

Seating herself securely on the bathtub rim, she brought the shower head close against her groin. Mac's laughing eyes embraced her from a wish. Through force of will she brought him to her arms, and in her longing she recalled his touch.

The water gushed and bubbled around the gaping emptiness between her thighs. She contrived her lover so convincingly she cried his name aloud. "Oh, Mac," she sighed.

Silent sobs shook her body inside out as she collapsed to her knees against the hard floor of the tub with the shower nozzle still pressed to her crotch. The alchemy complete, she sat spreadeagled in the tub, teary-eyed. Then dried herself and went to bed.

Alone.

15

"Well, you lucked out," said E-Z as he held the door for her. "If you've got to stand bus duty, best time for it is the short week before a holiday."

"Oh, it wasn't all that bad," said Aggie. "Besides, I hardly get to see you any more."

"Well, now you know where I been hangin' out," he said. "Look for me wherever the forces of darkness and evil threaten truth, justice, and the American way."

She laughed easily in his company.

"Teachers get short shifted of bus duty couple a' times a year. I'm out there all the time, rain or shine."

"You must be doing something right," answered Aggie. "It's been blissfully uneventful lately."

"Knock wood," sighed E-Z, stopping to rap on a wood door. "Don't tempt fate, girl. We're overdue!"

"I prefer to think we're over the hump," said Aggie as they continued down the locker-lined corridor. The crowd was thinning as the students found their way to their home-rooms. Late-comers were still slamming lockers and scurrying to beat the bell.

"That's because, like most women, you're unduly optimistic. It's a fact of life, you know, that for every small step forward we take two steps back. American education's been on the decline for decades. It's not working."

"Oh, I don't know," she answered. "I prefer to think we do a pretty good job with the bulk of the student body in spite of our problems . . ."

"See what I mean? You refuse to accept the reality of the situation. It's like we're trying to float a sieve. We keep bailing and plugging up the holes, but truth is . . ." He shrugged his shoulders with an ironic smile, as if trying to thrust off a great weight. "Truth is, we're all sinking, and not a life boat in sight. We're going down with the ship."

She was about to say something defensive and contradictory when they rounded the corner of the corridor that cut past the main entrance.

"Oh, no," wailed Aggie, breaking into a run. "What happened?"

The trophy case had been vandalized, the Christmas decorations destroyed. The tree was lying on its side in a tangle of garlands and snowflakes.

Old Mr. Farley swept glass and glitter into a large metal trash bin, while Coach McCarthy and several of his scarlet-shirted team members retrieved their trophies from the debris.

"Johnny, Ed, Dwayne," said the coach. "Go on to homeroom. We'll finish up here."

"Geez, coach," commented Johnny. "What a mess. Why would anyone do a thing like this?"

"Just some freaked-out druggie, I bet," said Dwayne. "Or maybe somebody who got cut from the team."

"Have to be some kind of prevert to take a piss in our trophy," said Ed. "Every time you try to do somethin' good or important around here, someone fucks it up."

"OK, guys. On to class," urged the coach gently. "Thanks."

But as they turned to leave, rage registered on Mac's face. "I want to know who's responsible for this," he growled, turning on E-Z. "I want someone to account for this. Those bloody bastards should have their hides nailed to the barn door."

"When did it happen?" asked E-Z, surveying the carnage.

"I found it like this when I came in this morning," answered Vance. "Some time during the night, most likely."

"Why the hell would anyone do something so senseless and destructive?" asked Aggie. "Why?"

"No tellin', honey," said Vance. "I'm really sorry, Aggie. All your beautiful work . . . It looked so nice. Bo's in there calling maintenance."

"How much of this is salvagable?" she asked.

"Just a few things seem irreparable," he replied. "The team's new trophy is still intact. Some soap and water, a little glue . . ." Anger and frustration showed in the cording of his neck muscles and the hard-edged glint of fury in his emerald eyes.

But it was the first time Aggie had had occasion to speak with him since . . . since Dixie.

"Hey, I'll help out here, honey. Why don't you go on? You'll be late."

"Yeah," agreed Aggie. "I'm gone!"

"Wait, I'll walk with you," offered Mac.

"I'll bring you whatever ain't broken up outta this mess a' decorations," called Farley.

"Thanks a bunch," she grinned, through clenched teeth. "There's not much I think I'm going to use again. Just chuck it all and call it a loss."

"See what I mean?" said E-Z. "Take up one stitch, and two more come undone. There's no way to get ahead."

"What'd he mean by that?" asked Vance.

"I don't know," she answered as they made their way toward her door.

"Hey, Sadie Mae," said Vance. "I've been wanting to talk to you."

"Coulda fooled me," she retorted. "I was sure you were avoiding me. There's no reason to feel guilty."

"Guilty? The only thing I'm guilty of is not lockin' that door. Look, I know you're probably disappointed in me, and I'm really sorry. But I'm glad it was you. It coulda been somebody who could do me some serious harm. I don't know how I could have been so careless . . ."

"Hey, you don't have to explain to me," interjected Aggie. "You don't owe me any explanations or apologies."

"Aw, Sadie Mae. It was nothin' but a little funnin'. Nothin' serious. Just a little fun and games is all."

"Everything is just a game to you, isn't it?" asked Aggie irritably. "A bone-crunching assault across a muddy field for another five yards . . . a cheap slut like Dixie . . . a backroom blow job. Jesus! I hope it's worth whatever it is you're getting out of it."

"Yeah, it is," said Vance. "It's good being a winner. On the field, in the sack," he grinned. "I admit it. I love to score. But I've been up front about it. And I've given you the right of first refusal, so what are you so pissed about?"

"You assume I care at all!" said Aggie, glad they'd

reached her door. Pete had opened it for her. Probably sprung the lock with a credit card again. Sandy was taking attendance and everything was rolling right along as usual. He followed her into her classroom and the impact was immediate. Some of the students simply smiled, that kind of smile that said something was happening. ·

"Hi, coach," smiled the girls, flirting with Mac.

"Right on, coach!" encouraged the guys snidely.

He acknowledged their attention like a visiting pontiff blessing his flock. He was aware of the attention his visit had aroused and played it cool.

Aggie was suddenly uncomfortable under their collective curiosity.

Vance sat in her chair while she went about the business of her homeroom, self-consciously acting the role of teacher.

The kids were also showing off. Mac's presence in her room had its effect on the class as well, and as they exited on cue in a body at the sound of the bell, someone snapped off the light, leaving the room in sudden semi-darkness.

"Dammit!" said Aggie, switching on the lights. "Somebody's always screwing up."

"I thought your kids were exceptionally well behaved," said Vance. "What's you're secret?"

"I flog them regularly," she smiled.

Her first-period class was drifting slowly into the room as he rose to leave.

"Well, I'm glad we're speaking to one another again," said Mac, flashing his heart-melting grin. "You'll be at the party tomorrow night?"

"Sure. Gomez and I have a little number we've rehearsed."

"I'm looking forward to it," he answered. "Why don't you and your date plan on sitting with us?"

"I'm going with Gomez."

"You mean he's your date?" asked Mac incredulously. "What happened to that cop you'd been seeing?"

She didn't want to get into it with him. "He's out of town," she lied.

"You broke up with him, right?" he asked, seeing through her deception.

"Not exactly . . ." she stammered.

155

"Why Gomez, Aggie? He's hardly capable of appreciating a lady like you. Hey, you know, there's this fella, nice-lookin' guy, down here scouting my boy Ben. He's been askin' if I knew any unattached gals. I could arrange for you to meet him. He'd fall all over himself to get a date with you . . ."

"Thanks, I've already made my plans," she replied.

"What a waste," he said, shaking his head.

Aggie rallied to Nandy's defense. "Gomez is witty, educated, well travelled, and charming," she said. "I think he's rather good company."

"No argument, Sadie Mae. Gomez is good company. But he's a lousy excuse for the real thing. What really went down with you and your bear?" asked Mac, unconvinced.

"I think we came to the crossroads, and proceded in different directions," she answered evasively.

"Well," he said, sounding almost pleased. "Anytime you're in the mood for the company of a *man*"—he winked one of those seductive green eyes—"you know where to find me."

"Next time I'll knock," she said as he left her room.

16

Gomez had a battered suitcase stuffed in the back of the Chevy when he arrived to pick her up for the party.

"What is that? Are you planning to stay all weekend?" asked Aggie.

"My costume," said Gomez. "Wait till you see, Aggie. Where's yours?"

"Right here in my bag. I threw a little something together." Her oversized handbag held a slithery wisp of grass skirt, her white bikini, and a string of imitation orchids.

"A very little," said Gomez. "you'll be the hit of the party."

"That's me," she kidded. "The sex symbol of the faculty."

The neon marquee in front of the motel read ALOHA, ARCADIA. They parked the pink Chevy in the lot and made their way to the Polynesian Room. They could hear the music drifting from the ballroom as they approached the entrance where Jimmy Joe Wingate manned the hospitality table dispensing name tags.

He was also acting as bouncer and about to evict Dixie and her very uncomfortable-looking young man.

"Look, lady. I don't want to get into a thing with you about this. He ain't old enough to be admitted to a place that's servin' liquor. Not no place in this whole state. Now, you gonna take my word for it or should I get someone else to explain it again?"

"And I told you that he's with me," complained Dixie, "and we've got reservations."

"We'll arrange to return your money, ma'am," Jimmy replied, his patience wearing thin.

"Well, I never!" huffed Dixie, backing down. "We'll think of something better to do."

Dixie walked right past Aggie and Gomez with Wayne in tow like Mary's little lamb, and the look she gave them as she passed was worth a thousand words.

Aggie was suppressing a giggle as they presented themselves to Jimmy Joe at the door.

He looked surprised to find them together. "Señor," he said, handing Gomez a paper name plate. "Can you imagine that broad trying to bring that kid in here? There's no accountin' for the nerve of that—"

He was about to continue with some choice expletives, but the scowl on her face stopped him.

Her white gown, wrapped around her like a sarong bared her suntanned arms and shoulders. He offered to fasten her adhesive name plate to her breast with an undisguised lewdness that stripped her naked.

Gomez ushered her past with the graciousness and courtesy of a gentleman and won her unspoken gratitude.

"I see they've put you right to work, Mr. Wingate," said Gomez. "I hope you get a chance to enjoy the party." By injecting his portly frame between them, he sheltered Aggie until they escaped Wingate's view.

"That guy gives me the creeps," said Aggie. "I don't know what it is."

"He is evidently fond of you," said Gomez, leading her to a table.

"Like the Colonel's fond of chicken," she quipped.

The Arcadia faculty was an odd admixture of the old and new guards. The polyester leisure suits and close-cropped haircuts were in the majority, but there were a few modishly contemporary longhairs sprinkled through the crowd, a few beards and rimless glasses and young faculty wives striving stiffly for the sober formality of the occasion while sipping a cup of rum-laced courage.

There was also a sizable number of absent-minded professors, the usual retinue of little old ladies wearing dress-black orthopedics with support hose instead of the everyday tennis shoes, and the 'fros and corn-row styles of the black staff and their spouses.

Gomez, in jumpsuit and flowered pink shirt, looked like a chubby matador. But as he led Aggie around the dance floor, she was amazed by his grace. He was very light on his feet for so large a man.

"You're a terrific dancer," said Aggie. "I'm having a good time."

"Then why do I sense a sadness in you?" he asked. He had that keen perception of the professional educator and the awareness of a true student of human nature. There was, indeed, a sadness in her.

"It's my friend from King. You know Maddy? Every time I talk to her I become more concerned. She's a born teacher. I love just hanging out with her, Nandy. I listen to her tell how it used to be to be a teacher, and it gets me down."

"The way it used to be, or the way it is?" he asked.

"Both, I guess," she answered. "I've seen so many changes in the decade I've taught. It's just a constant adjustment to changes."

"And this makes you sad?" he asked. "The world needs to change."

"Why does everyone feel so negative about it then, Nandy? What is it that hangs so heavy over all our heads?"

"I don't think I understand the question," he replied.

"I'm not sure that I do either," she said. "I just feel so bad about Maddy. She offered me her job at King."

"Her job?" asked Gomez, still confused.

"She's leaving teaching. Opting for early retirement. After twenty-seven years. I don't know anyone with more courage than Maddy. Nor anyone who believes in education more than she does. And she is chucking it all in. Maddy and I are so close. We're so much alike, in spite of the difference in our ages. She believes in kids. She's spent her whole life bending herself into a pretzel to accommodate the establishment, just so they'd let her teach. She influenced thousands of young lives. Now, twenty-seven years later, she can't wait to walk away from it."

Gomez sat quietly, contemplating.

"What would you gain by leaving Arcadia, Aggie?" he asked.

"Well, I wouldn't have Muriel standing over me, for one. Maddy's is the only position in art at King."

"Ah, Muriel," said Gomez with new insight.

"Do you know what that bitch did? While registering kids for the new semester's classes, she told some of my students that my classes were closed. She deliberately shut some of my best kids out of my classes. And last week, I got tied up in the guidance office trying to unwind some of the red tape and reregister one of 'em . . ."

He guided her expertly around the dance floor. The band was composed of a music teacher at the piano, a guidance counselor playing tenor sax, and the auto shop instructor recruited from the ranks to stroke a set of drums.

"I forgot about a department meeting," continued Aggie. "So instead of telling me, she walks right past me into the main office to announce over the PA that I am to report to her room for the meeting. Now the whole building knows I missed a meeting, right? She goes out of her way to make me look bad, and I get so shook."

"I'm sure you are mistaken," he said. "It is just that *she* is trying to look good. She is a person with little imagination, so she must, how you say, live by the rules. That is not wrong, Aggie. Just different."

"You're so good, you make me ashamed of my evil mind," confessed Aggie. "I wish I had that kind of faith in human nature."

"You could take the job at King and make it your own department," he said. "It would probably be a good career move for you. Better conditions, better backgrounds and family conditions. What is keeping you at Arcadia?"

She avoided answering him. She searched the crowd and found Vance on the dance floor. His wife was a tall, earthy, outdoorsy brunette in a bright red gown, and it was easy to pick them out of the crowd. They made a striking couple on the dance floor, but in Aggie's waking vision, it was he and she, two figures formed in golden filigree. This red-dressed woman was an intruder here. This was a company party, and faculty wives were the visiting team . . . And Vance was playing it cool, and so was Jimmy Joe and his chubby spouse and all the other guys who'd ever hit on her.

They were served a standard Chinese menu of won tons and sweet and sour chicken and jello covered with pineapple chunks and shredded coconut, which was somehow supposed to convey a taste of the tropics.

Gomez got them both a third Mai Tai from the bar and, by the time they were ready to present their entertainment, everyone was drunk, or working on it, but, with a self-consciousness that made it a dull party.

"Time to liven this place up," said Aggie as they made their way to the dressing room they'd improvised backstage.

Betty in a diaphonous mumu was already there. So was Irv Fisbine from the math department, in an uncharacteristically loud Hawaiian print shirt and ukelele. He had practiced an impersonation of Arthur Godfrey. Four guys from Industrial Arts were harmonizing a barber shop quartet rendition of "Little Grass Shack," and one of the guidance counselors honed a stand-up comedy routine reminiscent of Henny Youngman.

Aggie elicited appreciative whistles when she emerged from the cramped bathroom, a tanned expanse of skin exposed between the hula skirt and the wreath of orchids.

But it was Gomez who stole the show. Several layers of yellow cellophane straw encircled his bare belly over a pair of size 42 red flowered shorts. A multi-colored, harlequinesque hair piece covered his thinning black hair. From his earlobes, oversized shell earrings danced inanely. The piece de resistance was a brassiere made of the two halves of a coconut shell, grotesquely set over his hairy, bare chest. He wore lipstick and his eyelids were bright green. He grinned from beneath his black mustache as they all cracked up over his get-up.

"Who does your hair, my dear?" asked Aggie. "Harpo Marx?"

"You're just jealous, because mine are bigger than yours," he laughed, shaking the coconut shells and setting his tummy trembling.

"I'm not sure I can go through with this, straight," said Aggie as they waited their turn to go on. "I think I'm losing my nerve."

"There's no need to be afraid, Aggie. These are our friends, our peers. We are here to have a good time and to try to become closer. What's the worst thing they can do, throw their food at us if they don't like our act?"

They began exactly as they'd rehearsed it. Gomez had a passably pleasant voice and sang and swayed to a lyrical rendition of "Blue Hawaii." It was Aggie's job to circulate among the male members of the audience and recruit a hirsute chorus line to back the star.

Mac backed her off with a panicky look. E-Z blanched with revulsion and refused despite his mate's good-natured urging.

It was the paunchy wrestling coach, a guy about thirty who also taught a hygiene class and seemed secure about his masculinity, who first agreed.

A good-looking black named Green was her second reluctant participant.

Mrs. Calloway was unsure whether to allow him to leave the table, but Bo was drunk enough to "join the team" and she knew she was almost there.

She went straight to Irv Fishbine's table where he sat between his "little woman" and Muriel Peterson.

Muriel's look of withering disapproval was not entirely wasted on her.

Her starting line-up selected, she helped them roll up their pants and tied their hula skirts around them. Then she dropped a paper lei around each of their necks and led them to Gomez for a hula lesson as the audience whistled and clapped.

Gomez gave blunt instructions. "Get those legs up, boys," he gushed. "Stick out the chests, so." He demonstrated by breathlessly elevating the coconut shells.

They finished the production number, a sloppy chorus line of tipsy guys high stepping to the tune of "Bloody Mary Is The Girl I Love," while Gomez and Aggie took their bows amidst the applause and cheers of their peers.

"Well, hell," said Aggie. "That was fun, but I'm glad it's over, and we can all get back to normal."

Bo took the stage to make some announcements and deliver a few closing remarks, and it was so much like a faculty meeting you could almost hear them all groan.

Aggie edged toward the bar as Bo delivered a sermonette about the great job they were all doing. It was imperative to deliver some soothing strokes, like cheerleaders at a game. They don't directly affect the outcome, but they make the players feel better while they're taking the blows.

Vance stood to acknowledge the group's joyous confir-

163

mation of his successes. He'd generated a lot of good PR for Arcadia.

She didn't need another drink, but ordered one anyway. What she wanted was a joint, to mellow out, but she settled for yet another Mai Tai, wondering why she felt so disoriented and somehow out of it. It probably had something to do with Bob, but she wasn't sure exactly how.

"That's some kind of outfit," sneered someone from behind her. "Ain't that kind of out of keepin' with your image?"

She turned to find Jimmy Joe standing beside her.

"Were you talking to me?" she said, sounding silly. There was no one else around.

"I'm not sure who you are," he challenged. "Is this the same *Ms.* Aggie Hillyer got the reputation a' bein' the local ice maiden? Here you are, showing up lookin' like anybody's idea of a sex symbol, unescorted . . ."

"I came with a date," she snapped, walking away from him.

"You came with a faggot," he laughed. "Hey, maybe that does fit in," he observed, stopping her in her tracks. "They say a lot a' them wimmin's libbers is queer. Izzat your problem?"

"Just what's *your* problem?" she snapped.

"Shit, I'm just wonderin'," he drawled. "There's a lot a' people in this state don't think queers ought to be teachin' school, ya know? Not that I'm one of 'em, now, mind ya. My interest runs in an entirely diff'rent direction." He was scanning her with that scathing stare. "It'd sure be a shame if a piece like you was wired the wrong way."

Suddenly conscious of her scanty outfit, she retreated, to make her way back to their dressing room to retrieve her clothes.

It was then she witnessed Nandy's unrehearsed performance. Bo was making his final announcement.

"We have another member of our faculty who's distinguished himself on a national level for his outstanding work with non-English-speaking students . . ."

She saw Gomez at the edge of the small dias, beaming as Bo described Nandy's efforts on behalf of the increasing numbers of Hispanic students attempting to overcome poverty and a language barrier to enter the mainstream of

American life. The National Teacher's Organization had voted him the Teacher of the Year. Was it only false modesty that had kept him from telling anyone about this honor? Or was it a deliberate attempt to maintain a low profile? And was it only because he was a little tipsy that he abandoned his good judgment as he mounted the platform again, still in his outlandish outfit? He accepted their polite applause with the enthusiasm of a warm puppy, snatching the wig from his head as he spoke.

"Thank you all," he said. "Gracias."

"Speech!" someone yelled drunkenly from the back. They whistled as he shimmied, the clown, compelled to seek their response.

"Speech," yelled several more, goading him on good-naturedly.

"If I had known this was going to happen, I would have worn my pants," he said, obviously surprised.

They laughed.

"You know, it's a great country, this America. All kinds of people living together, as we all do at Arcadia. We are living proof that people of all races and all nationalities can get along."

The audience applauded, poised for entertainment.

"The greatest thing about this nation is the freedom to be all you can possibly be," continued Gomez.

No, thought Aggie, watching. He's not going to do it!

"Whenever a group of people are singled out for persecution," he continued in his heavy Cuban accent, "all people are threatened. When a man's livelihood is threatened for what he is, what he thinks, what he says, then no man is truly free. When a few can dictate to the many and their bigotry finds the ears of the community . . ."

By now everyone in the room knew where he was taking it, and the air was turning icy. You could feel the temperature drop, and Aggie, in her scanty costume, shivered with dread.

He mentioned the news clippings, the woman who advertised on national TV what was, after tourism, the state's major industry, and of the pious legitimacy her name lent the witch hunt their campaign had become. His soliloquy elicited an embarrassing silence.

No one wanted to acknowledge what was happening,

and there seemed no way to stop him. He was like a juggernaut, rolling ponderously to his own destruction. And he was doing it in drag.

That's all I can take, thought Aggie. But as she started toward him. Gomez seemed to crumble. Suddenly he ran crying, from the room.

Aggie caught up with him in the parking lot. She pounded on the window of the pink Chevy until he leaned over to let her in. Her eyes were also wet.

"Didn't you forget something?" she asked.

"I'm sorry, Aggie, I didn't mean to run out on you," he sobbed.

"Why, Gomez?"

"I don't know why, Aggie," he confessed. "Now that I've done it, I still don't know why. Maybe it was just a mountain that had to be climbed. I'm sorry I spoiled your evening. You don't have to leave with me." His head was pressed against the wheel.

"I make it a habit to leave a party with the same man I arrived with." Aggie wiped her eyes with the back of her hand.

"Some man," he sniffed.

"Someone once told me you measure a man by the courage of his convictions," she smiled. "That must make you very much a man."

He picked up his head to grin at her. "C'mon, I'll take you home," he said.

"You're still forgetting something," she said, shaking her head.

He was puzzled.

"Your pants," she laughed, looking at his knobby knees extruding beneath his bloomers and shreaded paper skirt.

They returned, arm in arm, only long enough to retrieve his trousers.

When the pink Chevy pulled up in front of her duplex, she was still half naked and barefoot in the chill of the night air. Goosebumps played upon her bare body.

"Want some coffee?" she asked pleasantly.

"No thanks," he said, still down. "I think I need a good night's sleep instead."

She stood there, her shoes and clothing clutched in her arms, and watched him drive away.

A dark form emerged from the shadows as she approached her door.

"Bob," gasped Aggie.

"I didn't mean to frighten you," he said. "You're home early."

She shivered, stunned into immobility.

"Did you have a good time?" he asked conversationally.

She shrugged, feeling awkward in the scanty costume. She wished she'd had the time to change.

"I could go for that cup a' coffee your friend turned down."

It wasn't until they tumbled out of the shower together that she remembered to ask him where Bobby was.

"That sweet neighbor who keeps baking spice cakes is watching him for me," he answered. "I took him out on the boat today. He fell asleep as soon as his head hit the pillow. You haven't asked me why I'm here."

"I know why you're here," she answered, wrapping him in a huge yellow bath towel. She held him tight against her, enjoying the contact with his naked skin.

"You're assuming I've just come out to play," he answered, nuzzling her. "I believe you're taking me for granted, shug."

"Well, you sure taught me a lesson," she answered, trying to keep it light. She didn't make it. "I almost thought you weren't coming back."

He gathered her into his arms and kissed her tenderly before he answered.

"I wasn't sure I would, babe. Then I started to miss you and knew I had to give it another shot."

He reached for the jacket he'd left laying on a chair and extracted a small, gift-wrapped parcel. She knew as soon as she saw it what it would contain. The question she posed was merely a delaying tactic, to give her time to control the panic she was feeling.

"What's this?"

Bob lit a cigarette and slung his long-limbed frame casually onto her rumpled bed, his burly body, naked against rose-patterned bedclothes, vividly accentuating his masculinity. She wanted to jump into his arms and roll into oblivious satiation. She wanted to sprout wings like Icarus and fly from the window into tomorrow's sunrise. She wanted the ground to open up and swallow her . . . she wanted to do *anything* but open the little velvet jeweler's box that contained a diamond ring.

"I'm takin' Bobby back tomorrow," said Bob. "We're gonna spend Christmas with my mom. I'd like you to meet her at least once before . . . Hey, what's the matter?"

She was getting choked up.

"I hope to God you're about to weep with joy," he grinned. "Hey, shug, you'll like my ol' lady, she's a real old-fashioned, in-the-kitchen, dawn-to-dusk kind of mom. She's gonna be nuts about you. She's impressed as hell you're a teacher . . . we'll have a traditional down-home Christmas."

She was afraid if she moved a single muscle she'd begin to sob. He extended his arms to her, inviting her in, and still she stood immobile, resisting, wrapping herself in the damp towel as if to hide.

"Don't you like the ring? I was gonna wait and put it under the tree, but on the outside chance you were gonna turn me down again, well . . . I wasn't ready to risk rejection in front of my family."

He dropped his arms and his dark eyes registered a rising apprehension.

"Oh, Bob, Jesus!" she gasped. "I don't know what to say."

"Anything affirmative'll do. Listen, if you don't like it or it don't fit it's not gonna hurt my feelings none to exchange it. We'll go together soon's we get back."

"Bob, it's not that . . . it's beautiful."

A single stone set asymmetrically into a platinum band winked like a god's eye from its black velvet nest.

"The other one's got a whole bunch of little bitty diamonds and they kinda lock together, but you don't get that one till later," he grinned proudly. "Whether or not I wear one's up to you . . ."

"Bob . . ." said Aggie. And that was all.

It seemed a long time they just stared at one another. Then he got up and reached for his trousers.

"Where are you going," she stammered.

"Either I'm gonna help you get a few things together for our trip tomorrow, Aggie, or I'm gonna put on my pants and go home to my boy. I need to know where I'm at with you. I love you, dammit! I want you for my wife."

"Bob, I need some time . . ."

"The time is now. It's either yes or no," he replied.

He lifted the ring from its case and reached for her left hand. She hesitated, started toward him, a single gesture, a half step forward . . . and withdrew.

"Bob, be reasonable. This is all so sudden . . ."

"Aggie, it's no surprise to you after all this time . . . we love each other . . . don't we?"

"Yes, of course . . . but . . ."

"No, not 'yes, of course, but'! 'Yes, I'll marry you' is what I want to hear. Dammit, Aggie. Say it. It's easy, if you mean it. Just say 'Yes I love you and yes I'll marry you'."

The words formed on her tongue a thousand times as he buttoned his shirt . . . as he laced his shoes and pulled a pocket comb through his dark hair.

Still clinging to her bath towel like a security blanket, she followed him to her door. "Yes" molded itself on her parched lips and glistened in her teary eyes, but even as she saw him leaving she couldn't get it out.

"So long, shug," smiled Bob ruefully, disappearing down the stairs.

17

"You gonna be much longer, Miz Hillyer?" asked ol' Mr. Farley, fumbling his way into the room pushing an oversized broom.

"Soon as I finish entering these grades, Mr. Farley," said Aggie. She finished thumbing through the stack of drawings, jotting letter grades beside the names in her grade book, cussing under her breath.

"What's dat you say, ma'am?" asked Farley, looking up.

"I'm finding it hard to maintain objectivity and reduce art to a multiple-choice categorization on a scale of A through F."

Funny, thought Aggie, how no one ever referred to him as anything but ol' Farley. He hadn't always been old. She'd love to buy him a drink one day when she had time and ask him how it was growing up and going to school in the deep South.

"My classes! I've got to give them grades, and it's very difficult to be objective with a subjective area such as art," she began to explain.

Farley leaned on his broom, perplexed. "Tha's jes' raht ovah mah haid, Miz Hillyer. I caint hardly draw a straight line with a rulah!" he chuckled.

"There are very few straight lines in nature, Mr. Farley. It's making them wiggle in the right directions that's tricky," laughed Aggie.

"I guess you' the one ta' know 'bout that," he answered.

"Hey, Sadie Mae," said Mac, poking his handsome face in the door.

"Mac!" A spark ignited.

"Puttin' in a little overtime, huh?"

"Just about finished," she answered. "Come on in."

171

He moved a sheaf of papers and seated himself on her desk. "Actually, that's sorta what I came to talk to you about. Hey, Farley," he said to the janitor. "How's it goin'?"

"Jes' fine, coach. You made us proud, winnin' the state trophy like ya done. That was one helluva game," he said. "S'cuse me for sayin' so, ma'am, but that sure was one helluva game."

"Thanks a lot, Farley. Surely appreciate you sayin' so. Hey, man, can you come back later?" asked Mac. "I want to be alone with my girl."

"Jes' 'bout done, boss!" said ol' Farley, grinning.

"Why'd you tell him that? Poor gullible old man's about to believe you," asked Aggie as Farley left with his cart and broom.

"Do you realize, Sadie Mae," teased Mac, smiling "that everyone thinks I been gettin' some all along?" He looked her over just for practice, while she laughed self-consciously. "S'long's we got the name . . ." he began, running a finger up her arm.

The spark grew to a flame and spread its heat over her insides. "Season's over, coach. Haven't you had enough of games?"

"You're right, Ms. Hillyer. Henceforth I will approach you with the proper respect when requesting a favor."

She laughed, resigned to his ways. She was about to be manipulated, but she didn't care. Mac was setting her up for a little professional courtesy. "What's the problem, coach?" she asked.

"My boy Ben," he answered. "He needs to raise his overall grade point average. He needs an A in your class."

"He's been out too many days, Mac. The C I'm about to give him is an outright gift with his excessive absences. I can curve a grade, but he simply hasn't been here to do the work, Mac."

"No sweat, Aggie," he said, his green eyes engulfing her. "Just fill in a few days on your attendance register so it'll correspond to mine. I'll give you the days he cut that I know for sure he was in the building. Some of the time he really was with me, in the gym or out on the field. I'll give you my word, Aggie. If you'll back me up, you're covered."

"Mac," she blurted, confused, "attendance records are state documents. I've got Muriel breathing down my back as it is for far less serious matters than the falsification of an attendance document."

"Not to worry," laughed Mac. He seemed amused by her consternation. "This is not an unprecedented procedure, Aggie. We do this for kids all the time and with far less reason. Listen, honey," said Mac confidentially. "Isn't this right down your alley? You're the one who's always saying that the grades don't reflect a student's real status. This is a poor black kid who's made good. He's the years most valuable player, the hero of our victory at state. The PR alone is invaluable to the school Aggie. We only stand to profit from this, believe me."

"Has any woman ever been able to say no to you?" she asked, gazing into his eyes with devoted resignation. She opened her attendance register and started to make the needed alterations to grant the phantom Ben Hooper that ultimate achievement—having missed more than half the required course work, he'd nevertheless aced art. "If anyone asks me how Ben Hooper ever passed art, let alone got an A, I'm going to dump my attendance register in the Avalon River and claim total ignorance of the act, Mac," she said as he bent over her shoulder to help change her attendance sheet. "Even if we get him into a college on this fraud, how the hell's he gonna get through a college curriculum? He's not passing high school."

"All he's got to know how to do is sign his name to the contract and play ball, Aggie. He's leavin' the ghetto. He got his shot. It's an imperfect system, but it's the only one we got," said Mac.

She sighed, realizing he was right. She couldn't stem the tide with just a finger in the crumbling dike. "What if something happens and he can't play ball? He's got nothing else to fall back on."

"Folks who got something to fall back on fall back," he replied. "At least this one's got a chance. A lot of 'em'll never even get that chance. Few kids get opportunities like Ben's being offered, with or without an education."

"Somehow it just doesn't seem right!" she said. "There's something we just aren't doing right."

18

He was an ordinary man, the sort one chooses to represent the median or control on any sociological scale. He was neither short nor tall. He was of average weight, with ordinary features . . . not stupid but not incredibly bright, Randall Denison was, with just a small exception, a homogenously mediocre man. But to his roommate, Gomez, he was unquestionably beautiful. And like all men in love, he was sufficiently enamored to grant his beloved anything—almost anything.

"Aw, c'mon," he pleaded, "you came out of the closet. Now get out of the house. It's New Year's Eve, for Christ sake! You expect me to sit here and listen to you bitch and moan. I want to go down to the club and have a few drinks, a few laughs . . ."

"I really don't feel like it," answered Gomez. "I will cook us something"—he kissed his finger to express a consummate delicacy—"and to hell with calories . . . Hah? We have a good time here . . ."

"Bullshit to that! Look, it's gonna be jumpin' down at the lounge. You oughta come and meet some of the guys, let them get to know you. You got more reason than ever to go public now. There may come a time you'll need a few friends."

"I have friends." Gomez got defensive. "My friends at school, my students, the people who make me Teacher of the Year . . . how about it, hah? There is only one a year. These people will not let it change their feelings. You are too hard, Randy. You have no faith. I believe they will continue to accept me for my abilities."

"That's how come we get those calls we been gettin' in the middle of the night, huh? It's just another one of your

175

friends anonymously callin' in his support and understanding? When the hell you ever gonna learn, you dumb shit? The only people that will ever understand you is your own kind."

"Randy, my own, my life, do not torture me this way. I need some peace and quiet. I need understanding and patience from you more than anyone. Come . . . help me so we can eat sooner . . . I fix you a surprise."

"I don't get the kick you do out of feeding my face," retorted Randy. "Look what it's doing to you. You're blowing up like a blimp. They could float you over the stadium during the Orange Bowl. Why don't you straighten your head out and just accept what you are? Learn to live with it and like it instead of making yourself miserable and then stuffing yourself so you'll feel better. Me, I'm gonna go start this year happy. I'm movin' out the end of the month."

"You what?" asked Fernando, stunned. He looked like a little boy pouting from beneath an incongruous mustache. "What is this, all of a sudden?"

"It's not sudden, Nan. I've been leavin' for a long time now."

Randy wasn't there for supper, so Gomez ate both their portions, and cried himself to sleep.

"Kids asleep?" asked E-Z as his wife emerged from their son's room.

Liz Jordon nodded and smiled as she settled lovingly into her husband's lap. "Isn't it time to open that champagne?"

"I'd love to pour you a drink, mama," he answered, "but I'd hate to get up."

The fire crackled festively and etched them in rosy profile in the gathering dark.

"I always wanted a house with a fireplace," she sighed.

"I'm glad I could give it to ya, honey," answered E-Z, a man content at his own hearth.

"Me and the kids are so proud of you, honey. The new house, good school district, all that stuff under the tree—I am one lucky lady," smiled Liz. "God has surely blessed us. I mean it, honey . . . it means a lot to know the kids are gonna get a good start . . ."

He interrupted her with a kiss.

"I love you so much," she said.

"I'm gonna go get the champagne and get you drunk, woman," said E-Z. "And we are gonna have us one hell of a party."

"I'm so glad we decided to stay home tonight," grinned Liz as E-Z popped the cork and poured the bubbly into long-stemmed glasses.

"Who was it?" growled Jimmy Joe Wingate of the chubby blonde as she stormed back into the room.

"Our neighbors, complaining about the noise," said his wife. "I bet we're the only couple in town to get told to keep the noise down on New Year's Eve. You're enough to wake the dead!"

"It would take somethin' like that to get a little off of you," he retorted. "It's been so friggin' long since I got laid I forget what the hell it's like."

"Shet yo' mouth, James Joseph," warned Darlene. "You jes' shet yo' mouth. And keep your voice down lest ya' wake the baby. I got better things ta' do than walkin' the floor all night with her."

"Well, don't let me keep ya' from it," he answered. "I'll try to find a way to take my mind off the pain *that*'ll cause me. I'll find somethin' else to do." He grabbed his jacket from the closet and, pouring down the last of his Jack Daniels, staggered for the door with Darlene on his heels.

"Where are you goin', you bastard?" whined Darlene. "I'm missing the Boltons' party 'cause you didn't want to go out. Where you think you're goin'?"

"I'm goin' to find me some better company," he replied, slamming the door behind him. Darlene began to cry. "You're not goin' to leave me here all alone, J.J. Please, honey, I'm sorry," she wailed into the silence. "You'll get yours one day, you son of a bitch."

He stuffed the key into the ignition of his Dodge pickup, and the engine cleared its throat and turned over. Bumping a tricycle left unattended in his driveway, he backed over the curb and the truck lurched out into the street. A Country Western station blared from the radio as he headed the truck like a homing pigeon toward his favorite watering hole.

It was smoky and noisy and crowded with revelers when Jimmy Joe squeezed through to the bar and parked himself beside a redhead perched on a bar stool sipping a Daquiri through a straw. He looked her over with studied casualness and said hello.

She ignored him, finishing her drink with an audible slurp.

"Can I buy you another one of these?" he asked.

"I'd die of thirst first, creep," said the redhead, abandoning the bar stool.

"Whatever you're chargin', ya ain't worth it," he called as she melted into the press of bodies in the room.

"Still in there pitchin' passes, huh, hero?" said the bartender, setting a Jack Daniels on the counter in front of him. "I didn't expect to see ya' here tonight, good buddy. Your pals left here about twenty minutes ago."

"Where'd they go?" asked J.J., raising his glass.

"Probably out cruisin'," said the bartender. "Tanked up an' spoilin' for a fight. Lloyd got him a new shotgun for Christmas. He's probably blowin' out a few street lights downtown, or they're scarin' the be Jesus outta a few niggers and queers."

They both laughed.

"That Lloyd's a playful sonofabitch when he's had a few, ain't he?" agreed Jimmy Joe. "Sorry I missed 'em."

"If you hurry, you can probably ketch up with 'em at Lloyd's house. He said somethin' 'bout showin' off his new piece."

"That ain't the kinda piece I'm lookin' for, buddy," answered Jimmy Joe. Spotting another unattached woman approaching, he gave her the eye.

"Lookin' for some action, huh, sport?" kidded the bartender, following Jimmy Joe's eyes as they surveyed a shapely blonde. "That's a piece worth lookin' at, for sure."

"Looks a little like this broad we got where I work," said J.J. "This goody-two-shoes teacher with a set a' tits you gotta see ta believe. I know she likes me, 'cause when I first got there . . ."

"Look," said the bartender, cutting him another drink. When J.J. got to bragging about his conquests, he was good for an hour or more. "Why don't I jes' leave another one a' these for when you're ready. We're kinda' busy here tonight."

"Yessiree, sure got a great set a' knockers for a school marm, that's for fuckin' sure," muttered J.J., working up a drunk and a mental hard on along with the bourbon.

Aggie dropped a number-four sable carelessly across her palatte and rushed in from the terrace to answer her phone.

"Oh, Maddy," she said happily, "Happy New Year . . . I was going to call you later."

"I almost hung up. I was hoping you *weren't* home, darlin'," said Maddy.

"I was out on the terrace, finishing a painting," said Aggie. "I got so engrossed, I worked long past daylight . . . but I'm going to wait past midnight till I sign it," Aggie explained. "I can't always hear the phone out there."

"You mean you're going to *paint* all night? Alone? On New Year's Eve?" asked Maddy with a touch of outrage. "Why don't you come and join us for a little late supper, darlin'? You haven't even met Cliff yet."

"No, I don't want to barge in on a private party. I love you for asking, dear, but I'd feel like a fifth wheel. Besides, don't make it sound like being alone is some kind of punishment akin to solitary confinement or being dateless on prom night. The kind of job we've got, being alone is often a luxury to look forward to. And this is the first painting I've finished in months. I've still got to clean my brushes, take a bath—I smell like turpentine. Then, if I get bored, I can always finish correcting my midterm exams," she laughed. "You'd starve if you had to wait for me."

"If you're sure, Aggie."

"Thanks just the same. Go on without me," she said. "I've got my evening planned. But I'll drink to you at midnight, and count your friendship among my blessings."

"Aggie . . ." she hesitated, unsure. "You know I'd love to have you here . . ."

"I know, Maddy, I love you." And laying the phone back into its cradle, she ran to retrieve her paints from the terrace.

The temperature dropped to about 50 degrees as the

moon came up, rising bright and yellow like a slice of melon in a bowl of starry, deep blue sky . . . a sky stolen from a Van Gogh painting. Too cold to be outdoors, thought Aggie. It must be true about the blood thinning out in the warmer climes. This would have been a midwinter heatwave instead of a cold snap, back home, but she compulsively returned to her canvas. A touch of veridian, a spot of zinc white for highlight against the Mars black pupils, and the eyes focused. The image on the canvas came to life.

Dragging the easel into the room, she stood it up in a prominent position in the corner of the room. Not bad, she mused, admiring it. It really is like riding a bike or making love . . . you don't forget. That's not at all a bad resemblance, she thought with satisfaction. The figure on the canvas was blond and bronzed, his naked limbs extended toward an emerald ocean as green as his eyes.

"Don't go 'way, love," she said, blowing him a kiss. "I want to slip into something more comfortable for the signing ceremony."

She dumped half a bottle of her favorite perfume into her bath water and applied her makeup as meticulously as though she were stepping out, but her lace and satin gown had been purchased just for such an occasion in a lingerie shop that specialized in sensuous sleepwear.

Guy Lombardo was beginning his nostalgic journey down a musical memory lane, while the eye of the TV camera focused on the revelers amassed in Times Square, waiting for that sphere to drop on the rooftop proclaiming the new year . . . thousands of people gathered in a drifting snowfall and icy northern winds, freezing their buns off, compelled by some tribal instinct to have fun this night, no matter how they had to suffer for it.

A fireplace would be nice, she thought as she lit the candles and poured the wine.

Two glasses stood, winking golden bubbles on the table as she laid the remainder of the wine into a bucket of ice and broke out a lid of the stash Bob had laid in for her.

Vance's green eyes stared from the glossy wet canvas, and all the folks on television in Times Square screamed and applauded as Aggie raised a signature brush to affix her name to the portrait.

180

"Thank, you thank you, ladies and gentlemen," she giggled, taking a bow toward the screen. "And thank you, too," she sighed to Mac's image. "You'll never know what great times we've had together."

Rising on the bubbles and the smoke, she floated to the ceiling, where she and Mac danced a pas de deux in the best tradition of Fred and Ginger. Her pale yellow gown hugged her contours like butter melting on a sweet roll, and her skirt swirled high around her bare brown legs. Vance was garbed like the hero-prince from Swan Lake . . . and it was beautiful, as it always was, when she conceived him in her mind's eye . . . and it was all the more wonderful for being of her own creation. The second glass of wine went flat, untouched, as she pursued her dream into a gentle slumber.

The candle was nearly burnt out as she snapped awake, startled by the ringing of her doorbell. She switched on the lights, and, squinting into the sudden illumination, jumped up from the couch.

The bell sounded again, more urgently. Who could that possibly be at this hour? she wondered, noting by the clock in the kitchen it was half past two . . . only Bob, getting off a late shift, perhaps. No one else would call on her this late. "Who is it?" she called through the door apprehensively.

There was no reply.

Fear overtook her. She stood, frozen, unable to shake the drowsiness. The dope and wine had done their number on her head. "Who's there?" she asked again with what she'd hoped was a little more authority.

"It's me," said a vaguely familiar voice. It *wasn't* Bob. Jimmy Joe, she wondered? "What is it?" she asked.

"Open up, Aggie. I need help."

His garbled voice sounded different somehow. She looked through the peephole and saw Jimmy Joe slumped against the wall, holding onto the fire extinguisher outside her door. She unlocked the deadbolt but left the chain hooked.

"Mr. Wingate, it's nearly three o'clock in the morning! What are you doing here?"

"Lookin' for an all-night diner," snickered Jimmy Joe.

"Open up, Aggie. I can't make it home. I'm sick. I was driving by and I got pains. I may be having a heart attack."

Jimmy Joe's well-tailored suit was rumpled, his thinning hair mussed.

"How did you know where I live?"

"Let me in, Aggie," he pleaded, panting and groaning. "Just let me sit down for a minute."

"You're not sick, you're drunk. Go home to your wife, Mr. Wingate."

She began to close the door. But whether it was a deliberate ploy or the action of a sick man, Jimmy Joe fell against the door, his weight snapping the chain. The impact threw her backward into the room, the satin gown slid high about her thighs as she and Jimmy Joe lay sprawled, staring at one another from the floor.

She got up, indignant, pulling the garment about her protectively as though the fabric alone could shield her from his eyes.

"Now, don't be scared," he said, slobbering. "I just need a cup of coffee to get home on. You wouldn't want it on your conscience that you turned me out in this condition, would you?"

"How did you get here in the first place?" she was more angry than frightened. "How did you know where I lived?"

"I looked you up in the personnel files," he smiled.

"In case you ever needed a place to stop for coffee in the middle of the night," she snapped angrily.

He kicked the door, and it slammed shut behind him.

"If you ain't got any coffee made, I'd just as soon have a drink," he said. "Whatta ya' got to drink around here? Well, will you lookee here," he grinned, zeroing in on the wine glass. "Did you get stood up tonight, pea-pie? Whew, and a dope fiend," he hooted, noticing the lid and the roach. "I believe what we got here is one frustrated, desperate woman."

He reached for the glass, still full.

"Don't touch that," said Aggie. "Get out of here before I call the cops." Snatching the glass from his hand, she felt her rage turning to apprehension.

"Do that," he smirked, "and tell 'em to bring a warrant so's they can take this here funny ta'baccy you been smokin'."

He raised the wine bottle to his lips and drained it, then staggered toward the easel. "Hot shit," he laughed. "You do that? Now what would a gal who lives alone be doin' paintin' pitchers a' naked men?" He leaned closer. "He reminds me a' someone I know. Goes to prove what I been sayin'. A woman like you needs a man."

He advanced unsteadily toward her as she cautiously inched her way to her bedroom, and although she sprang the last yard in a single leap, he was on her, his shoulder to the door like a blocking lineman. "You're ripe for some real lovin'." His bulk was even harder to manipulate in his drunkenness, but he lurched forward rather like an eighteen-wheeler parked on an incline whose brakes had slipped and reached for her with both hands.

"Get out of here and leave me alone!" she shrieked. "Get out!"

"Now, you don't mean that," he whined. His eyes were bloodshot; a bubble of saliva dribbled from the corner of his mouth. "All got up in that outfit, I can tell you were getting ready for a big night. Be a shame to send you to sleep without a little . . . oh, baby," he smiled, tearing away the lace bodice of her gown. Her rage turned to terror.

Her naked breasts glowed pink-tipped and full-orbed for just an instant before she fell away from him, aghast. "Are you crazy?" she gasped. "You've got a wife and kids at home, a responsible position . . ."

"No one has ta know," he leered. "Come and gimme a kiss."

The thought of his mouth on hers was disgusting. She fought to maintain the self-control she needed to figure a way out of this. Holding the torn garment against her body, she inched toward the phone. Jimmy Joe's eyes never left her.

"Here pussy, pussy, pussy," he piped in a startling falsetto. "Come an' eat my bird."

He opened his fly to release a prominent erection.

By the time she reached the phone and raised the receiver he was on her. The nightgown fell away before the onslaught of his clumsy hands. Clinging desperately to the phone, she struggled in his grasp. Her pulse raced and her bare breasts heaved with real fear as she rolled, naked, from beneath his lumbering weight. He hit the floor and got up, mad. By the time he lunged again, his exposed organ flaccid and shrunken, she'd made it to the bedroom door. He grabbed her ankle and wrestled her to the floor again. As she felt his weight come down on her she brought both her knees, hard, into his groin and, jumping up, ran out of the room. She would have run screaming into the street had she not been naked.

Grabbing up the extension phone, she began to dial the police when she heard Jimmy Joe come staggering after her.

"No," she whimpered, her fingers shaking as she punched out each digit. "No, please, no," she cried as he overtook her. "God, please don't," she stammered through trembling teeth as he descended on her like those oversized monsters on the late show. His face contorted with liquor and lust, he grabbed and dragged her to her bed. With a drunkard's strength he pinned her beneath him.

She felt his naked cock against her belly and cried out "No!"

"Go ahead, little pussy. Pretend you don't want it. You don't fool ol' Jimmy Joe. You lil' do-good Yankee brung your sexy little ass down here to mess around with a bunch of underage niggers." A string of his saliva fell on her cheek and rolled down her neck.

She swung her right fist up into his face but he caught her arm and pulled it fast behind her.

"Jimmy Joe knows the real reason you ya'll come . . . 'cause all them pansies and perverts up North don't know how ta handle a hot-blooded woman."

He descended on her mouth like a piranha. His breath was so rancid with drink she wanted to puke. He began to hump and heave unsteadily. His beard stubble scraped her face.

No one's ever forced it on you before, she thought.

Jimmy Joe rutted like a hog as he struggled to penetrate her. And then, almost imperceptibly, his prick twitched ineffectually against her inner thigh and died in a milky drizzle.

Taking advantage of his moment of weakness, she used her second wind to roll him off her body and grasp with her released right hand a heavy metal ashtray. The blow caught him on the left temple and did something strange to his expression. Then he rolled over and fell, bleeding face up, on her pastel pink percale.

Weak-kneed and nauseous, she made her way to the bathroom to wash his slime from her skin. She remembered as she stepped, dazed, into the shower that the front door still stood wide open. What next . . . drag him out? Lock him in? With her? Alone? Could she get him out of there alone? Certainly not down a flight of stairs without detection. She needed help. She didn't want Jimmy Joe discovered in her apartment. Not this time of the morning. Not in her bed, bleeding from his empty cracker head.

Who to call in the middle of the night to help her remove a drunk? She knew she'd never bring herself to call Bob again. Not tonight. Could Maddy help her with that weight? she wondered. No, no. If they dropped him he might really hurt himself. Mac? God, no. He's the last person she wanted to know about it.

Gomez, she prayed, dialing his number. His machine took the call. He was out for the evening. She cast an anxious glance at J.J., hoping he was, too.

With the receiver still pressed to her ear, she pressed out Bob's home number, suddenly desperate for the sound of his voice.

"Hello!" She nearly shouted into the phone. "Bob?"

"No," said a feminine voice. "He's asleep. Do you want me to wake him?"

"No," answered Aggie. "It's not that important," she said, her voice aquiver with pain. It took another minute to recover from the shock.

Well, who's left? she thought. Who'd she trust well enough to impose on with a favor of this magnitude?

"E-Z," said Aggie into the phone. "I hate to wake you this early in the morning," she apologized, "but I've got a real problem."

"What is it, mama?" asked E-Z, only half awake.

She began to explain . . . But she only stood there, shivering, sobbing into the phone.

When she ushered E-Z into her bedroom a short time later, Jimmy Joe lay sprawling with his limp penis exposed,

185

leaking a trickle of blood from his forehead and snoring soundly.

"Land a' Goshen, honey," mimed E-Z, an impertinent grin invading the corners of his lips. "If it ain't Massah Jimmy Joe Wingate, the Third!"

He stood there, staring, a big hand propped on each hip while she gathered her wooly robe around her. She told him what had happened. "He was drunk, E-Z. And ugly," said Aggie.

"Mos' white boys is ugly, chile," he smiled, adding, "I could a' tol' you right off this dude was bad news."

"He's lucky I didn't kill him," she spat. "Please, E-Z, do something. He's messing up my sheets."

"I'll put him in his car and drive him home, but you'll have to follow me in my car." He fished Jimmy Joe's keys from his pocket and tucked his privates back in his pants. "Here's my keys," he said, hoisting Jimmy Joe over his powerful shoulder. "He'll wake up parked in his own driveway and think he imagined the whole thing. Well, let's get him out of here so's we can all get some sleep."

"I'll throw on a pair a' pants while you're loading him into the car," answered Aggie, grateful for his comforting presence. But as he headed for the door with his burden she called to him. "E-Z?"

"Yeah, honey?"

"He saw my stash. He knows I smoke."

"What's he gonna do? Tell people he came here to assault you and saw your dope?"

She sighed, relieved.

"Just don't get *me* mad at ya," he kidded.

She smiled, and it almost hurt. Her jaws had locked with fear, and a smile came slowly . . . painfully.

"Don't worry, honey. Your secret's safe with me."

19

Birds chattered in the towering tree tops on the east lawn of the Arcadia campus, all the birds that found their way to the temperate winters of the South.

Beyond the fence, the traffic of the street droned by, remote and nearly unnoticed by the students spread out on the lawn, their drawing boards across their knees, intent on capturing the peaceful, pastoral setting with charcoal or pencil.

"See how this plane diminishes to a vanishing point off the surface of the paper? It's really important to remember the fundamentals. Try this now," instructed Aggie. "Close your eyes and visualize the object. That's it! Now hold the image—open your eyes—and try to duplicate your vision using simple lines on your paper. Good . . . that's it! You're getting a fine grasp of the principles of perspective," said Aggie, looking over the young artist's shoulder. "Lookin' good," she said as she moved on to the next one.

Sheila Morrow sat propped against the trunk of a gnarled oak, the sunlight filtering through the branches, casting a lacy pattern of light and shadow across her beautiful face.

"Not bad," said Aggie, looking down to the drawing Sheila held on her lap. "Just one thing . . ."

"You mean the tower," said Sheila. "Yeah. I knew it didn't look right."

"Well," answered Aggie, "you're having some trouble with your perspective. See?" she pointed out the mistake. "You've shown me the top of the tower. It's way above your eye level. You wouldn't be able to see the top plane from here. Watch!" She picked up one of Sheila's books

188

from the pile beside her and held it above her. "What part of the book do you see?" asked Aggie.

"The underneath," answered Sheila.

"Right. Now get up," ordered Aggie, "and tell me which part you see."

She smiled as comprehension overtook her. "From here I can see the top," she said. "Things sure look different when ya get up on yo' feet, don't they? You can see a whole lot more than when you're down in the dirt. One a' these days, I'm gonna' see the top a' the tower. 'Cause I'll be sittin' on the top a' the worl' lookin' down."

"I know you will, honey," Aggie agreed.

"I guess I needed someone ta point mah dumb face in the right direction. You made it easier for me, Ms. Hillyer. Make a difference somebody give a damn about ya. At first, I wondered why, but it don't really matter. Remember when you got on my case to go out for the Queen's Court? Well, I never tol' you why I decided to go for it."

"You don't have to tell me," replied Aggie.

"No, I wanna say. I feel like I owe ya. Remember the day you and that man a' yours took me home?"

"Yes," said Aggie. It seemed so long ago.

"Well, there I was, comin' on ta' him, and all's he had eyes for was you. He must love you a whole lot."

Aggie's eyes stung suddenly.

"Ben's kinda simple. He really don't know a lot about life. But he play ball like a bat outta hell. He got a good future. And he look at me that same way . . . not like I'm a piece a' dirt, but like your man look at you. Ben Hooper love me, that big ol' dummy really love me, too."

Aggie gave her a heartfelt hug before moving on.

"Hey, Hilly," yelled Pete Santini from across the lawn. "You seen Beck?" he asked, approaching.

"Not today," said Aggie. "I thought she was absent."

"She wasn't in school today," answered Pete. "I know she wouldn't cut your class."

Pete and Becky Gaynor had been what the kids called "tight". Since that day she transferred into Aggie's class, the shy, quiet little girl had clung to Pete Santini, staring at him lovingly from big brown eyes awash with sadness. They were a curious contrast, the exuberant Italian and the timid little mouse.

"I've looked everywhere she could possibly be," said Pete.

"She'll turn up soon, safe and sound," said Aggie, crossing the lawn with Pete by her side. "Aren't you supposed to be in class?"

"We got a sub in math," he answered. "She let me out. I told her I had to help you. I'm worried, Hilly," said Pete solemnly. "Beck never got home last night."

Aggie spotted Dixie Beaumont hobbling across the grass on skimpy high-heeled sandals.

"You're presence is requested in Bo Calloway's office," said Dixie caustically. "I'm supposed to cover your class. Lord, how come you bring the little brats out here in public?" she scoffed. "Ain't it safer to just stay in the room?"

"Not if you're studying perspective," snapped Aggie. "What's this all about?"

"Some girl from this class! Her father's here and makin' quite a fuss. They got all her teachers in there. Better hurry. I didn't know where to look for you. Everybody else is already there."

"I've gotten down on my knees and prayed for that girl," ranted the Right Reverand Gaynor.

Muriel scowled as Aggie took the last empty seat in the crowded room. Like the pillars of Stonehenge encircling a sacrificial alter they sat listening, shamefaced, while the orator skipped not a beat of his recitation.

He seemed too old a man to be father to a young girl Becky's age.

All Becky's teachers were present: Al Ruffner, a quiet, elderly man from the science department; Elston Dunne, the social studies instructor whom everyone suspected of Marxist leanings; Helen Armstrong from the physical education staff, her masculinely muscled legs exposed beneath red gym shorts.

"What she needs is discipline," stormed her father as though from a pulpit. Becky's sobs were the only other sound in the room.

Seated beside Muriel were the girl's Dean, Beulah Pruitt, and a silent stranger with her trembling hands tightly folded in her lap whom Aggie assumed to be Mrs. Gaynor.

Jimmy Joe Wingate presided in Bo's absence.

". . . but He was wounded for our transgressions, He was bruised for our inequities; the chastisement of our peace was upon Him; and with His stripes we are healed. Isaiah 53:5," Reverand Gaynor quoted, shaking a fist excitably.

"Reverand Gaynor," began Jimmy Joe, "if you'll just settle down."

Aggie stole a look at his solid face, the mark still visible beneath the thinning shock of hair that fell across his forehead, and hated him.

"Settle down," shouted the red-faced man. "Our children are falling like flies . . . falling by the wayside. There's no respect for age, for authority . . . spare the rod and this is the predictable result. You'll have anarchy in the schools, in the streets. Well, by God, I won't allow anarchy and disobedience under my roof!"

"Reverend Gaynor, we are concerned with a student cutting classes, not an uncommon occurence, but ah don't think we're talkin' about an uprisin' of the adolescent masses here. Now, let's jes' stick to the subject."

Aggie tried to piece together the situation. From snatches of dialogue she was able to determine that Becky had managed to get herself locked into the school yesterday. Nor was it the first time she had been missing all night. And though she had spent the night in the building, Becky had apparently been cutting the majority of her classes for the last three weeks.

While the adults in the room took turns reciting attendance statistics, Becky sat in the midst of the congregation, crying, wiping her nose on the back of her hand.

Becky was new on Aggie's class list, and had not cut a class nor presented any other problem in the three weeks since being transferred from Muriel's class, and when it was her turn to speak, she said so.

"It certainly won't help her to make excuses for her," shouted Reverend Gaynor, jumping to his feet.

"Perhaps a bit of kindness and understanding would help perform the miracles you seek," said Aggie. "Becky's been no trouble in my class . . ."

"You must be one of them do-good bleedin' heart liberals that believes in coddlin' kids," raged the pastor.

191

Becky's face was red and swollen; she choked on her tears, verging on hysteria.

Jimmy Joe threatened to press charges for breaking and entering or malicious mischief; Becky's father alternately directed his verbal abuse against the school and his hapless offspring, whom he promised would "get the Devil beat outa her."

Mrs. Gaynor offered her daughter no solace. An occasional tearful hiccup was the only audible contribution she made.

That's all I can take! thought Aggie. "If no one has anything more to say on the subject," she said, rising, "perhaps you'll all excuse us while we compose ourselves."

She pulled a wad of clean Kleenex from her purse and laid it in Becky's lap. Then, placing her arm gently around the girl's shoulders Aggie led her from the room.

Muriel's eyes were the last thing Aggie noticed before she left, and the shocked silence that had even befallen the preacher.

"She told me how you got her out of there, Hill—" Pete began. "Miz Hillyer," he finished.

"You don't have to start getting formal with me now," answered Aggie, sipping tea.

"I want you to know from my heart," said Pete, "that I appreciate it. Thank you!"

"Don't thank me yet," said Aggie. "We haven't heard the last of this. There'll still be a piper to pay, count on it."

"Someone ought to put that hypocrite away," hissed Pete, anger replacing compassion in his eyes. "He just wants Beck back so he can manhandle her again."

"Pete," wailed Becky, beginning to cry again.

"Christ, Becky! You gotta tell somebody," said Pete. "Next time he could kill you."

"Pete, she's been upset enough today. Lay off for now," interrupted Aggie.

"So's he can get away with it again? Ask her why she ran away in the first place. Go on! Ask her!" shouted Pete.

"No, Pete, please, no . . ." sobbed Becky.

"Trust me, Beck. Hilly's OK. She's good people. Tell her, Beck." Now Pete was crying too. "Tell her how he comes into your room at night . . . tell her about the things he does to you. I love you, Beck," cried Pete, "and I'm scared 'cause I don't know what to do."

Aggie stood frozen, watching the scenario unfold.

"Pete, that's enough now," she said, setting down her cup. "We're all upset. Becky's going to make herself sick if she doesn't calm down."

"She'll be dead," yelled Pete, "if someone doesn't do something."

"No more, Pete," sobbed Becky, again.

"No, Beck, no," said Pete. "Don't let him off the hook again. Fight him, Beck." He embraced her.

Aggie watched, fearful of the fury in his usually cheerful face.

"He's carzy, Hilly. The man's some kind of monster. He started climbin' into Beck's bed when she was in the fourth grade. Then he'd beat the shit outta her for temptin' him with the sins of the flesh. Once, when Beck's mom got in the way, he broke her back. Laid her out. But he keeps gettin' away with it, 'cause the ol' lady's such a twit . . . and Beck's so scared of him," said Pete, looking into Becky's tormented eyes.

"Is that true?" asked Aggie, aghast.

Becky shook her head, tearfully denying Pete's words.

"Pete, you can't go around making sordid accusations against a man"—Gaynor's hateful face flashed back to her—"a member of the clergy," she finished lamely.

Pete grabbed Becky, bending her abruptly across his knees, and yanked her T-shirt up her back. The delicate, pale skin was covered with puffy bruises and festering welts. It looked as though she'd been flayed with a strap or rod. *He was wounded for our transgressions. He was bruised for our inequities*, thought Aggie.

"Did your father do this to you?" asked Aggie.

"Yes," wept Becky into Pete's blue denim lap. "My father did it."

For we must all appear before the judgment seat of Christ, she recalled from some remote corner of her head.

"Is that why you ran away?" she asked again of the distraught girl, "and stayed all night in school, 'cause there was no place else to go?"

"We're gettin' married soon's school's out. I'll have a good job in my dad's lumberyard. They already told me I could marry Beck if I just waited till the end of school."

Becky raised her bloodshot eyes to Pete's face and sniffed.

"There must be something we can do till then," said Aggie. It crossed her mind that she really ought to return to the conference, but knew as well that Becky's fate had already been determined. They would decide among themselves how best to deal with Rebecca Gaynor.

Muriel would let her know. She was certain that in some fearful way, her own fate was sealed as well. She alone would bear the brunt of Muriel's wrath.

She ran a clean rag under the cold tap in the slop sink and was pressing it to Becky's eyes when there came a knock on the Dutch door.

The red-gold beard split to a smile and the azure eyes beamed radiantly over the top half of the Dutch door.

"May I help you?" she asked.

He wore a tan leather sport jacket over a T-shirt and jeans. Someone's new teaching intern, thought Aggie.

"Are you the teacher?" he asked, somewhat surprised.

"I'm Ms. Hillyer. What can I do for you?"

"I'm a transfer student, ma'am," he said, introducing himself. "Daniel Mitchell." He handed her his transfer papers. "I guess I'm kinda dumb about the way you do things down here," he apologized. "I had trouble finding you. Have I missed the class?"

"No, Daniel," she answered. Something in his accent, not a Southern one, sounded startlingly familiar. "They'll be here in a minute."

"Minstrel," said Daniel. "They call me Minstrel. I didn't mean to interrupt. I heard voices . . ."

"It's all right, Minstrel. Well," she said skimming his transfer forms. "You're from New York. So am I!"

"Maybe we can talk about home if I get homesick," he smiled.

"For sure," said Aggie. "I'll be right with you."

Closing the Dutch door, she returned her attention to Pete and Becky. Aggie affixed her scrawled signature to two open-ended late passes.

"Stay with her till she calms down," she said to Pete.

"These'll get you back in class. Becky, honey," said Aggie to the sobbing girl, "we'll get you some help. I don't know how yet, but I promise we'll do something."

When she returned to her room, the handsome young stranger was seated on top of one of the tables near the window. The plaintive melodic sound of a flute floated through the half light of the room. When she approached, he stopped playing and turned to look at her. Perhaps it was the beard that made him appear older.

"Don't stop," she begged, smiling. "I'm enjoying your music. Now I know why they call you Minstrel."

He laughed, a low, throaty laugh that bubbled warmth and enthusiasm.

"My magic flute ma'am," he said. "A melody to pass the time or turn a frown around." He raised the flute to his bearded lips and piped another tune. The song rose in the silence like a flight of starlings, breaking toward the open sky, filling her heart with gladness. Like Pan, he piped his haunting tune in an enchanted forest of empty furniture.

Then, like the wail of a tomcat, the passing bell scattered the silvery sound.

"I'll look for you tomorrow, Minstrel," said Aggie.

"Till tomorrow, ma'am," said Minstrel, tucking the magic flute inside his jacket.

It wasn't until sixth period that a student messenger found her on the east lawn to deliver Muriel's memo summoning her to a departmental meeting after school.

Muriel was waiting in her room when Aggie presented herself at the door.

"Come in, Agnes," said Muriel. "Be seated."

She didn't say please. She didn't waste time on amenities.

"I'm sure you realize that Rebecca will be suspended from class for two weeks for her misconduct," she began without preamble.

Aggie wondered, at the wisdom of a system that meted out a punishment identical to the crime. They would suspend Becky for two weeks for cutting classes. Two weeks' suspension would force Becky into an untenable position. It would mean automatic failure in most of her classes.

"That leaves us with the problem of what to do about you," she continued. "You seem to have accrued a number of infractions, none of them individually serious."

Her voice was as dry as crackling parchment.

"But taken as a whole," she continued, withdrawing a yellow legal pad, "they seem to indicate an attitude problem."

Somehow she'd managed to keep a running record of every time Aggie had been late to class, every time she'd written a student pass to cover a kid of hers tardy to someone else's class, the impromptu Christmas party they'd organized . . .

"And of course," continued Muriel, "parties in the classrooms were expressly forbidden, in addition to which, the rules specifically state there is to be no food or beverages consumed in the classroom."

"But that wasn't a planned party," protested Aggie. "Some of the kids in my classes simply brought some stuff, soda and chips and things . . . why there must have been a dozen parties put together on the spur of the moment . . . very few of the faculty enforce that rule."

"While I am chairman of this department, Agnes, we will observe *all* rules."

"And all this garbage about being three and a half minutes late to class if I've been conducting classes outside the room, well, what have you done? In three years, you've been watching, waiting to spring this."

"For the past three years, Agnes, you've been a probationary teacher at Arcadia. I will be called upon to evaluate your performance. Now, about this last little detail," she continued, adjusting her rimless glasses on her beakish nose. "I can't find anything specific to cover the situation as it occurred this afternoon. But certainly, taking that student out of a conference—right out from under our noses—after her parents had gone to the trouble to come in to express their concern for her." Her indignation was the strongest emotion she'd displayed in the two years Aggie had known her.

"That parental concern you speak of is expressed in the home by a father who physically and sexually abuses that girl," said Aggie.

"Don't raise your voice to me, Agnes," said Muriel, the beginnings of a smile forming on her thin lips. "It is not my intention to discuss the fantasies that this student contrives outside of school—nor yours. Though the spectacle you made of yourself at the Christmas party was certainly no credit to the department. Be that as it may," said Muriel, about to deliver the final blow, "I've decided in light of your conduct today, I must advise Mr. Calloway of my inability to recommend you for permanent, full-time employment. I have further suggested that a disciplinary hearing be conducted immediately by the administration to determine your fitness for teaching. Faculty with a disregard for the rules produce pupils with a lack of respect for law and order."

Aggie heard her as though from a bad dream.

"Your conduct today was at the very least an embarrassment to the art department and to Arcadia," she continued.

But Aggie no longer listened. The extra hours, the additional work she'd taken on herself, the devotion to her charges beyond the demands of duty were of no account. Muriel had been accumulating the debits for three years.

"I must therefore recommend that your tenure be withheld," said Muriel.

Tenure, thought Aggie. It hadn't occurred to her that Muriel had the power to withhold her tenure. It just hadn't been important to her. Tenure was the sort of security teachers like Muriel fell back upon. Tenure was a way to stay in the system. Tenure was granted to any teacher who managed to survive the system for three years, and having been granted, assured the employment of educators who'd stopped trying—of those who no longer had anything to offer.

Was it over for her? Aggie wondered as her eyes began to burn. She rallied for a rebuttal, but the words caught in her throat. She would not give Muriel the satisfaction of seeing her cry, but the bile rose on the back of her tongue and her stomach turned over.

By the time Muriel dismissed her, red spotches began to appear on her arms and neck.

She found her way to the ladies restroom on the first floor, where several female faculty members had gathered in the anteroom for a bit of after-school socializing.

"Aggie," called Betty as she entered, "have you heard? We've been sold out. They settled for only seven and a half percent increases for the coming year. They signed another

197

two-year contract, and it's not retroactive to September."

Half a dozen women filled the available seating space in the small room. Aggie saw them through a haze of tears.

She passed through the far door to the tiny room with its sink and two toilets.

"Aggie, this is important," said Betty, following her in. "Aren't you interested . . . Aggie . . . what is it?"

The knot in her stomach had let go, and the retching began. Leaning over the stained ceramic seat, she puked till she got dry heaves.

It was there that Gomez found her. She heard him bustle in, explaining to the ladies as he invaded the sanctity of their lounge.

"Don't worry about me. I'm just one of the girls," he squawked. "Where is she?" he said to the women assembled there.

"In there, puking," offered Betty. "What's going on?"

Gomez burst through the bathroom door.

"What are you doing here? How'd you find out?" she asked weakly.

"Bad news travels fast," he replied. "One of my kids was in the office next door and overheard."

The red patches on her arms and body had become hives, and her head hung weakly over the john.

"Aggie, honey," said Gomez. "Don't worry, Aggie. You've got friends."

He cradled her gently in his bearlike arms.

"She's getting me kicked out of school, Gomez," wept Aggie. "It's over. No more classes, no more Hellions, no more kids."

"No, no, Aggie. You are a good teacher. All the people who count know it."

He rocked her, seated there on the floor with his back to the toilet.

"I never stopped to think, Gomez," she sobbed, "that they could kick you out like that. Nobody cares about the kids . . . just the rules. All they care about is the rules. They don't care about people. They don't care about anything that counts. Like that awful weapon, that neutron bomb, you know, the one that destroys all life but leaves the buildings standing?"

"It's always been like that, Aggie, there's no room to be different in a place like this," said Gomez.

His eyes were moistening too.

"We both made a mistake, Aggie," he continued. "We both thought we could change the system. Perhaps in another time, in another place."

"Nandy," she sniffed, "do you think it's true? That those who can't, teach?"

She was genuinely scared.

"Nandy," cried Aggie. "If I can't teach, what'll I do?"

20

"So they settled on a contract they're unhappy with after working for a whole year without one . . . and they keep us overtime to tell us how we all got shafted," she bitched, her long hair bouncing indignantly as she wound her way through the maze of corridors toward the exit.

"What did you expect?" sputtered Gomez, hurrying to keep up. "But didn't you say you were going to join? It could be a good move, Aggie. They could be a valuable ally, in case you need a lawyer."

"I couldn't, Nandy. It would be hypocritical to join an organization I don't believe in because Muriel's threatened my job."

"Where does that stand, as of this time?" he asked.

"Bo's holding up the paperwork. When I approached him about it, he said something vague about not wanting to make waves. He thinks it's a trivial thing that ought to be solved within the department."

"As it rightly should. But how to reason with Muriel?"

"That's the one *I* have trouble with."

"I wish I could think of a way to help you. You know I would do anything . . . but I have made my own bed of nails."

"What's wrong?" asked Aggie.

"No big thing, really. Worse things have occurred . . ."

"Lately?"

"Today," he replied. "I leaned over a boy's shoulder to tell him something—I don't even remember what. He acted like I had a disease he could catch from me. He acted like I was going to make him dirty because I touched him. He called me a name." Gomez's eyes began to tear.

201

"Oh, Gomez," she gasped. She worried she could not console him. "I'm sorry. I don't know what to say. They're kids, Gomez. They don't know. We've got to teach them. People like you and me, we're here to teach them."

"No more, Aggie. I don't know if I can take it anymore. I get calls at home in the middle of the night—obscene notes in my office mailbox . . . It's not just the kids, Aggie. Kids learn from grownups. How can we expect kids to understand what their elders cannot? How can I teach a kid anything after he's been taught to hate?"

She struggled for an encouraging word to counter his self-pity but came up empty. Her morale had been flagging too. "You can't just give up," she offered lamely. "You're too important."

"You're fooling yourself," he replied. "I could make a fight of it. I've already lost my pride, my professional dignity, and my lover. What's left to sacrifice? Did it ever occur to you to ask yourself if it's worth it? What do we end up with? Money? No, no. Our own union screws us on our contracts, you'll never do better than simply survive. The kids, hell, they don't really care. A few along the way, perhaps . . ."

"I've never heard you talk this way," said Aggie, somewhat alarmed by the depth of his despair. "You're a born teacher, Gomez. Everybody knows that. And you're a warm and loving person. Doesn't that count?"

"Only if you're careful to express your love in acceptable ways. Wake up, Aggie. It's over for me. Things haven't been the same for me since Christmas. I did a foolish thing. I thought if I was a superior teacher I could compensate for being only half a man. They won't let me forget! There is very little gaiety in being gay, I'm thinking."

"I've had days I didn't think I'd make it through, Gomez. It'll pass. It will all be over in another few months, and you can begin anew—make a fresh start. This thing will blow itself out. By next September no one will remember, no one will care."

"There won't be another September for me, Aggie. I'm leaving Arcadia."

"You don't really mean it. What else will you do?"

202

"You mean what will I do when I grow up?" The grin that accompanied the question was devoid of humor.

"Yeah! People were always asking me what I was gonna do after I got out of school. Funny, isn't it? I never did get out of school. Hey, Nan. It's almost dinner time. How about we stop at Vinnie's and split a pizza and a pitcher of beer. You'll feel better after we've eaten."

He reached around her to push open the heavy steel door and they descended the steps to the faculty parking lot.

"I always feel better after I have eaten," he joked. "Why do you think I have this?" asked Gomez jovially, hugging his plump stomach.

She laughed and looked at him, but Gomez had stopped short a few paces behind her.

"Where did you go?" asked Aggie, turning back to see.

But Gomez was struck speechless, horror and hopelessness written across his face. He approached her with uncertain steps, and staggered past, unblinking and unresponsive.

"What is it now? Change your mind?" she called. "Gomez?" She followed him with her eyes across the parking lot. They both stared, disbelieving, in the direction of his car. Scratched into the fender of the perfect paint job of the pink Chevrolet was a crudely scrawled F-A-G.

Gomez dropped to his knees on the pavement, his dark eyes streaming.

"Oh, Gomez, don't! Darling, please don't," she pleaded, holding his face against her breasts. "I don't know what to do for you, Gomez. Get up," she begged. "Please get up."

He continued sobbing. He cried so hard his breath caught and rattled in his throat.

She struggled to raise him to his feet, but he was dead weight against her. She felt helpless, unable to offer adequate consolation to match the depth of his grief.

"That's good," she said as he righted himself at last. "You're gonna be fine, Gomez. You're gonna be OK."

His eyes were dull and unseeing.

The terror rose anew inside her and constricted her throat and bowels. She realized it was a critical condition and was afraid of her inadequacy to see him through the crisis.

"I'll take you home," she insisted. "Come on, Gomez, we're going home," she shouted, pulling on his inert arm. "You can't stay here, Gomez."

"I'll get home by myself, Aggie," he finally answered. "Forgive me, but I have to go the remainder of the way alone."

"I won't let you be alone in this condition," she cried. "We're friends, Gomez, remember?" Her mascara was burning her eyes.

"There are things in a man's lifetime he must do alone," said Gomez. "Goodbye, Aggie, and thank you—for everything." He threw his battered old briefcase into the defaced Chevy and positioning himself slowly behind the wheel, he pulled away.

It seemed like a long time until she could move, and then her arms and legs felt leaden and listless. Putting each foot heavily before the other, she trudged blindly across the lot to where the little 'Vette sat waiting. It took a long time to find the key and fit it to the lock. It took longer still to insert it into the ignition through her teary eyes. She finally backed the car carefully out of its parking space and toward the gate, shaken to the core of her being.

"Hilly . . . Hilly, wait!" came a voice from behind. Glancing in the rearview mirror, she saw the red T-shirted figure bounding, limbs akimbo, across the blacktop.

"Hilly, I been lookin' for ya," he panted, still breathless.

"Not hard enough! *I* was in class today," she answered, a sarcastic reference to his ditching art again.

"I really got a good excuse this time, Hilly."

"I'm really not into hearing it right now, Pete. Honest to God, I can't handle it now."

There was nothing she wanted that moment so much as a hot bath and a hot meal except, perhaps, some sleep.

"Please, Hilly—Ms. Hillyer," he corrected, contrite. "It's really heavy shit."

"It must be," answered Aggie, noticing the altered address. "You only call me Ms. Hillyer when you want somethin'. Listen, Pete . . ." she began, looking for a polite way to put him off. She wasn't in the mood for pubescent pranks.

"Becky's run away, again."

204

"Oh Pete," said Aggie, "She'll turn up. Don't worry!" She suddenly saw real fear in Pete's brooding dark eyes.

"This time she's gone," answered Pete. "I've looked everywhere, called everyone she knows. She took some clothes and left a note." He swallowed hard and set the roach clip under his Adam's apple trembling. His eyes were red and weary. He handed her a folded penciled note.

Dearest Pete,
  I wanted you to know that whatever happens to me, that I love you too much to put all my trouble on your head. I need to find a way to stop feeling so dirty and ashamed. Honey, tell Ms. Hillyer thanks anyway, but I just couldn't wait. When I get to where I'm going, I'll call and let you know, because then they can't make you tell where I've gone.
All my love 4 ever,
Becky XX
P.S. Tell Ms. Hillyer goodbye for me, because she was my second best friend, you being the first.

"Get in the car," said Aggie, handing the note back to Pete.

They cruised the neighborhood around Arcadia, recrossed the distance to the small white church and adjoining cottage of the Reverend Gaynor, idled vainly before the homes of Becky's friends while Pete rang bells and repeated the same useless questions.

"Where now?" asked Pete, returning glumly to the car.

"Back to my place," she answered. "It's time I made a call."

Darkness had fallen, but the air was still warm and heavy. Few stars winked their way through a heavy cloud cover.

She had trouble remembering the number, but when the desk sergeant answered at the Avalon Police Subdivision he recognized her voice.

"Sorry, honey, he's working . . . Out cruising the neighborhoods. Can't come out to play till after midnight."

"This is business, Larry," answered Aggie. "I need a cop! I'd just appreciate it if you'd send someone over."

"Anyone in particular?" kidded Larry.

Aggie was in no mood to be amused, but it was true she had an overwhelming urge to see Bob.

Rain drummed restlessly against the highway and rose again like steam from the heat stored in the pavement. The moon raced silver thin like a boat tossed on a sea of angry clouds. Muddy water flowed in a brown eddy along the edge of the pavement where it ripped away the sandy soil and scrubby brush and sent a river of debris along the shoulder.

A fragile figure in jacket and jeans dragged a satchel of her pitiably few possessions into the shelter of the overpass. Removing a bandana from her bag, she wiped her teary eyes with it before she tied it around her rain-drenched hair.

A car approached, its lights a pair of eyes piercing the dark, ominous and threatening, but the car didn't stop. The elderly driver was probably as fearful of the dungareed figure lurking under the overpass as was the youngster huddled there.

What a night I picked to run away, thought the young girl, trembling as much from cold as fear. I'll have to take a ride, at least till I get out of town. She had twenty-six dollars and change hidden in her sock. Not much security for an uncharted journey on the open road . . . and she was getting hungry.

Becky sat, undecided and afraid, awaiting her fate. It was not long in coming. It came rolling to a stop under the underpass in a dark green van with out-of-state plates and a couple of guys with a bottle. She didn't want to go with them. All her instincts told her otherwise, but she was young and alone, and they were so enthusiastic and insistent and there was really no way to say no.

"Look, Pete," said Aggie. "She's not dumb enough to be out in this. She's staying with someone we've overlooked. She'll call you when she's ready."

"How come the cops never called us back?" asked Pete.

"Probably because there's nothing to say," she answered. "We would've heard by now."

"We should have heard by now!" said Pete.

"You should call your folks," suggested Aggie. "They're probably getting worried."

"They'd just tell me to come home," answered Pete.

"That's probably not a bad idea," she replied.

"Not till I see Beck," said Pete grimly, working his way anxiously through a large bag of potato chips.

She began to gather up the remnants of their sandwich supper, just for something to do, when there came a knock at the door.

"Who's that?" gasped Pete, jumping up. She knew, but was just as startled. Now that the man was outside her door and she had to face him, she was suddenly, what . . . scared? nervous?

She opened the door and saw him standing there, his dark eyes serious under the visor of his uniform cap.

It was Bob who finally spoke.

"How've you been, Aggie?"

"Fine, just fine," she lied, stepping aside to let him enter. His partner followed him in. "Hi, Joe. It's been a while," said Aggie. "I was about to make another pot of coffee."

"Man, I never thought I'd be glad to see the fuzz . . . began Pete. "The police," he corrected. "Have you found her?"

"I think we ought to talk alone, shug," said Bob softly, looking at her. He followed her to her bedroom as he had so many times. They faced off awkwardly.

"I was beginning to think you weren't coming," said Aggie.

"I almost didn't," he answered. "Don't take this wrong, Aggie, but you're not looking good. What the hell are those splotches on your arms?" He took her hand to get a better look before she had a chance to pull away. "What is that?"

"Nothing!" she snapped. "Nerves, an attack of hives. I've been getting a little strung-out over all this." She threw her hands into the air.

He knew her too well to accept excuses. And she'd run out of patience with his don't-get-involved and I-told-you-so speeches.

"Have you seen a doctor?" he asked.

"Yeah!" she confessed. It was good to have someone care. "He confirmed what I already knew, Bob. It's just nerves. As a matter of fact, he gave me a prescription."

"Tranquilizers?" he asked, pursuing the same line of questioning.

"Yeah!" she answered. "Why?"

He removed his hat and seated himself on the edge of her bed.

"Because I see a familiar pattern developing," said Bob. "You're beginning to remind me of your old friend, Maddy."

Silence rushed to fill the void between them.

"That's not what you came in here to tell me," said Aggie. "What is it you're trying not to have to say?"

"I'm trying to think of a way to tell you what I know."

"You found Becky?" asked Aggie, brightening, but only briefly. There was no joy in Bob's demeanor. "What is it, Bob? What's wrong?"

"We got this kid that came in tonight. Everything about her checks out, including old abrasions and contusions on the body. They haven't found her purse or clothes yet, or got a positive make—"

"The body? Bob, what happened to her?"

"Aggie, in the nearly two years of our relationship this was the one thing I couldn't cope with. You're like a sponge. I see you sitting here absorbing all the pain and problems of these kids . . . covered with hives . . . popping pills . . ." He looked searchingly into her troubled eyes.

Somehow she seemed to sense the answer she sought. She felt her stomach heave.

"I didn't say for sure the kid we got downtown's the one you're looking for, shug. There's a chance it's not your girl at all."

"One of the things about our relationship I found difficult was the way you always tried to shelter me from the grim realities of my world." She felt as though she ought to take a tranquilizer, but would not venture it in front of Bob.

"What I'm about to tell you is not very pretty, shug. You're not gonna like this one at all. Matter of fact, if

208

you've got one a' them 'mellow outs', maybe now's a good time to take it."

"Becky's dead, isn't she?" said Aggie woodenly.

Tears collected in her constricted throat and her voice wavered.

Bob nodded.

"How'd it happen?"

"She was hitchhiking on Highway 41. Looks like she was picked up by more than one perpetrator . . . raped, then bludgeoned. Cause of death was a blow with a blunt instrument. That's all we know so far."

She fell face down on the bed and sobbed.

"Aggie, stop!"

Poor child, poor wasted life. Rest in peace now, Becky. No one will intrude on your dreams now.

"We'll find them, Aggie. We'll put them away," said Bob, reaching for words to console her.

"Will that stop it?" she cried. "Will that stop the hurting and dying? Will that bring Becky back?"

"I never know how to answer that," said Bob, touching her shoulder gently. "Don't cry, shug. Cryin' can't undo this senseless thing."

"Someone's gotta cry for 'em, Bob. Someone's got to care and someone's got to cry for these children."

"Maybe you're right," he said.

It wasn't until she heard Pete wail like a timberwolf baying in the wilderness that she could set aside her own grief.

"I told him we weren't sure it was her," offered Bob's partner defensively. Pete was doubled over with the pain, horror contorting his face into a grotesque mask.

She ran to embrace him, to offer solace and comfort, but he was inconsolable.

"Aw, Hilly, she never even had a chance to live," he sobbed. "He killed her. He killed her as sure as if he'd done it himself. Where's Beck? I wanna see her," he yelled, livid with unspent rage.

"Listen, son, I don't think you ought to go down there tonight, as upset as you are . . . and her folks are bound to be there now," said Bob gently.

"We were gonna be married," choked Pete, barely able to extract the words. "I loved her," he sniffed. "I loved her . . . more than anyone else ever did."

"I'm not sure I can arrange it . . ." began Bob.

"Then what the hell good are you?" challenged Pete. "Who the fuck needs you? Where were you when my girl was gettin' beat to death, pig? Bustin' some kid for possession?"

"Pete, please, stop," begged Aggie.

"Why don't you let us take you home, son?" asked Bob.

"I don't need you to get me home," shouted Pete. "I don't need to come rolling home in a pigmobile. I don't need nothin' from no cop." He turned to Aggie. "I didn't even get to say goodbye." He was crying as he ran out into the rain, and the last she saw of him was the inscription screened on the back of his red T-shirt. 'When I'm gone, man, fuck 'em,' said the symbolic finger on Pete's back.

"I'll wait for you in the car," said Joe, following Pete awkwardly out the door.

"I'll be right along," said Bob. "Are you OK, shug?" he asked.

"I'm . . ." She was having trouble finding her voice.

"It's one of those I-wish-I-knew-what-to-say times," said Aggie.

"I've had a bunch of those since last I saw you," he replied. "I've practiced a thousand reunion speeches you've never heard, planned a dozen dinners we've never shared . . . rolled over in my sleep and called another woman by your name."

"Bob, don't," she pleaded. "This isn't the time . . ."

"I know," said Bob. "I don't know if the time will ever come again."

21

The insistent summons of her clock radio finally dispersed the terrifying nightmares that invaded her drug-induced sleep, and she awoke with a start to find she was still wearing yesterday's rumpled clothing. Having slept so soundly she should have awakened rested, but her head ached and her eyes hurt.

She should have been hungry, but her stomach was queezy, and her foul-tasting mouth dry as cardboard. She considered calling in sick, but fixed herself a screwdriver for breakfast instead and found her way to the shower. As she stripped off her sweaty clothing she noticed the rashes had reappeared and spread across her neck and down her belly, and she was aghast at the haggard face that stared at her from the bathroom mirror.

"My God," she said aloud. "What's happening to me?"

She needed a long rest—a change of scenery perhaps. She would call her folks—make plans to spend Easter up North—get away for a while. That's why teachers had all those holidays, wasn't it? The pressures of the profession demanded frequent periods of R&R. Who was it that had told her, or had she read it somewhere, about teachers who worked in high-stress situations, suffering the same psychological symptoms as shell-shocked soldiers who'd spent too long under fire in Vietnam?

She was just suffering from battle fatigue, Aggie assured herself as she daubed flesh-toned liquid on her neck. Her rash was becoming more difficult to camouflage. Maybe they'll think I'm going through a second adolescence and mistake it for acne, she thought, grimacing at her own reflection.

She popped a couple of aspirin with the remainder of

her liquid breakfast and the last of the tranquilizers from the vial on her night stand before hurrying out the door.

God, how her head throbbed! And the sun already so hot through the windshield that her makeup melted into a mask of sweat on her face. She switched on the radio and bore down on the accelerator impatiently. The needle rose on the speedometer as the small car took the railroad tracks without an instant's hesitation.

She heard the siren and saw the flash of red lights in the rearview mirror as the police car pursued and overtook her. She curbed the 'Vette despondently and rolled down the window as the uniformed officer approached.

"Pardon me, ma'am," he began, "but I've been following you for a while—"

"Yes, officer," she interrupted, fishing in her purse. She handed him her driver's license and registration.

"Didn't you see me signaling you?" he asked. "You were burning up the road." His swarthy Latin face looked stern.

"I'm sorry, officer," she answered contritely. "I'm late for work," she added with disgust. That's all she needed today. First a traffic ticket, then Muriel to contend with for being tardy. Christ, maybe she should have stayed in bed.

The mustached policeman began delivering a lecture on the laws of the open highway. He looked so familiar, she was certain she knew him.

"Hillyer," said the cop, perusing the papers in his hand. "I thought you looked familiar. I don't forget such a beautiful face so quickly. I got an eye for beauty," he smiled.

She squinted at him through her oversized dark glasses, trying not to lean close enough to let him smell the liquor on her breath.

"Jesus!" he blurted.

"What?" She was having trouble focusing her eyes and her memory.

"Hey-soos!" he repeated carefully. "We met, oh, several months ago at the game, remember?"

The images emerged slowly from her muddled mind.

"I was working. You were with my buddy Bob."

"Yes," said Aggie, forcing a smile. "I remember now." A shooting pain ran up the back of her neck and she winced.

"Hey," said Jesus, sticking his head into the car, "are you OK?"

"Yes, yes, I'm fine," she replied. "Just late for work and worrying about it."

"Look, I'm not gonna cite you this time. Just drive carefully, all right?"

"Thank you," said Aggie as he returned her documents. "I'll mention to Bob we met and how kind you were." She wondered if she'd ever get the chance.

"Listen, I don't want to butt in, but maybe you better take it easy. You don't look so good. You sure you can drive?"

"Fine, really," she said straightening. "I'll be more careful." She put the car in gear, remembering to signal before pulling off the shoulder.

The first bell was sounding as she raced up the steps, two at a time. The halls were already clearing as she propelled herself down the corridor toward the office.

Martha was removing the faculty attendance sheet from the bulletin board when Aggie burst through the door.

"Mercy," gulped Martha, "you startled me. Thank heaven you're here. We've got a problem with personnel this morning. The substitute I contacted to cover Mrs. Schwartz's home economics classes hasn't gotten here yet, and Señor Gomez hasn't even called in. I just don't know what we'll do. This is very unlike him."

"What was that about Gomez?"

"Well, he's usually so reliable," answered Martha. "He's never done this, *never*! Didn't even call for a substitute. You don't look well either, dear. What's that rash on your neck?"

"Nothing," said Aggie. "Just nerves. Have you tried calling?"

"My, yes, there's no answer there. Mr. Wingate is covering his first period. I'll simply have to find someone else after that. Miss Peterson is in your room," offered Martha. "Thank heaven I can cross your name off the crisis list this morning."

Don't count on it, thought Aggie as she headed for her room. The second bell had sounded and the halls were clear of all but the last few stragglers, all hurrying as she was. Muriel in her room. Was she to be spared no indignity on this ill-fated day?

Martha's voice cut through the nearly empty corridor before she even reached her door.

I PLEDGE ALLEGIANCE . . .

Bile broke against the back of her throat as her haphazard breakfast assaulted her system. The force of the light that hit her eyes when she removed the glasses nearly sent her reeling.

TO THE FLAG . . .

The nightmares that had racked her through the night returned. Gomez wouldn't go AWOL without reason. Where was he?

OF THE UNITED STATES OF AMERICA AND TO THE REPLUBIC . . .

He must be ill, she thought. Perhaps he went to the doctor. Sure, he went to a doctor. She'd have to make another appointment.

FOR WHICH IT STANDS . . .

She'd have to make an appointment to get some more tranquilizers with that doctor downtown who was so loose with his prescriptions. Perhaps he could give her something for her headaches, and that awful rash—

ONE NATION, UNDER GOD . . .

Poor Gomez. He must be very ill. Or perhaps he dropped his car off this morning and got hung up.

INDIVISIBLE . . .

Sure, she said to herself to dispel her uneasiness. Everyone knew how much he loved that car. He was embarrassed to come back here with that awful epithet engraved in his fender. He's probably signing in with Martha right now, thought Aggie, unconvinced.

WITH LIBERTY AND JUSTICE FOR ALL.

Aggie entered her room. Every student was standing at rigid attention. No one was giggling nor passing notes nor playing cards behind the sink. Not a single spit ball or paper plane littered the freshly swept floor.

"You may be seated, class," said Muriel.

They descended in to their seats as a single person, and in unison, turned their eyes to her.

Aggie met Muriel's gaze across the room and felt her knees tremble in spite of herself. Then suddenly in the pregnant silence, something struck her funny about Muriel's pedantic scowl. She started to giggle, but bit her tongue and swallowed her pride to put an end to the unpleasant scene. Tension crackled through the silent space between them, but before Muriel could speak, Aggie rushed to fill the void.

"I'm sure we all appreciate Miss Peterson's appearance here this morning," she said straining to speak. "Could we offer her our thanks?"

"Thank you, Miss Peterson," piped a chorus of hesitant voices tremulously.

Muriel crossed the room to confront her imperiously. "We'll discuss this matter of your tardiness after sixth period, Miss Hillyer," she said with an air of agitated authority.

"After school," agreed Aggie. You arrogant ass, she added in her throbbing head as Muriel made a dramatic exit.

As she left, the class came alive.

"Boy, are we glad to see you," said someone with an audible sigh.

"We were afraid we were gonna have her in here all period," said someone else.

The crowded room began to teem with spontaneous activity.

"I'm sorry I'm late today," she said. "Let's not waste any more time."

Minstrel appeared from the door of the Cave carrying her mug filled with steaming black coffee.

"I was afraid you were sick," he said, handing her the beverage.

"I'm OK," she said. "Thanks for this."

"Ms. Hillyer," interrupted an anxious adolescent with a mouthful of braces. "I need a number-two brush from the storeroom."

Aggie began to fish for her key before she realized that the door was already open. "How did you get in there?" she asked of Minstrel.

"I'll get the paint brush for you," he offered in answer. "Want me to lock up your purse?"

She handed it to him. "You've learned a lot from Pete," she said.

"We all learn from one another," he answered.

Upon emerging from the Cave he came to sit beside her, as he often did, and vocalized again a concern for her health.

Someone had put a poignant ballad by Roberta Flack on the phonograph, and the pupils all settled into their usually animated ambiance.

"What's that rash you've got all over your skin?" asked Minstrel solicitously.

"Acne," she retorted. "I'm experiencing my second childhood."

"You're not old enough for a second childhood," he cajoled.

"If you only knew," she answered, beginning her rounds. She attended to the students who most urgently needed her help, then returned to her desk to sit down.

"Now I know you're not well," said Minstrel, rushing to her side.

She gulped down the last of her cold coffee, a chill raising goose bumps on her skin.

"I'd go get Ms. Peterson if I dared," he offered. "Do you want me to call someone?"

"No!" she snapped.

His concern was becoming annoying and she felt guilty for her lack of appreciation. She was grateful when the dismissal bell finally left her blissfully alone.

By the time the lunch bell sounded, she was perspiring profusely, certain she was running a fever.

This is ridiculous, she thought, mopping her hot head with a clean cloth from under the tap of the slop sink in the Cave. I'm not gonna get through this friggin' day this way.

"Is it OK if we work in here while we eat?" said someone at the door.

Aggie jumped and turned to find two of her fourth-period pupils peering over the storeroom door.

"Not today," she answered. "I was about to leave. I have something very urgent to attend to."

"You can lock the door when you leave," insisted the student. "We'll look after things till you get back."

Aggie acceded and, leaving the two girls to their art work, fled to find E-Z Jordan.

"I've got to talk to you," said Aggie.

"I was just going to get some lunch, sweetie," E-Z answered, pulling his office door closed behind him.

"This is awfully important, E-Z."

He hesitated long enough to see the apprehension in her eyes.

"I hope you'll take this in the spirit of constructive criticism," said E-Z, ushering her back into his office, "but you look awful. What the hell is wrong with you?"

"Has Gomez shown up yet?" she asked, ignoring his question.

"Not that I know of. Martha dug up another sub just last period, I believe." His next question registered alarm. "Is there something I should know?"

"Yesterday someone vandalized his car. An obscenity had been scratched into the fender. He was very upset." She could feel a salty sting against her aching eyes. "Something terrible has happened to him," she sobbed. "I know something awful is going on."

He handed her a box of Kleenex across the desk and turned away for a moment. When she met his gaze again, she was angry at what she saw there. "Don't you care, E-Z?" she cried. "You, of all people."

"That's not what's really bothering you, Aggie. You're upset about the kid. You gotta right to be angry, Aggie. It was a terrible thing . . . but let's not let all that anger get us paranoid over every act of minor mischief that goes on around here."

"It's not like Gomez to just not show up. He's not like that."

"I think you're letting your imagination get away with you, honey," he answered. "You're letting yourself get all upset over nothing. Gomez got the blues over the irresponsible act of a senseless kid. We've got three thousand kids to worry about, and another hundred faculty . . . we can't go overreacting to every little thing."

"Little thing," she repeated, appalled. "You didn't see him, E-Z. This is no little thing."

"So, he'll take the day off, and they'll slap his fingers for the infraction when he returns tomorrow, and that will be the end of that," snapped E-Z. "You'll see. By tomorrow you'll see I'm right. I'm not so sure you ought to be here. Have you got a temperature?" he asked approaching to touch her temple.

"I'm just sick with worry," she said, shrugging him off. "E-Z, I'm scared. We've got to do something. I've got this horrible feeling . . ."

"Martha called his place all morning," said E-Z. "He's not there."

"Suppose he's sick," answered Aggie. "Suppose he's sick and can't come to the phone."

"Aggie, you're not being reasonable. What is it you're asking of me, girl? What do you want me to do?"

"Go find him," she ventured. "Please."

"Say what? You're the one that's sick, girl. I've got a group of black parents coming in this afternoon about that suspension business, and I still don't know what I'm going to tell them. Now you want me to go racing around town looking for your fairy prince?"

"So that's it!" she said, rising. "That's the truth of it. I never thought I'd hear such a statement of callous prejudice from your lips."

"Prejudice," snapped E-Z. "What do you know about prejudice. When you've lived inside a black skin as long as I have you and me can speak of prejudice. I've spent half a lifetime trying to instill some pride and dignity in a generation of hopeless little bastards from broken homes. I've spent my career trying to build an exemplary image for a bunch a' kids who don't know you can be black and be a man. A guy like Gomez makes a normal man uncomfortable, Aggie. Most of us can't identify. I'm sorry as hell he's having a hard time. But he brought it on himself. I can't afford to get involved with self-defeating causes that don't concern me. Don't tell me you're too color-blind to notice, but I'm the token nigger in the administration. I've got a family and a future to consider. And a battle of my own to fight. One that's already begun. I've been sitting here all morning rehearsing evasive diplomacy in order to try to fool a pack of prying reporters into believing this grand social experiment we call integration is actually working. You want to worry over somethin', try my problem."

"Tell Martha I need a sub to cover my classes, will you?" she sniffed against a soggy Kleenex.

"You gonna go home and get some rest?" he asked. "You look like you need it."

"No," she replied, "I'm going to go look for Gomez."

"Man, you're really askin' for it," said E-Z, leaning back in his chair. "The trouble you got comin' down on your head. Leavin' this campus and leavin' your classes, especially with the staff shortage we've got today, would be a bodacious blunder, baby. You got a department chairman that is not exactly known for a forgivin' nature."

"I'm already in trouble," said Aggie. "What difference . . ."

"The difference," stormed E-Z, "is that all she's got against you now, perhaps, is that you've been a bit zealous on behalf of some of your students. That is *not* the same as being guilty of a dereliction of duty. There are rules, Aggie . . . we live by the rules or we don't survive. The system demands obedience . . ." He looked at her worried face and softened.

"Look, I'm sorry," said E-Z more gently. "I'm a little uptight myself today. If you'll just hang on until I finish with these people, I'll jump in the car and take a run over to Gomez's place, OK? That delegation is already overdue."

"Oh, E-Z," she said, forcing a smile, "I knew I could count on you. You'll let me know immediately?"

"I'm still thinking this is a fool's errand," he answered "But if it will ease your mind, well——"

"E-Z, I'd be so grateful."

"I'd be grateful if you'd just go home," he said. "You don't look like you're gonna make it."

"I can't," said Aggie. "We've run out of understudies. I've got another couple of matinees this afternoon and no one waiting in the wings to go on. By the time a sub arrived it'd be the end of the day anyway."

"What are you trying to prove, pushin' yourself this way? You look like you're about to have a breakdown."

"Don't worry about me. I know the script by heart. I can't stand up my audience. The show must go on.

"There was a time I thought what we did here would make the difference," she said, her hand on the doorknob. "But we're all getting caught up in the game. The myths we invent for our students and the hypocracies we contrive for the sake of our public image."

"No one ever said the system was flawless."

"No one ever told me how ineffectual it actually is either," answered Aggie. "Some of the best educators I know are nothing but so much carnage. The system just chews them up and spits them out like raw meat. After we've sacrificed the best of our numbers to this destructive monster you call the system, what hope will there be for the kids?"

"If it were anyone but you, Aggie . . ." said E-Z, walking her to the door.

"I'm indebted to you," she began.

"You don't owe me nuthin'," he interrupted, smiling resignedly. "Except maybe lunch."

"If I ever get to where I can swallow past the lump in my throat, you've got a deal," she answered, attempting to smile.

Letting herself into the art room, Aggie discovered that the girls had gone, but the storeroom door was partly ajar and the light was on inside. Then she heard the wistful wail of Minstrel's flute.

"How'd you get in here?" asked Aggie, entering. "No, never mind. I don't really care. I'm glad you're here," she sighed falling into a chair.

"I was worried about you," he said, pausing for air before beginning another passage. The song poured out of the

221

slender silver stalk like water gushing from a hidden spring. Propped atop the pile of packing cartons, he looked like a satyr who strayed from the Elysian fields of Olympus.

"Why?" she laughed, lighting a cigarette.

"'Cause you looked so upset this mornin'," said the young man earnestly as he lowered the flute to his knees. "You looked like you'd lost your best friend."

She turned away abruptly and rummaged her handbag for a comb.

"Have you eaten?" he asked.

"No," she confessed. "I had business in the Dean's office."

Sometimes she was certain Minstrel was capable of reading her thoughts. In his extended hand was a big red juicy apple. "An apple for teacher?" she laughed gratefully.

He beamed like a bearded cherub, reacting to her appreciation. "Maybe to keep the doctor away."

She bit off a chunk of the succulent fruit. It tasted so sweet on her swollen tongue, but it took a super normal effort to swallow past the lump in her throat. The apprehension that had gripped her over Gomez's disappearance wouldn't let go. She gave up the apple. "Perhaps I'll save this for later," she said, attempting to erase the fear from her ravaged face with a covering of cosmetics.

"Remember I told you I sometimes helped the maintenance crew clean up the convention center after the concerts and all?" he asked.

"Um-hm," she murmured as she smeared lipstick on her parched, dry mouth.

"Well, I got to know some of the other people who work there," he boasted. "It pays to have connections."

"Yeah," she agreed, wondering if E-Z had left yet. She found a bottle of eye drops in her handbag and threw her head back to apply the solution to her eyes. Her face was still puffy, but some of the redness was gone.

"These are really good tickets I got," said Minstrel excitedly.

"Yes," she agreed, catching up to the conversation. "That's a real break. They're probably hard to get."

"Impossible is more like it," he grinned. "Practically impossible. Two seats to the concert tomorrow—why, they've been sold out for months."

She tried to remember which group was playing the downtown auditorium, certain he'd told her and that in her preoccupied state she hadn't heard. She returned to her despondent thoughts while Minstrel rambled on.

"Yessir," said Aggie with lame enthusiasm as if she knew what she was talking about. "That's gonna be one hell of a concert."

"Are you sure?" he asked.

"Of course," she answered, without hesitation, unaware of what she was agreeing to.

His grin was in such severe contrast to her despair they looked like the player masks that symbolize comedy and tragedy.

Her fourth-period art class was already drifting into the room as Minstrel pocketed his magic flute and made for the door.

"I'll see you tomorrow," he said with enthusiasm as he split.

"Yeah, tomorrow," she said. Then, realizing her mistake she added, "Tomorrow's Saturday."

But Minstrel was long gone.

Fourth period was a surrealistic assemblage of disembodied voices and floating shapes. With a determination of will that was quickly waning, she made the right moves, but like a Zombie rousing from the sleep of the living dead. She was tiring of the effort. The fifty-five minute class period seemed of an infinite duration. She wished she'd asked Minstrel to stay and help.

Where was E-Z? Why wasn't he back? Why was he torturing her this way? It was Muriel, not the dean, who entered the room with the fifth-period students.

"Muriel, I know we have things to discuss but this isn't the time."

"We'll discuss this *now*," snapped Muriel. "I remind you that I'm the chairman of the department."

The throbbing in her head that had slowly settled to a dull ache now flared, searing the inside of her skull like a fire brand. Her empty stomach growled, gripped with a cramp.

"Dean Jordan has requested that I look in on your class again, Agnes. You are to report to his office. *Now!*"

Aggie turned and ran without another word toward E-Z's office.

He was waiting, withered and somber, when she arrived.

"Well?" gasped Aggie, out of breath. "Did you find him, E-Z?"

"I never got to Gomez's place, Aggie."

"E-Z, you promised. I've been on pins and needles all afternoon."

"Sit down, girl," said E-Z, gently stern. "What I got to tell you is gonna hurt more than pins and needles. The cops were here just now. We got another messy problem."

Cops? she thought dully. She struggled to maintain her composure but was losing the fight. She contrived impossible excuses to explain away what she already knew to be.

"He's dead, isn't he?" she asked calmly as though she were inquiring about the weather.

He turned his back before answering. "His building super smelled the gas this morning and called the cops. They'll want to talk to you. Happened last night sometime. From what you told me, you were probably the last one to see him alive. Christ," spat E-Z vehemently. "Who'd ever have thought he'd kill himself?"

"He didn't kill himself, E-Z. We did it. All of us. We killed him with pretense and apathy. We all killed him. We killed the Gaynor girl the same way." Her voice was flat and lifeless, belying the pain that wrenched her heart.

"That's a lot of fatalistic bullshit, Aggie. We make conscious choices . . . decisions that affect our lives. I'm sorry as hell he's dead, but let's not forget he died by his own hand. He's the one who made the decision to go gay, he's the one who chose to parade his perversion publicly, and he's the one who snuffed out his own life."

"Gomez didn't choose to be gay," cried Aggie. "He couldn't have been other than he was any more than you could, E-Z. Any more than I could not be as I am."

"I know he was a friend of yours, Aggie, and you're entitled to be upset. But don't go layin' guilt on *my* doorstep for this. You know, when Hank was killed, I carried a lot of guilt. Everytime I picked up a newspaper, I just couldn't help feeling guilty. I didn't feel much remorse, 'cause he was a bigoted bastard and a drunken bum. But I was carrying the guilt for his senseless murder on my own head, 'cause the poor asshole who wasted him was the same color as me. *I* didn't choose my condition. Gomez did."

"Oh God, E-Z, I'm so tired," sobbed Aggie, "I'm so sick and tired of all this shit."

"Go home and get some sleep, Aggie, before you fall on your fanny. We'll deal with it later. We'll get it all squared away Monday morning."

But she was already on her way. "Tell Muriel I can't make the meeting," she said as she left.

22

Aggie could hear her phone ringing as she turned the key in the lock. She raced in and picked it up.

"Oh, Maddy. I'm glad you called."

"You sound different, dear," came Maddy's reply. "Is anything wrong?"

"Probably took the stairs too fast and I'm smoking too much," she answered, pulling another cigarette out of the pack. "I just got in."

"A date?" inquired her friend.

"Hardly," sighed Aggie. "Another funeral. For someone who hates funerals, I've sure been to enough of 'em lately."

"Gomez?" asked Maddy.

"Gomez," answered Aggie. "I had to go. The place was packed with kids . . . his kids sure loved him. You know, I was talking to this man at the funeral . . ."

"You've met someone," said Maddy.

"No," sighed Aggie. "He was the funeral director. Know what he told me? Gomez had his whole funeral arranged more than a month ago. Almost like he'd been planning it. Like he knew . . ."

"Listen, honey," said Maddy earnestly. "I've been around a long time. Maybe that entitles me to offer a little wisdom I've accumulated over the years. There are several ways to cope with this institution we refer to so grandly as 'the school system'. You can spend your career swallowing your pride and your tears, lulled by a false sense of security or some romantic ideal, in which case you may survive to retire on half salary, with perhaps half your sanity intact. Or you can swim against the current till your heart bursts with the effort, in which case you'd be wise to make

227

prior arrangements as did Gomez, in his innate wisdom."

"God, what depressing alternatives."

"There's another way," said Maddy, "if you've the courage."

"What's that?" asked Aggie.

"Walk away," answered Maddy. "No, don't walk. Run!"

"Strange to hear that from you," said Aggie. "My elders have always taught me that courage entailed facing your responsibilities and making a stand in the face of adversity."

"Fact is, if you take up a position on a railroad trestle, sooner or later the Super Chief is gonna mow you down. It would be fatal to believe you could stop it with positive thinking."

"What will become of the kids if we all just up and leave?"

"Whatever they want to become. Some will drop out, or fail out, or be thrown out. Others will graduate, make lives for themselves, marry, have kids, and send them to school. And some of them, as some of us, will die before their time. And what we do along the way will ultimately have very little relevance to the realities of life beyond school. I don't know what the answers are, honey. I only know it's bad and getting worse all the time."

"They hired another teacher and he was on the job in less than a week, Maddy," said Aggie. "Just like that."

"Doesn't surprise me a bit," answered Maddy. "With the turnover I've seen these last few years, I expect the teachers' colleges will improve the process till they can produce us to be as disposable as Kleenex. A school is a transient society, Aggie. The students come and go within three years, and lately, so do the faculty."

"Then why did you stay with it all these years?" asked Aggie, needing desperately to know, sensing somehow that the answer could help shape her own destiny.

"There's an old joke," said Maddy, "about the guy who joined the circus and ended up sweeping up after the elephants."

"If the punch line has to do with getting out of show biz . . ."

"That's the one," said Maddy. Aggie could almost see her gentle eyes, smiling, but there was no way to lift the weight of sadness. She needed something—anything—to bolster her morale and her flagging faith.

"What you're looking for is miracles," said Maddy.

"Aren't there any miracles left?" she asked, near tears.

"The miracle, my dear," answered Maddy, "is that any of us survives it."

It wasn't the alarm that roused her from her insensate stupor, but the door bell. She snatched up her robe.

"I'm coming," she called.

Her tongue was thick and her head as big as the Goodyear blimp. "Minstrel," she gasped.

He stood there freshly scrubbed and smiling.

"What are you doing here?" asked Aggie, aghast. She smoothed her hair self-consciously and rubbed her aching eyes.

"Don't you remember? I just asked you yesterday. I helped them set up the sound equipment for the concert and they gave me the tickets—"

"Oh, yeah, the concert," she said as he followed her inside.

"Yes, ma'am," he answered, his handsome young face becoming concerned. "Did you forget it was this afternoon?"

"I guess I did," she said, pulling the robe around her.

"Well, begging your pardon, ma'am, but how long do you think it'll take you to get ready?"

A thread of memory was unraveling in her addled head. Oh, my God, thought Aggie, what have I gotten myself into? "What time is it?" she asked absentmindedly.

"It's only about three," answered Minstrel. "I thought we'd get something to eat first, but it's a good idea to get there early to find a parking space," he explained.

Oh, Jesus! How am I gonna get out of this? thought Aggie, agitated. "Minstrel," she began, trying to be gentle. "I misunderstood. I didn't realize you meant for me to go with you."

"Hey, that whole talk we had about lovin' the same kind a' music, sharing memories of our home town . . ."

"You've a right to be angry," said Aggie. "I was upset. I've been very down lately . . ."

"Because of that teacher? The Spanish guy?" asked Minstrel.

"Among other things," she nodded. "I'm really sorry, but I'm afraid you'll have to excuse—"

"Hey, listen," he interjected. "I understand. But I think you're makin' a big mistake. There's no better way to take your mind off your troubles than to get out and have some fun."

She was about to protest, but his young face was so exuberant that she was suddenly tempted. She leaned against the door, staring at him in the dim light of the hallway. Her hair hung in stringy wisps from a knot on her head. Her arms and chest were peppered with hives. She felt like hell and probably looked worse. "There's no way I can be ready in time."

"Sure there is," said Minstrel, smiling. He wasn't about to give in. "I'm early," he said sheepishly. "There's plenty of time. We can even get a couple a' burgers on the way."

"This is insane," said Aggie. "By the time I get dressed—"

"I know what," he interjected, his grin indicating he'd taken her indecision for acquiescence. "Why don't I go get us something to eat here while you get dressed? Nothing fancy," he added, looking casually mature in new blue denims and that tan suede jacket he wore the day she met him.

Before she could voice an objection he took off down the stairs and was gone.

Downing another swig of vodka laced with orange juice and another Valium borrowed from Maddy's well-stocked reserves, Aggie stepped into a hot shower attempting to reassemble her reason. How was she going to let this misguided kid down gently? Minstrel was so sensitive, so intense. She smiled in spite of herself—the warm, soothing liquid fingers were massaging her skin, augmenting the thoughts of her serious young admirer. Ridiculous, thought Aggie, guiltily relishing the idea of herself as the object of the affections of a much younger man.

Well, she resolved, better to make a clean break of it. She would be as gentle with his feelings as she possibly could, but she must put a quick end to this matter. She couldn't possibly go to a rock concert with a student.

It was ridiculous, she said to herself as she pulled on a

pair of slim-legged jeans, to even consider such a preposterous idea. It would only delay the inevitable end of such misguided attention, she admonished the image in the mirror as she pulled a brush through her freshly washed hair.

By the time Minstrel got back with a bag of burgers and fries, she had her speech prepared and rehearsed, calculated to spare his feelings, while leaving no possibility of his misunderstanding her rejection of his attentions.

"That was a terrific concert," said Aggie. "Really good group."

"Aren't you glad now I talked you into it?" asked Minstrel. "I'm really glad you had a good time."

"Love your van, too," said Aggie, looking around at the interior of the cozy compartment.

"Hey, thanks a lot," he grinned proudly. "I did most of the work on it myself. Only thing is, I'm gonna have to give it up for something smaller when I go back to the city, or I'll never find a place to park it. You know, there are people in New York who've never gotten off the expressway? They just spend their entire lives driving around because they can't find a place to park."

He had her giggling like a grade schooler.

"It's true," kidded the serious young man without a trace of a smile to give himself away. "Know how many people have been born in the back of an old Chevy 'cause their parents couldn't find a place to park?"

"No," laughed Aggie, encouraging the lunacy. "Tell me."

"Not as many as have been conceived in an old Chevy, because their parents *could* find a place to park, I'll bet," he laughed. "Aw, I thought I'd have chicks falling all over me when they caught sight of this rolling crash pad, but it just seems to scare them off. Maybe they figure a guy with a bed built into his vehicle is too much of a threat . . . as if all a guy's interested in is just jumping their bones."

"Which, of course, is entirely untrue," said Aggie.

"Well, not entirely," said Minstrel, his smile emerging from the soft brown beard. "But mostly I just use it for getting off by myself. It's very comfortable for one person—or two people, actually, but only if they're close. If you're lookin' to impress the ladies, though, you're better off with a bullet like your 'Vette. I'll bet that thing really moves. Is it comfortable?"

"For one," she teased, "or two if they're really close." They both laughed. "But it's not the car for making out. There's no bed. Not even a back seat. But if you're trying to make out with girls, your problem isn't your car, it's your companions. Why don't you date girls your own age?"

"Last girl I took out thought the BeeGees were classical music. Girls are kinda silly, you know?"

"Yeah, I know, I used to be one."

"Aw, you're puttin' me on," he replied. "You know what I mean. You must think the same thing of me . . . that I'm just a dumb kid."

"No," Aggie answered. "I think you're sensitive and sweet. I think you ought to give the girls another chance at you."

"Maybe the truth is," he confessed, pulling a joint from his jacket pocket and placing it between his lips, "that I'm incapable of handling rejection." He popped the cigarette lighter from the dashboard and held it to the tip of the grayish roll, sparking a bright ember in the dark interior of the van. "Aspiring to someone so far above me seems to make it bearable somehow. I mean, you're so far beyond my reach that it's OK, somehow." He pulled on the smoke, filling the cab with the smell of burning hemp, and guided the vehicle deftly along the darkened highway. "God, I'm amazed I had the guts to say that," he mused, releasing the toke, slowly smiling. "Go ahead, take it," he urged, passing the stick.

"No thanks," she said, trying to sound casual and in control. "I don't . . ."

"Don't what? Don't smoke dope? I've been painfully honest with you," said Minstrel earnestly. "I know you do because I smelled it on you and I know you want to because of the way you watched people passing them at the concert. Is it just that you don't want to turn on with a kid? I know there's no way I'll ever end up with you," he said, "but can't you help me preserve the illusion for an evening?"

A wall of guilt and shame sprung up between them and she furrowed into the seat, feeling suddenly small and unworthy of her responsibility for anyone's deportment, including her own.

"Does anyone else . . . ?"

"Know? I don't think so. Not from me, anyway. I'd never say anything. Not even to Pete, though he's so sharp I'm amazed he missed it. I didn't see any reason to call it to his attention."

He took another hit and held it out to her once again, like a challenge as much as a gift. "Trust me," said Minstrel, and his eyes said *Please*.

She reached for it timidly and pressed it to her lips. It was burning hot and uneven, popping as the seeds burnt. "Ow! That's hot."

"You should have changed your mind before it got so short," he said. "When'd you get into dope?"

"Not till college," said Aggie. "Compared with today's kids, my generation were late bloomers."

He reached for a knob on the panel behind the wheel and pushed a tape into the machine, and they were rolling to the haunting strains of a symphony by Rick Wakefield.

"How come you're not seeing anybody?" he questioned. "Still hung up on that cop?"

"What is this?" she wailed, taking a long drag. "An interview or an interrogation?"

"Neither," he laughed. "Why?"

"The answers I give may depend on it. You're making me nervous."

"Sorry. I won't do it anymore."

"How did you know about the cop?" she asked, taking another hit and passing it.

"I asked. You can find out anything you need to know if you ask the right person."

"Yeah? What else do you know?"

"I know this roach is gettin' too short to get a hold of while I'm drivin'," he said, passing it.

"I've got a clip in my purse," she said, fishing for it in the dark. "If I can only find it."

"We're almost to your place. I'll roll us another one."

They pulled into a spot alongside her white sportscar. Light-hearted and light-headed, she hopped down and shot off across the parking lot at a full run toward the playground at the far end of the complex.

"Hey," yelled Minstrel in pursuit. "Where are you going?" His long muscular legs easily overtook her. By the time he did, he understood. As Aggie lowered herself gingerly into the leather sling swing, Minstrel was making like Tarzan on the jungle gym.

The sky was bright with a multitude of stars and the air was heavy with the scent of orange blossoms from the grove beyond. Laughing like little children at play, they passed the time in joy, sharing an innocent intimacy along with another joint under the trees in the orange orchard.

"That was more fun than the concert," said Minstrel. "You ready for a fast game of Frizbee?"

"Are you kidding?" asked Aggie in mock incredulity. "I'm ready for a rest cure in a geriatric ward."

"Now you're kidding," he answered, his blue eyes gleaming in the glow of the roach. "I don't see you as old, but I was aware of your discomfort earlier. I was so proud you were with me, and I got this feeling like maybe you were embarrassed."

He looked so serious, his eyes beginning to dilate, penetrating her private thoughts with their piercing earnestness.

"Lest we forget," sighed Aggie, "I'm nearly old enough to be your mother."

He laughed heartily and passed the roach directly to her lips as he explained.

"Not nearly. My mom's probably old enough to be *your* mother. I was a change-of-life baby. I came along when they'd already given up hope."

"I'll bet they spoil you rotten," teased Aggie.

"Yeah," he agreed. "But there are drawbacks. The year I turn twenty one, my dad will be seventy . . . if he makes it."

"What do you mean?" asked Aggie, inhaling and holding it.

"Aw, I probably got no right to complain. Up North, my dad had his own business. He was one of these self-made men, you know? But he always had the time and energy to spend on me. We used to go camping, fishing, up into the Adirondacks. He was so full of life. Then he retired and came to Florida. Now all he seems to be doing is waiting to die."

"I'm sorry," said Aggie, realizing how little she knew about him. "What's your mother like?"

"She's a lot like you, actually. She's bright and creative . . . she wanted to be a pianist, but she ended up giving piano lessons because women didn't pursue careers in her day. I think she kind of felt cheated."

Aggie felt a sudden kinship with this woman she'd never met.

"She was beautiful when she was young," said Minstrel. "She had long, dark blond hair . . . a lot like yours. And your passion for the arts. Not just music, but all the arts. She took me to museums—the Met and the Modern—to concerts in Central Park, to Broadway shows . . . I don't think she likes it down here much either, although she'd never say anything. I think she misses New York too."

"Are you homesick, Minstrel?" asked Aggie.

"Yeah, but not for long. Come June, I'm gone."

"You mean you're just gonna leave?" She was surprised by her own question.

"In a manner of speaking," he answered. "I've been accepted at Julliard to study music."

"Oh, Danny, I'm so happy for you," said Aggie, flinging herself onto his neck to embrace him with abandon. He smelled of marijuana and musk, and an emerging maleness that startled her. His beard brushed her ear and burned with a white hot bolt of instant guilt. She began muttering embarrassed apologies till he stopped her.

"Please don't," he chided. "Don't go paranoid on me and spoil it all."

"I think I better go . . . and so should you."

"You're getting all uptight over nothin'," he said, grabbing her hand. She pulled away more abruptly than she'd intended.

"Nothin'! Nothin' but running around smoking dope with a student. I could get arrested for what's happening here. I'm the one responsible. I'd lose my job . . . I'd never work again. There's not a school in the country that'd ever let me near their kids again."

"Damn narrow-minded of 'em," he slurred, still laid back, stoned. It was having an irritating effect on her. She was rushing, rising too fast, and nearing a hysterical peak.

235

"Hey, calm down. Mellow out . . ." said Minstrel, taking out a pack of rolling papers and a pouch of green-brown filler. There was a slight breeze stirring the scent of the orange blossoms around like a floating euphoria, and in the face of his overwhelming serenity she felt suddenly silly. Minstrel spilled some herb into a Double-wide and laid the baggy down on the ground, but before he could clasp his fingers around the paper the breeze had grabbed up the pot and wafted it away. He bunched up the paper with a choice expletive and then it was his turn to be apologetic.

"Are you getting paranoid 'cause I'm your teacher?" she teased.

"Yeah," he admitted, smiling sheepishly.

She took the papers from him and climbed up into the thorny branches of the orange tree. He joined her there in the shelter of its scented branches. Dumping a neat line of dope into the paper, she grabbed it with a practiced precision and almost in a single gesture rolled a neat joint.

"You do that better than anyone I've ever known," said Minstrel admiringly as he took it from her hand.

"We artists are known for our manual dexterity," she quipped.

"Flutists got great lips," he bragged, relicking the glue along the seam of the joint. "I'll have this dry in a minute." He blew on the wet paper gently.

"Don't go getting any ideas," she chided.

"I've already had the idea. It's the experience I'm lacking. How about teaching me?"

"Are you crazy? I've never fucked a kid in my life.

"Well, then," he grinned, setting the joint into the grinning wreath of beard. "How about teaching me to roll a joint?"

"All I'm gonna do for you tonight, guy, is make you some coffee to sober you up and send you home to bed. And I warn you," she cautioned, climbing down from the tree. "You lay one finger on me and you're dead."

"Promise," he grinned. "I was just trying to get up the courage to ask you if I could call you by your first name."

"Anywhere but school," said Aggie.

23

"I simply can't stand by and pretend it never happened. This thing has hung over me like the sword of Damocles. I'm simply asking for a definitive statement from you regarding my position and my future here at Arcadia, sir," said Aggie with the deference due one's employer.

Bo Calloway leaned back in his vinyl desk chair and folded his hands across his ample vested belly. The walls were cluttered with framed documents and nostalgic photos of football teams all the way up to the oak-beamed ceiling. Arcadia's colors were clearly evident in the heavy-handed decoration—the oversized windows that were a starkly overwhelming feature of each room at Arcadia were here camoflaged with costly red velvet draperies; expensive, randomly patterned carpet of claret and gold muffled the sounds of footfall and voices.

The large oak desk was littered with memorabilia and the overflow of trophies from the bookshelves whose leather-bound volumes had been bought by the inch and never read. It was an environment created to impress and intimidate, as if the occupant were seeking to bolster a secret insecurity—like the eccentric, mischievous gnome who built an Emerald City so he could install himself as the Wizard of Oz.

With a class ring gleaming from one hand and a wedding band from the other, Bo rubbed himself up and down like a big cat scratching and issued his pronouncement like a doctor telling a patient who'd been told her disease was terminal that the whole thing had been a big mistake.

"Muriel's a high-strung woman, Aggie, and kind of set in her ways, but she's been with me a long time. She's extremely conscientious, and well meaning in her way.

Now, on the other hand, I've a feelin' you're just as temperemental. Well, maybe bein' artistic has somethin' to do with that. You're young and new, and filled with all sorts of exciting ideas, and what's more important, the kids are crazy about you. Now, I feel confident two bright, educated ladies like yourselves can find a way to work this out. After all, we're all on the same team."

"What is it you're suggesting, Mr. Calloway?"

"I'd just forget about it, if I were you. Muriel will settle down and this whole thing will just blow over."

"I'm willing to do whatever is required of me in the performance of my duties here, but I can't function at my optimum while under this constant harassment. If Muriel's filed formal charges against me, I feel I've the right to know specifically what I'm being accused of so I might answer the charges or correct my behavior."

"Aggie, now I've told you there's nothing to it. Muriel gave me a bitch sheet that amounts to no more than a bunch of chicken shit. Now before this gets out of hand, I'm tellin' you, just find a way to stay out of her way." He was becoming irritated. Bo had little patience with insoluble problems, as this one was becoming. "Keep a low profile, so to speak," said Bo, recovering his composure and smiling slyly as he looked her over. Bo had not made eye contact during the entire conversation.

"That's all you can offer then? To continue subjecting myself to her threats and petty annoyances?"

"The only alternative is a good recommendation and my best wishes for successful employment elsewhere," said Bo. There was an uncomfortable silence, then she rose to leave. "I have every confidence you'll find a way to deal with your problem, Aggie. Now, I want you to know I've advised Muriel to exert her authority a bit more judiciously. I'd hate to lose you. You're a valuable member of our team."

She felt as though she'd been given a pat on the head and a fast brush-off. There was certainly no help forthcoming from Bo. She and Muriel had been exercising great care in avoiding one another. When their jobs and physical proximity forced them into conversation, it was strained and elaborately formal. And somehow, just knowing that the enemy was waiting in ambush left Aggie tense and

239

emotionally exhausted. It was with gratitude rather than irritation she faced a conference day with only three meetings scheduled, all of them in the morning. Out of an entire classload of over a hundred and fifty kids, only three parents had taken advantage of the opportunity to meet with their children's teachers, and one of those didn't show up. Of the two that did, both had kids who were at the top of their class and had just come to collect compliments and hear what an asset their offspring were to themselves and to their school.

The only students evident in the sparsely populated corridors were the ones earning a few brownie points helping their teachers with classroom chores or back paperwork.

Aggie spun the combination lock on her mailbox and found a note from Muriel, demanding yet another audience, when out of the far edge of her peripheral vision she spotted Vance McCarthy coming down the hall. His red visored cap was pushed casually back on his head; his long, tanned legs covered the distance in graceful, easy strides.

As Aggie watched him approach, waving, two young girls appeared out of nowhere, and, flanking him on both sides, accompanied him down the hall. One of them was tall and lissome, with long, carrot-colored hair. The other, dark and plump, wore a T-shirt that announced I'M A VIRGIN, and, written beneath it in smaller print, the disclaimer BUT THIS IS A VERY OLD T-SHIRT. She may have been all of sixteen and giggled a lot.

The redhead held an elaborately enameled box which she handed Mac as reverently as a supplicant delivering up a sacrificial offering before a deity.

But for a sidelong glance at Aggie they hardly acknowledged her presence, focusing their collective devotion on Mac.

"These are for you, coach," sighed the redhaired girl with obvious adoration. He took the tin gingerly and pried it open. Homemade sugar cookies lay neatly layered in paper lace doilies on aluminum foil.

"Why, thank you, Karen. Any special reason?"

She blushed. Her friend giggled.

Mac popped one in his mouth and bit off a chewy chunk. "Mmmm, fantastic, I didn't realize you could cook, too, honey. Here I thought you were just another pretty face," he teased.

Thanking her, he extended the open box to Aggie. "Try one a' these, Ms. Hillyer." He addressed her formally as was their custom around the students.

She tasted it dutifully and extended her compliments.

The girl was not overly interested in her opinion. She was devouring Mac. There was a note that went with the cookies. Mac promised to read it in private, and the girls took their leave, reluctantly.

"A student who'll come to school on her day off to deliver a box of cookies is definitely in love. Does this happen frequently?"

"Fairly," said Mac immodestly. "Want another one?" She shook her head.

He helped himself once more before closing the tin to read his letter. He began to chuckle.

"That funny, huh?" asked Aggie casually, concealing her rampant curiosity.

"Mm-hmm," he nodded. "Some of the stuff I get'd singe your eyebrows. 'Some a' these lovesick little ladies are so anxious to give it away it makes my head swim. Listen to this:

DEAR COACH VANCE, ETC.
YOU PROBABLY HAVEN'T NOTICED, BUT I'M HEAD OVER HEELS IN LOVE WITH YOU. YOUR SHOULDERS AND YOUR BROAD, HAIRY CHEST THRILL ME. YOUR SMILE AND BEDROOM EYES SHAKE ME LIKE A HURRICANE. I NEVER KNEW THAT I COULD FEEL THIS WAY ABOUT AN OLDER MAN, BUT SINCE YOU CAME INTO MY LIFE, I CAN'T BE SATISFIED WITH THE—"

"I don't think she intended that anyone else hear that," interrupted Aggie.

"Really gettin' to you, huh, Sadie Mae?"

"It really is very personal. When a young girl is in love," began Aggie, gazing into his smiling green eyes, "she doesn't want it spread—"

"That ain't love, honey," he interjected with a snide little

241

chuckle. "And if she keeps writing hot shit like this to guys the information ain't all that's gonna get spread. I wonder what she meant by 'older man'. That must be a mistake."

He crumbled the note into a compact little ball and flung it toward the trash can in the corner, sinking it with the skill of an ace.

"She really did lay it right on the line, didn't she?" smiled Aggie.

"If I just wasn't a man of such high moral principle and integrity," he said with a deprecatory amusement she found endearing.

"Your principles and integrity don't extend to putting the make on art teachers or librarians," she said pointedly.

"You still upset about that little incident in my office?"

"Why should I be?" countered Aggie. "It's your affair."

"Not any more," said Vance. "The lady in question has gone and got married."

"Married!" she gasped. "I don't believe it. When? Who?"

"You mean you haven't heard?" he chided. "How does all this stuff get by you? Everybody else seems to know. She up and married that kid. What's his name? That Wayne character. I hear they went up to Alabama last weekend. Calloway's tryin' to keep it under wraps till he can figure out what to do about it."

"God, every hot-blooded kid in the building is gonna think it's open season on teachers," she said. "You've got to admit that's rather . . . Christ, I can't even think of a word. Unbelievable is all that comes to mind. I know what *he's* contributing to the relationship, but what could a sixteen-year-old kid see in a woman her age?"

"She gives great head," said Mac.

"And you're left holding the cookies," laughed Aggie jubilantly. "Serves you right."

"Well, it left an opening in my social schedule, but I'm about to begin auditions for a replacement if you're interested."

Mac's finger traveled the perimeter of the underside of her jaw. They stood, poised, facing one another with the look of eager readiness that has precipitated the mating dance of lovers throughout time. She wanted to fall into his

242

arms, lose herself in the feel and the strength and the scent of him, drown in the cool oceans of his sea-green eyes.

"I'm not interested," she lied, making her way toward the main office. He fell into step beside her.

"Don't you know if you tell a fib your nose is gonna grow all outa proportion to your body? Or is it your titties grow all out of proportion to your body?"

"I'm not fibbing," she sputtered indignantly, embarrassed at having been found out. "And leave my 'titties' out of it."

"Look, Sadie Mae," he said, suddenly serious. "You can be honest with me. I know you've thought about it cause I've caught you staring me down with that same hungry look that that little redhead had in her eyes . . . the look of an unfulfilled, lonely woman."

She turned to face him down with all the defiance she could muster. "Why you conceited, presumptuous . . . *chauvinist*," she finished for want of anything more vile. "You assume because a woman is unmarried and past thirty, all she lives for is her next lay. Well, let me set you straight on a few things . . ."

"Hey, don't go flying off the handle, honey. I can live with the fact that you turned me down. I've even accepted that asshole Wingate succeeding where I failed. But it has nothing at all to do with . . ."

"What?" she exclaimed, wincing.

"I don't blame you, honey. I know his type appeals to a lotta wimmin, and I'll admit I was p-o'ed 'cause that bastard lucked out with you. I've been hoping the guy that got *your* cookies"—he shook the tin for emphasis—"when you were ready would be me."

"What the hell are you talking about?" she asked, confused.

"Your carryin' on with Wingate. I'm forgivin' you for breaking my heart. Please pay attention. There'll be a quiz at the end of the week," he quipped.

"Mac, me and you, that's improbable. But me and Jimmy Joe Wingate is so far-fetched it's laughable. Why would you think such an incredible thing?"

"Because he came in the morning after with a hangover and a lump on his head, smiling from ear to ear, to collect the Pussy Ki . . . scholarship fund," he corrected. "Four hundred and seventy-five bucks, most of it mine."

"And you believed him?" she asked, her lip beginning to quiver.

"Smilin' like that, in his condition," grinned Mac with a broad wink, "made his story very believable."

A shiver went through her. The undersides of her arms and chest began to itch. She wanted a pill. She wanted a drink. She wanted to scream with rage. She wanted to die of shame. Turning away so he wouldn't see the tears start, she fled from him to the sanctity of her own room, but as she ran down the empty corridor her tears had been distilled to a pure fury. It was not to her own room that she proceeded with angry steps sounding grimly on the granite flooring. It was to the office of the vice principal, Jimmy Joe Wingate, to demand a showdown. She stood, shifting impatiently until he hung up the phone and turned to face her.

"Why, Miz Hillyer, what a pleasant surprise," he gushed, gazing at her with the slick eyes of a snakeoil salesman. "Have a seat!"

"I don't think so, Mr. Wingate," answered Aggie approaching the desk. She raised a fisted hand high and slammed it on the desk top with a resounding bang that set the objects on its surface clattering.

"How dare you!" she fumed, her rage collecting like storm clouds across her face. "How dare you slander my virtue, impune my professional reputation. You egotistical, baldfaced, lying—"

"Now just a damn minute." He rose to face her. "I don't know what your beef is, lady, but you come in *my* office, you behave yourself."

He sat back down, and glared at her.

"Now what is it you wanted to say?" asked Jimmy Joe.

"You know what I'm talking about," she answered. "Don't sit there and pretend you don't know, you unspeakable . . ."

"Uh-uh," he cautioned smugly from behind his desk.

"You arrogant bastard," scoffed Aggie. "How can you sit there so smug after what you've done to me! You invaded my home in the dead of night, assaulted my person . . ."

"Let's not forget who assualted who," snapped Jimmy Joe, interrupting. "Had to tell the boys I fell outa bed," he winked conspiratorially.

"And then you add insult to injury by spreading vicious lies." She flushed with righteous anger, thinking of the self-denial she'd submitted herself to for the sake of her ravaged reputation.

The look of Jimmy Joe's face was a clear indication he hadn't anticipated being found out.

"And on top of that, you're a thief," shouted Aggie indignantly. "I think there's a matter of $475.00 you pocketed fraudulently."

"Well, if it's the money, that ain't important. We could plan on spendin' it together. After all, by rights it is half yours."

"You insensitive . . . animal," sputtered Aggie, her temper totally out of control. She could think of no words to counter his cruelty. There could be no meeting of minds here, no concession to truth or respect for fair play.

"You tight-assed liberated Northern wimmin' make me sick," he scowled, his lip curling. "You get so wrapped up in yourself you forget what a woman's for." A snide smile bent the corners of his mouth. "You wouldn't be half bad if you learned to control your temper." He touched the sensitive spot on his forehead tentatively.

"Now come on, sweet stuff," he chided sarcastically. "Why don't you just climb off your high horse an' admit you could do a far sight worse than catch the eye of a guy like me. That ol' windbag Muriel wouldn't give you a hard time no more. I could help you get a better class schedule, a bigger supply budget—do you a lotta good."

He came around the desk and tried to touch her, but she shrunk from him as though he were contagious.

"You won't get away with it. I'll expose you for the liar and thief you are," she sneered.

"Yeah," chuckled Jimmy Joe. "Fat chance anybody 'round here's gonna buy it though. Most folks'd rather hear a good story than listen to a bunch of excuses. Anyway, who cares?"

"I care. It's my life we're speaking of here. I care very much."

"Well, what do you want me to do about it now, go

245

stand in the courtyard and make a public confession? You want money? Is that it," he bellowed. "Will that make you happy?" He pulled a wad of bills from his pocket and strewed them across the desk.

"I don't want your dirty money," she hissed. "I want the truth. I want my name cleared, I want an apology, and I want the restitution I deserve."

"You're outta your mind, woman," sulked Jimmy Joe. "Ain't no way."

They stared at one another across an unbridged abyss.

"Well, what now?" he smiled. "What are you gonna do about it?"

"First chance I get, I'll go to your wife. I'll see she, at least, knows the truth."

"Hey, wait just a minute, hold it, now," yelled Jimmy Joe, coming out from behind his desk. "You can't get away with this . . ." But there was no one listening. Letting the door slam deliberately behind her, she ran, frustrated and angry, down the hall.

In another moment she was sobbing on the broad shoulder of Dean E-Z Jordon. Somehow, she managed to relate the sequence of events with some degree of clarity through her tears.

"E-Z, what'll I do?" she wailed.

"I was hopin' that dumb gossip would just die on the vine. Now you know it's not gonna make any difference to those of us who care about you. Nobody in their right mind would believe that crap."

"Mac believed it," she whimpered, only half resolved to his consoling charm.

"Oh, so that's what's bothering you." He grinned broadly. "It ain't what Jimmy Joe's done to ya, it's what the coach thinks of you that counts. Well, seeing as I'm the only one who knows the truth about what really went down that night . . ." His dark eyes turned merry. "If you'll release me from my vow of silence, maybe I could square things with Mac for you."

A smile of gratitude broke through the sorrow.

"Oh, E-Z," she said with renewed hope. "If only you would. Now all I've got to do is figure out what to do about our Mr. Wingate."

"I'm afraid my word don't carry much weight with

him," drawled E-Z. "We don't get along real well. There's somethin' about that guy I never did take to. Would you really tell his wife?"

"Nah, there's nothing I can do about him. And from his position, he could squash me like an ant. Between him and Muriel, I feel like a shuttlecock at a badminton game, and there's no sense taking it to Bo. It does no damn good. All he cares about is how good we look to the world outside. I'm just glad there's still a few good guys like you around."

"Man, you sure look glad as hell," he teased, "with that chin of yours dragging down on the ground. How heavy is that torch you're carryin'?"

"Torch?" asked Aggie.

"Hey, now, don't try to fool ol' E-Z, honey. He sure has got a thing with the women, that man."

"Yeah, I guess he does," said Aggie, rising to leave.

"One more thing, because I love ya," he said. "I don't want to cut down the coach. He's a good man, fine athlete, and a friend a' mine. I don't know what you think you see in him, but maybe if you got close up, it somehow wouldn't look the same.

"Why don't you make peace with Mac before it's too late and you're left hangin'?" asked E-Z.

"What?" She wasn't allowing it to register.

"Didn't he tell you he was leavin'? Honey, where you been hidin'? Maybe you be burnin' out. You really ought ta get off all that shit you're into."

His warning rang an ominous note as she wearily retreated into the cave.

Vance McCarthy poked his head in the door of the Cave, his perfect white teeth set in an endearingly guilty grin. "You shouldn't leave your door unlocked when you're in here alone," he said. "No tellin' whose apt to walk in here with lust in his heart."

"You come with lust in your heart?" asked Aggie.

"And an apology on my lips. What can I say, Aggie? I feel like an ass. How about letting me buy you lunch?"

"I brought my lunch today."

"Why don't you save it for supper and let me pop for a few cold beers instead? Or whatever else you prefer with a great big juicy steak and onion rings. Do you like onion rings? Can't order onion rings unless we both eat 'em."

She'd been making a cup of instant coffee and stood feeling stupid with the spoon of dry brown granules poised in mid-air.

"You mean, just you and me?"

"Unless you plan on asking a chaperone. I promise I won't jump you in public. Who the hell you think I am, Wingate?"

She dumped the coffee into the mug and turned her back on him to pour in the hot water.

"Hey, I'm sorry. That was a shitty choice of words, Aggie. I want you to know, too, I'm sorry as hell about what you've had to put up with from some of the folks around here. If there was anything I could do about it, you know I would. All I can do is speak for myself. If I've caused you any grief, for any reason, I'm truly sorry."

"How come you never told me you were leaving?" she asked.

"I was about to, but I never got the chance, Sadie M— Aggie," he corrected. "It's a coaching position up at the university. It's a great opportunity for me. Is that terrific?" he asked enthusiastically. "And I think we got a buyer for the house. I spoke to Sharon this mornin'—"

"I'm happy for you," she interrupted. She was no more anxious to hear about what Sharon was doing than she was to hear about Jimmy Joe.

"Hey, come on," urged Mac. "We haven't had a chance to just sit and shoot the bull in a long time, and who knows when we will again. We could both use a few laughs, and I'm starved."

"I've really got too much work," she protested. "The kids messed up the screen for the prom posters and I wanted to clean up the place a little . . ."

"Now, I'm not takin' no for an answer," said Mac, dumping her newly made coffee down the slop sink. "We're gonna make one little stop by my office so I can put my pants on, and then we're gonna go eat."

The midday sun beat white hot against the windshield, outlining his profile in a brilliant radiance. His sheer summer shirt emphasized the muscular contours of his torso and framed the gilded planes of his sun-bronzed chest and throat. Trimly fitted tan trousers outlined the gentle flex of his leg on the gas pedal as he guided the bulky wood-panelled station wagon onto Eastern Avenue.

"I don't suppose it's very classy to admit it, but I'd really prefer a beer," said Mac, passing her the nearly empty wine bottle. She finished the wine in one pull.

He took a sharp corner and she fell against him. He smelled faintly of a pungent, bittersweet cologne. The fabric of his shirt felt cool and slick on the back of her neck, and she made no effort to move away. Instead she reached down into her cleavage and withdrew a joint wrapped in pale blue Kleenex. Mac pulled her close against his side and observed with keen interest while she pulled the lighter off the dash and ignited the pot.

"Jesus, Aggie, you been carryin' that on you in school? Suppose it fell out of there?"

"Be no way to tell where it came from," she said, holding the toke and settling comfortably into his armpit. "But I'd have hated to lose it. It's the last one I've got. I was going to leave a little early and go to the beach this afternoon. But I'd rather share it with you."

"My vices are limited to beer, broads, and contact sports, honey, and not necessarily in that order. What does that shit do for you, anyway?"

"It feels good," she admitted. "It blunts the pain you can't fix with a Band-Aid or an aspirin. But mostly I just like it," she laughed, lifting on the rush. It was good stuff, a fast high . . . and, coupled with the sensate movement of his body pressed to hers, unbearably erotic as well.

"It also makes you horny," said Aggie playfully, pressing it to his lips. "Have a hit."

"While I'm driving? You got a death wish, Sadie Mae? And there's no way I'll guarantee your safety if I do something to get me horny while I'm alone with you."

"As long as you keep one hand on the wheel," she laughed. "Well, I'm not about to offer twice. More for me."

"It's got a kind of a strange smell up close, doesn't it?" he asked, watching her smoke with piqued interest.

"You've never done dope, have you?" asked Aggie as the realization dawned. "There's no reason to be scared of it. It's no more deadly than a couple a' beers, except it doesn't hit ya on the back of the neck like a mugger. It's a much nicer feeling than drunk."

"How long does it last?"

"Not long enough," she replied.

The Moody Blues were doing a number on the radio when they pulled into his private parking spot behind the gym, and she asked him to stay long enough to hear it out, deliberately delaying the end of her romantic interval. She was having too good a time . . . The roach was smoked about halfway down. She was about to tap out the ember when Vance reached for it and brought it hesitantly to his lips.

"To think I was there the first time you turned on," she chuckled. "I'll remember this occasion always." Vance took a draught as ineptly as any nonsmoker, and started to cough.

"Here," said Aggie, unable to cover her amusement. "Let me help. All you have to do is breath in deep." Turning the roach backward she placed the cherry end carefully into her own mouth and exhaled a stream of smoke down his throat. He did better with it off the shotgun. As he released his breath, he leaned in closer and suddenly their lips were locked, and his tongue was slick against her teeth and sweet against her tongue and she was transported into another of her fairy-tale daydreams. By the time they'd smoked the roach down they were making out like teenagers at a drive-in. Aggie was bent back against the seat and Vance's face was pressed between her breasts.

"Mac, stop! Suppose someone should see us?"

He came up quickly, his expression panic-struck, and got out of the car. He was tucking his shirttail into his belt as he came around to open her door. The view from her window was full of his groin, and she was certain by the look on his face as he helped her alight that he'd caught her looking, again.

"I feel like a truant, sneaking into school this way," confessed Aggie, grinning. "I've got some eyedrops and some stuff for your breath in my purse."

"I can't believe I'm still hungry after that meal I just ate," said Mac.

"One thing I forgot to mention about pot," she whispered, struggling to suppress a snicker. "You've got your first official case of the munchies."

"Is that some sort of social disease?" he asked.

"Yeah, come to think of it," she laughed.

"Lucky I've got cookies in my office," said Mac.

A bell rang, unheeded, in the strangely silent building. "You know, this place really is creepy without the kids," observed Aggie. "If that's the fourth-period bell, we're late."

"Late for what?" asked Vance. "You got no classes coming in and half the faculty probably won't get back from lunch. I wouldn't be here if I hadn't promised a few of the guys on the team I'd mess around on the field with 'em this afternoon."

"We might have been missed."

"By who?" asked Vance.

"Whom," she chuckled.

"Whom the fuck cares?" he retorted. "That's what you get when you hang out with teachers."

"Thanks for lunch," sighed Aggie, about to take reluctant leave of him. "I really enjoyed it."

"You're not leaving!" he exclaimed. "You're not gonna get me ripped like this and take a walk. I can't be trusted alone."

"I've got to go back to work," she answered as he guided her firmly into the Phys Ed office. "Mac, where are you taking me?"

He inserted a key into a door she'd always thought was just a closet, and pulled her into a room about the size of one, crammed with apparatus. A small Jacuzzi occupied one wall; a door to the toilet, another. The center of the room was occupied by a table on castors, its vinyl surface covered with a paper sheet. Mac's red and yellow uniform lay across the only chair. The air was heavy with the mingled odors of disinfectant and mildew and that curiously erotic scent of masculine sweat. The only illumination in the musty cubicle filtered down from a sooty skylight overhead.

Locking the door behind them, he turned to embrace her. *No* was the word left unspoken when his lips stilled hers. *No* was the syllable sounding the percussion of her pounding heart echoing in her head. *No* underlined the fear and guilt written in her eyes before her heavy eyelids fell, but as he explored her face and body with his lips and hands, her arms crept tentatively around his neck, and the only sound that escaped was a whispered sigh: "Oh, Mac . . ." She felt as though she were being lifted, carried away, floating toward the bright light seeping from the ceiling. The small room spun as Aggie levitated under his touch as if under a sorcerer's spell.

With his hands cradled gently under her buttocks, he set her down on the training table, his tongue tracing a saliva slick along her inner thigh. Then the word exploded like a gunshot. "No! Mac, not here, for God's sake. This is going to be awfully hard to live with."

"Relax," he whispered, the hiss of the snake in Eden. "You know there's no one, no place, needs you as much as I do right this minute." Mac casually began to undress as he spoke. She lay propped on her elbows, enjoying the view. Nude, his body was a Grecian bronze, each limb in concert in its every move, as incongruous with his surroundings as a Rodin in a public restroom.

All of Aggie's reasoning powers went into a state of malfunction, attempting to cool her body's irrational reactions. Even as he undressed her, she was offering her body and her objections simultaneously.

"My God, not here. We can't, Mac," she gasped against his ear. "Please don't," she pleaded, glad that she'd worn her lacy lingerie. A creamy swath of skin encircled Mac's groin and buttocks, and she noticed for the first time the single imperfection on his sculptured form—a jagged, ugly scar laced its way around his hip and back. She reached to touch it and winced. He moved with deliberate slowness as he exposed her warm flesh to the cool of the air; his eyes were intense and remote as he ascended the table and straddled her. His testicles were as well formed and pink as Easter eggs burrowed in a nest of straw-colored curls; his erect organ rose like an obelisk. Flexing his muscle its full length he preened for her. Aggie was certain lightning would suddenly travel down the skylight and strike them down . . . and it did . . . only the fable didn't really tell it like it was . . . it wasn't like this . . . not Mac . . .

he filled her field of vision, blocking her view of the sky-light high above her on the ceiling . . . maybe all this was just a wet dream and she'd wake up in a proper bed with Prince Charming. Silhouetted in the dimness, the contours of the golden prince resembled a large vampire-frog who'd descended on her chest to suck the life from her body . . . Her mouth was parched . . . the drug had run its course and was letting her down. Her throat constricted as his penis probed her palate, gently at first, while she tried to adjust to the physical discomfort and failed. Fighting for air, she spat him out, the bile rising in the back of her throat . . . Mac's hand gently, tenderly smoothed her cheek and ear and neck, then clenched a fistful of the tender nape hairs, repositioned her face to accommodate his urgency . . . "Hang on, Sadie Mae, I'm at the point of no return," he cried.

The training table was traveling around the room on its castors, sounding a rhythmic squeal of rubber wheels against the concrete floor.

Tears slid down the back of her nose and closed off her intake of air . . . her jaw ached and her hair tore in his fingers as he flung his pelvis hard against her head.

"A little more," croaked the frog, "just a little bit more," and then let go the first rush, then again, and again, and yet again in a wild crescendo . . . Mac I'm choking . . . Mac, don't hurt me, oh my darling, oh my God, he's coming . . . OH MY GOD! I'm drowning . . . suffocating . . . dying . . .

Aggie lay inert, outlined in sweat on the wrinkled paper sheet, listening to him urinate beyond the open door of the cubicle, equanimity returning slowly as her senses readjusted. It might all have been a nightmare, a bad drug trip but for the perspiration running down her skin and the acrid, bitter taste of semen in her throat. She heard the toilet flush, water running in the sink, and his voice sounding distant and hollow.

It took fully a minute to lift her heavy head and prop her leaden torso on her stiff, cramped arms, and yet another to raise herself up to sit, trembling and dizzy, to watch him wash—a big, golden alley cat, licking himself clean, his eyes gleaming with the pride of conquest. He wrung a clean towel under the tap and attended her, passing the cool cloth across her breasts and belly covetously, possessively, finding the touchstone of raw nerve endings from which still emanated the heat of unspent passion. Seeking love, she'd been abused.

Ravished.

His lips upon her forehead were cool and healing. Holy, like a benediction. "You're fantastic, baby, just fantastic . . . Aggie, honey, I didn't mean to come in your mouth."

She clung to him weakly, like a child who'd been disciplined, seeking the reassurance that this pain had been inflicted in the name of love.

This is gonna hurt me more than you because I love you.

"Was that great, Sadie Mae? Was that terrific? Wow, you've got a hickey on your thigh."

He finished mopping her down as perfunctorily as if he'd just finished the dinner dishes and stood, poised and smiling, as if awaiting an answer.

"Are you asking me if it was as good for me as it was for you?" croaked Aggie, finding her voice. She reached tremulously for her clothes to cover herself, then ran for the toilet and puked.

"I've had to intercede for you with a parent this afternoon, Agnes," said Muriel, peering primly over the lenses of her rimless spectacles. "This day has been set aside for the specific purpose of allowing parents access to their children's teachers. It was not intended for the convenience of the staff."

"I'm very sorry," she began. "I didn't have any appointments this afternoon, Muriel, or I wouldn't have . . ."

"You were to be on call in your classroom, regardless."

"It'll never happen again," promised Aggie, contrite with guilt and humiliation. She wasn't fit to survive another mental manhandling. All the other department heads had let their staff have the afternoon off. It was as much a streak of sadism as dedication that inspired Muriel to call a department meeting after school on a conference day.

"Now, this request for a special event that you've submitted to the administration," clucked Muriel officiously. "What's this all about?"

"Something the kids requested," she explained, afraid to show too much enthusiasm lest her plans be quashed.

"You really must remember that these requests must come through channels. Mr. Wingate handed it back to me for approval prior to his authorization. It displeases me that you chose to submit it without discussing it with your immediate superior."

"We seem to be suffering a breakdown in communication," answered Aggie. "Since it isn't strictly a department event, the student in charge of the project just submitted it directly to the office. There was no slight intended."

"And is it that rag-tag ring of radicals and troublemakers you've assembled to take charge of the project?"

"Now just a minute," said Aggie, rising defensively to the insult, then checking herself. The Hellions were planning a celebration of brotherhood, a spring rite for the students to share their music, crafts, legends, and dreams. They were calling it Unity Day, and several other teachers were already organizing their events for a day-long carnival in the courtyard by the cafeteria.

"Muriel, this has already generated a lot of enthusiasm and goodwill among students who were hardly speaking to one another a few months ago. Surely you're not suggesting the art department pull out. We should be at the helm of this endeavor to promote goodwill among our staff and students," she suggested gently.

"Exactly my feeling," answered Muriel. "I've informed the administration that in order to insure the success of an event of this magnitude this late in the year, it is imperative that a firmer and more disciplined approach is in order. I have offered my organizational abilities to this endeavor and would caution you to put a greater effort into your curricular responsibilities."

"Are you suggesting that you're going to take me off my own project?"

"I'm suggesting nothing. I'm informing you that the only way I will consent to this department's participation in this art festival is under my own direction. I've no intention of letting your radical and unrestrained ideas promote an event that reflects unfavorably on myself and this institution. Those are my terms and they are nonnegotiable. Now, for the next item on our agenda—"

"No way in hell," said Aggie.

"I beg your pardon, young lady. What was it you said?"

"I said I'm not having it. I'm not accepting your terms. I'm not gonna tell my kids they're getting benched for the only game of the season."

"I don't think you know the trouble you're in, Agnes. It is by my willingness to be equitable and fair-minded that you still hold your position here."

"My position here, Muriel, is flat on my back with your foot in my face and I'm sick of it. I've had it," Aggie said, surprised by the grim resolve in her voice.

"How dare you!" gasped Muriel, sucking air like a goldfish that's flopped out of its bowl. "You'll pay for this," she threatened. "You'll not get away with it. I'll have your job."

"And just let me tell you what you can do with it," said Aggie.

"Aw, Maddy, where are you? Maddy, I need you," she cried, pounding on the window, but the house was dark and the locked door unyielding. "Please, Maddy! I need someone to talk to 'cause I think I'm flippin' out and I don't want to be alone. Please, Maddy, where are you," she sobbed, sitting desolately on the steps of the cottage.

The moon rose fresh and pale like a slice of lemon lying in a bowl of black caviar, and the trees that lined the highway clutched at the sky like the last handhold of a drowning swimmer. The 'Vette ate the road like a piranha sucking up an eel.

There was only one more place to check if she could remember how to get there—the Holiday Inn on the far side of the airport. Maddy had taken her to the bar there once last spring.

The sign appeared in neon as she rounded the turn.

VACANCY and DANCING NIGHTLY for the convention of computer salesmen in attendance. Would this be where she'd find Maddy?

She parked the car and smoothed the crumpled gabardine of the suit she'd worn all day, then found her way to the bar. The music was loud and the lights were low. Maddy was not there.

"Can I buy you a drink?" asked a voice behind her.

256

"I'm looking for a friend," she answered, startled. He was tall, handsome, and well groomed.

"I can be a friend," he said, extending a hand. He introduced himself and began apologizing for his boldness, then repeated his invitation.

"Thanks, I don't think I'm in the mood," she answered. "I'm about to leave."

"Join me for a little one," he pleaded. "For the road."

She let herself be persuaded. The software salesman from Atlanta plied her with a succession of Southern Comforts until she found the solace she'd been seeking this night, in a motel room in the arms of a stranger.

24

Summer comes almost unnoticed to a land without seasons, so subtly, so imperceptibly you could miss it unless you had a need to know.

The sun still rose each morning as abruptly as a cracked egg hitting a hot griddle.

The mighty, muddy Avalon, swollen slightly with the spring rains, slithered like a great snake bloated with a fresh kill, slipping surreptitiously among the cypresses that trembled, cringing, and clinging to the shore.

The winter birds departed, and the summer tourists began arriving by air and by sea and by land. The airports swarmed, and the marinas hummed and the highways jammed and backed up by the mile. Tempers ran short in the sizzling sun.

Insects that had hibernated for an intense period of procreation emerged in copious numbers. Mosquitos swooped in endless Kamakazi assaults on hapless victims with their sweaty skins exposed in deference to the oppressive heat. Paired love bugs, hooked by their backsides, flew at the windshield as Aggie pulled her white 'Vette out of the parking lot. She kneaded the knob of the gearshift lever, sensually, as one would massage a lover, and pressed firmly on the accelerator. But instead of four sure-footed steel and rubber tires spinning swiftly for the getaway, the 'Vette lurched and limped and finally came to rest at the curb not two hundred yards from the gate.

A police car was parked on the far corner and a uniformed cop was sauntering casually toward her, crossing against the light.

Bob, thought Aggie, pleased and grateful. But it was not Bob.

He tipped back his visored cap and removed his mirrored glasses, smiling.

"Can I be of assistance, ma'am?" asked the officer.

"I seem to have gotten a flat tire," explained Aggie dejectedly.

"That tire's been cut, ma'am," he said, bending to look at it. He was fortyish and pleasant-faced. Not nearly as dashing in his uniform as Bob, she thought idly.

"I'd be glad to help you with that if you've got a spare," he said.

"Thank you," said Aggie, handing him the keys. "What a lucky coincidence that you were around."

"No coincidence, ma'am," said the cop, bouncing the spare against the pavement to test it. "We've had a rash of these cases recently. Last night they got the tires and windshields of seventeen buses at the transportation center. They've had to run half the kids in the school district on split-shift hauls. Haven't you noticed?"

"Tardy students don't attract a great deal of attention in the greater scheme of things," said Aggie. "I've been pretty busy wrapping up my art show for tonight."

He fitted the jack and raised the car. "You folks are planning a great big party here this evenin', are you?"

"Sure thing! The kids have worked very hard on it. How many buses are they bringing over here?"

"As many as they can lock up on the back half of the senior parking lot."

"There aren't enough parking spots for students now. That's not going to go down well with the kids," said Aggie.

He loosened the bolts and removed the wheel. "Seems to me that that's just too damn bad, if you pardon my saying so, ma'am," he answered. "We're too blessed concerned with our kids bein' happy instead of bein' good. What we need to do is take a harder line with 'em. Make 'em buckle down and mind their P's and Q's. I'm not crazy about this busin' business myself, but you don't see me goin' out and vandalizin' public property. It ain't the buses what's at fault. It's the damn kids. 'Stead a' lockin' up the equipment, we oughta be lockin' up the little bastards what done it. Say, this tire's been punctured, not slashed," said the cop with amazement.

"It doesn't surprise me," said Aggie. "If it had been cut, why would they have stopped at one tire? Why not the soft top? Why not rip off my tape deck? Besides, officer, I can't think of one of my kids with a reason to want to hurt me."

"Kids don't need a reason," he answered, fitting the new spare in place while Aggie stood by helplessly. "Not the kind of kids that would do the things I'm talkin' about. Far's I'm concerned, we should just let 'em get doped up and wipe out each other. These gangs that come up like rats out of the sewers of this city, nearly every one of 'em a doper. We'd all be better off without 'em."

"You're not serious," said Aggie, handing him the lug wrench so he could tighten the bolts on the tire. "The trouble is that the police only see the bad kids. They're not all like that, you know. I've known some really wonderful people who just happened to be kids." She smiled inwardly as the impact of her statement came home to her . . . "some of my best friends are kids" . . . it was as automatic as breathing to be defending her kids against the bigotry and hatred of outsiders. It was a constant source of consternation and amazement that there were people in the world that didn't instantly melt in the presence of a small animal or a kid.

"Say what you will," said the cop. "*I* wouldn't want to be alone in a room with thirty or more of the little bastards. I don't know if I could drag myself out of bed in the morning if I knew that's what was waitin' for me, especially if I looked like you," he said, rising again. "You don't happen to have a rag, do you?" he grinned, dropping the defective tire into the trunk.

"Use that towel in there," offered Aggie.

"It's clean," he said. "I'll ruin your towel."

"It's OK," said Aggie. "It's the least I can do for you after all you've done. I only use it when I go to the beach, and I'm not gonna get there today."

"How come you're so late leavin'?" he asked, wiping grease from his hands with her towel.

"I had to finish setting up an exhibit for the festival tonight," she replied.

"Expecting a big crowd, are ya?" he asked.

"I sure hope so," said Aggie. "Why don't you come?"

"I'm not working tonight, ma'am," he said. "I drew the

afternoon shift this round. Besides," he grinned, "I got a wife and two children."

"You've got kids?" she asked, wondering how it was possible a man who hated them so much had any. Probably mistakes, she mused. That's what teachers get— somebody's mistake. This cop was probably an unwanted or overdisciplined child . . . or abused. "Bring them along," said Aggie. "If you look me up I'll show you around. Youngsters love coming to high school . . . it's a real treat for them to see where they'll be go—"

"Are you kidding, lady? Bring my kids here? I couldn't bring *my* kids *here*. It ain't safe."

The river flowed dark and deep beneath the Cypress grove, shrouded with a black lace veil of mourning. The river carried its sadness to the sea, somber as a funeral procession.

The night wind held its breath, withholding its cooling touch from the summer-scorched landscape, a silhouette in black on black under the deep stillness of a starless sky.

The oncoming glare of headlights was blinding through the windshield as the sportscar sped swiftly across the railway trestle that spanned Southbound 41.

In the orchard that lined the highway, the blossoms had fallen and the unripe fruit promised a rich harvest.

Somewhere a clock ticked like a waning heartbeat, winding down the final hours of the school year.

Above the glow of neon from the shops along the avenue, the clock tower of Arcadia thrust an upturned finger in an obscene gesture against the imperturbable ceiling of the sky.

Arcadia forever . . . the recurring refrain of a thousand signatures on the leaves of a leather-bound yearbook.

These things we shall remember when the madness lifts . . .

Alone on the dark road, Aggie worried because she'd failed to drop off the tire. There was something very insecure about driving at night without a spare.

The lot was full and the street clear of illegally parked cars . . . only because of the police cars conspicuously stationed at both ends of the block. The buses stored for safekeeping had eliminated a lot of parking.

She presumed on Mac's good nature and parked the precious 'Vette in the private, protected grotto behind the gym, and deemed it safe enough to leave the top down.

There was no moon to light her way in the darkness as she carefully locked her purse in the trunk and pinned the key in her bra. She picked her way cautiously through the empty courts and corridors to the auditorium where the festivities were due to begin.

In the interior the courtyard lights burned brightly and the choir rehearsed acapella, polishing their performance for the evening.

The Home Ec instructor briefed her hostesses. Young girls in evening gowns prepared to serve coffee and guide visitors to the restrooms when necessary.

Fat ladies in white uniforms and hairnets were pouring huge vats of angel cake batter into pans to bake and eventually frost with gold icing and red peppermints.

And, in the patio, hung from fences and pinned to portable bulletin boards, an exhibit of artwork, the handwrought treasures of a year's creative endeavor. Cartons covered with construction paper held ceramic vases and sculptures of paper mache as splendidly displayed as museum pieces. It was a formal, rigidly traditional event. Not the sort of thing she would have planned to commemorate the occasion. Hers would have been an entire environment, an experience to symbolize a renaissance of spiritual love and brotherhood.

"Aggie," said Mr. Fishbine from the math department. "Have you seen Mr. Wingate this evening?"

"No, I'm afraid I haven't, Irv," answered Aggie. "What's wrong? You look perturbed."

"He's needed on stage. He's to make the announcement about the scholarship fund, and no one can find him."

"What award, Irv?" asked Aggie.

"Why, the one for Señor Gomez," explained Irv. "He was to make the announcement, since he contributed the initial donation. Five hundred dollars toward the pursuit of higher education for a student of Latin descent. Isn't that wonderful? I'm surprised you haven't heard. He's a generous man, but doesn't suffer an excess of humility. If we can't find him, someone else will have to make the presentation in his place," said Irv, shaking his head and turning away to continue his search.

Aggie smiled jubilantly. It's the pussy kitty he stole, she thought. It couldn't have gone to a better cause.

"Miz Hillyer," yelled a pink-gowned young hostess across the court, "the wind blew down some of the pictures on the far fence. We need some masking tape to put them back up before all the people come out here."

"Hold the fort, Stacey," she answered. "I'll have to get some from my storeroom and the keys are in my car."

She retraced her steps through the corridor to the parking lot where she'd left her car and spotted E-Z speaking to a school security guard.

She couldn't resist sharing the good news, and signaled him from across the lot. The security guard left to make his rounds of the building as E-Z ambled toward her. He was dressed up in tie and jacket, and looking good.

"Have you heard?" she chirped, unable to contain the joy.

"Hi, Aggie, hows it goin'?" he said. "Have I heard what?"

"About the scholarship fund."

"Yeah," he said. "I thought that would make you happy."

"You knew?"

"You might say I was the first to know," he smiled mysteriously. "Even before he did."

"This was your doing?" she said. "I should have known." She reached up to hug him.

"You're gonna set tongues waggin', girl," he said, grinning with satisfaction. "I can't go bailin' you out all the time, now," he cautioned. "There's a bunch of disasters just waitin' to happen tonight."

"Oh, E-Z, how can you be so gloomy and pessimistic on such a lovely evening," Aggie rhapsodized. "Ah, sweet justice. God's in his heaven for sure. All's right with the world."

"Now, don't go gettin' carried away, girl. Best you be on your toes and keep your eyes peeled for trouble."

"You're such a worry wart," she chided playfully. "But you're better lookin' than usual."

He laughed. "What the hell you doin' out here?"

"I've got to get my room keys from the car. We need some tape."

"You're not supposed to be in that part of the building, Aggie. You want me to go get it for you?"

"No thanks, E-Z. I can do it. You've probably got enough to do tonight."

"You're right about that. There's some sort of sabotage going on with the buses. Gang activity. Go along now. I'll be by in a while to see what a great job you've done with the exhibit."

She fetched her key and wound her way back through the darkened maze of corridors. As she approached her door, she thought she heard footsteps sounding softly behind her.

Just an echo, she berated herself as the goosebumps rose on her skin. The echo of her own footfall in the vast, empty hall.

The building was eerie . . . full of bad plumbing and rats skittering through the walls.

She had trouble inserting her key in the lock in the dark. Snapping on the lights, she flooded the room with the weird greenish glow of fluorescents.

Unlocking the Cave she opened a cabinet and found she had to open a new carton of tape.

Was that a noise from the classroom beyond? She was hearing things. She took down an x-acto knife and cut open the carton. There it was again . . . a subtle sound of someone moving. Another rat, probably. Then, unmistakably, she heard it again.

"Who's there?" asked Aggie, entering the room with the blade still in her hand. "Who is it?" she asked again. No answer. Then the room lights were extinguished and she was left standing, scared and immobile, in the darkness. Then a voice, no more than a whisper . . . the rasp of a file on metal or the hiss of a tire deflating.

"It's an ol' friend, teacher! An ol' friend," the disembodied voice rasped.

"Where are you?" called Aggie, searching the silhouetted forms of the furniture and equipment stacked around the room. "Who are you?" she repeated with a mounting sense of terror, edging toward the door. "What do you want?"

"We have some unfinished business, teach."

"Let's just shed some light on this situation," she began, mustering her courage. Reaching for the light switch and touching something . . . something organic, slick, alien, and she instinctively recoiled from it.

The intruder struck a match and ignited the end of the cigarette clenched in his snarling lips. The glow from the flaring match showed her his face for the first time.

"Ernie!" she gasped.

"Pride, bitch," he snarled. "How many times I got to tell you?"

He flipped the match at her without extinguishing it, the bright arc of flame landing on the paint-stained floor, still burning. Her foot shot out automatically, crushing it out.

"For a teacher you sure are a slow learner," came the throaty voice. He lit another match and then another, pitching them toward her, his eyes gleaming with hate.

"I told you what was gonna be, teach. I told you what could happen to you if you went pokin' your nose into other people's business."

"Pride," she stammered. "Please stop! You don't know what you're doing."

He tossed another lighted match into the darkness. This time it hit her dress, scorching the fabric.

"You're crazy!" she yelled as she strove to see the damage in the dark. "You know that, you're crazy, Ernie. You need help," she finished in a softer tone.

"Shut up!" he shrieked like a gunshot into the emptiness of the blackened chamber. "You just shut up. I'm through listening to you and the whole lot of ya, teachah!" he spat, making the word sound like an obscenity. "You and the cops and the social workers and all the other shit that they stuff down my throat tryin' to help me. You call puttin' me in that hole the juvie pigs run is *helpin' me?*" He struck another match.

"Pride," she uttered cautiously, "you've got to listen. This room is filled with paper, paint, flammable liquids like turpentine and acetone . . ."

"I don't 'got' to listen to you, teach," he sneered. "I don't never have to do *nothin'* again unless I want to."

She saw his eyes as he kindled another match, smoldering with a malicious, terrifying glint . . . a dreadful reflection of the pain and prejudice that rendered him immune to another's suffering.

The match flew, a scarlett arc across the blackness, and landed on a stack of newspapers. It caught, spread as the two of them faced off. He was a large, hulking, overpoweringly physical young man. Her chances of besting him in a physical bout were negligible.

A tongue of flame rose from the pyre of paper, tearing away a small chunk of darkness.

"Pride, please," she pleaded.

"Please?" he intoned. "I kinda like the sound of that. Let's hear it again, teach. 'Please.' Only this time on your knees," he said, coming toward her. " 'Please', teachah," he ordered, grabbing for her. She felt the slim steel blade of the razor still clutched in her trembling hand and, with a swift thrust of fear, lashed out at him. A fine red line severed his silk shirt.

Pride recoiled, stunned, as crimson oozed from the wound. She could hear him cursing as she bolted for the door and flung herself into the gloomy corridor.

Then there was a flash beyond the open doorway and a pillar of smoke shot into the corridor, chasing her as she ran down the hall.

BREAK GLASS IN EMERGENCY said the neat white letters on the red firebox set in the wall.

She pulled the lever that set off an alarm, cutting away the sinister silence with the earsplitting sound of a bell, magnified many times, somehow a welcome, familiar sound in the empty corridors of Arcadia.

"What's happening down here?"

It was another reassuring sound, a voice so welcome and so right here in this place. She rushed toward it, running breathlessly into the arms of E-Z Jordon.

"E-Z!" she gasped. "It's Ernie. He's in my room. The fire . . . we've got to go back . . ."

"Come on," he said, pulling her toward an exit. "This place is about to go up like a tinderbox. We gotta get out!"

The adults that had sat stolidly in the auditorium to hear the administration extoll the virtues of Arcadia panicked. They ran, screaming and stomping all over one another in their hasty exodus. Those that found their way out through the rear exits trampled the portable bulletin boards, crushed the sculptures and pottery under foot as they fled.

Some found their kids and managed to escape the scene in their cars before every access to the building became blocked with police cars and fire trucks. Others stood around in the parking lot, restless and frightened. Others—some said it was kids—vented their rage on the fleet of yellow buses standing silently in the student lot.

The equipment arrived quickly. The street was braided with firehoses, the pavement in the parking lot was already flooded halfway up the hubcaps of the cars caught inside. There, under the palms, an endless cordon of cops tried to control the crowd while sooty-faced men in slickers hosed down the ancient edifice, fighting to contain the fire.

"What's happening?" she cried as E-Z escorted her to safety.

"What the natives call urban renewal," he answered.

"How can you kid at a time like this?" she sobbed as they pressed through the people milling around on the soggy lawns.

"It's the only defense I got against insanity," he answered.

"E-Z, there's a kid in there," she said, snapping out of her trance. "That kid Ernie, Pride, you know, the one with the gun during Homecoming, remember? He's in there. He's still in there and we've got to get him out."

"You can't go in there," he yelled. "If he's in there, they'll get him out. It's not for me and you to do, girl."

"We can't just leave him there!" she screamed, breaking away from him to run, near hysteria, toward her room.

"Aggie, stop it! Just stop it!" he snarled. "That kid tried to kill you!" As they grappled, she began to babble and sob. E-Z put a big hand on each of her shoulders and shook her, hard. "Stop it, Aggie. Stop it now!"

"Oh, E-Z, help me. I'm not gonna make it."

"Come on, now, girl. Let's get our act together. We gotta get this crowd of maniacs under control and we can't do it if we're gonna go flyin' off in all directions."

"Burn, baby, burn," chanted someone on the far side of the crowd.

BURN, BABY, BURN, echoed the crowd.

"Evacuate the area," yelled a cop on a bullhorn as the human flood swirled around him like an eddy. "Disperse and evacuate. You are hindering the efforts of the fire-fighters. Evacuate the area."

"Where'd you park your car?" asked E-Z, guiding her through the crowd.

"Behind the gym," she answered.

"I'm gonna try to get you out of here," said E-Z. "Do you think you can get home alone?"

"I'm not leaving, E-Z," she said stoically. "I can't leave."

"If your car's still there and we can get it past the gate, you're going home," he stated firmly. They broke through the noisy throng and found the little white car still tucked safely into the dark recesses of the spot in back of the gym. He shoved her behind the wheel.

"Get out of here, Aggie. Go home!"

"No, E-Z. Let me stay. Please," she wailed, struggling to stand. "Please let me stay with you . . . I don't want to go home alone. I'm afraid to be alone."

"Aggie, I haven't got time to argue with you. Let's move the car, at least."

He shoved her, trembling, into the passenger seat. "Where's the keys?" he asked, positioning himself behind the wheel and adjusting the seat to his overlong legs. "Come on, girl, the keys," he yelled.

She unpinned them from inside her dress and passed them to him. He turned over the engine smoothly and backed the car out of its shelter.

A riot had erupted in the lot and the cops were flailing wildly into the crowd with nightsticks and helmets, but they were only succeeding in promoting further panic.

"Move that vehicle out of here!" yelled a cop as young kids scattered before their onslaught.

"We're trying, officer," shouted E-Z. "Just help us out of here!"

They rolled a few more feet, cautiously, avoiding the fleeing pedestrians.

"POWER TO THE PEOPLE," yelled a young black, raising a clenched fist in front of the windshield.

Along the eastern facade of the building, the stained glass windows blazed a rainbow swath across the lawn with the brilliance of the fire that burned within. With a pop like gunfire, one of them exploded in the intense heat. It shattered and fell into the shrubbery beneath.

From the pit of the obelisk of the clock tower, a cloud of smoke ascended against the firmament, and the neon haze that lit the skyline was overwhelmed by the blaze of flame.

"Arcadia's burning," gasped Aggie to no one in her fearful solitude.

They left the car in front of the porn shop on the far side of the street, and hurriedly picked their way toward the Arcadia campus.

STUDENT POWER, screamed the crowd. GIVE US BACK OUR SCHOOLS. POWER TO THE PEOPLE.

The refrain echoed like the sound of thunder. The glow of the flames had begun to subside, but the smell of smoke hung heavy in the warm night air.

A harassed cop swung a night stick and caught a young Negro on the jaw. The kid yelped and fell. "We need more help," yelled the cop to a comrade. "When are those reserve supposed to get here?"

"I hear there's a local group of volunteers on their way," yelled his uniformed friend.

"This is getting unbearably ugly," said Aggie, grabbing E-Z's arm as they rolled slowly toward the main gate.

As they broke through the police line by the curb on the far side of the street, a large blue flatbed truck came careening down Eastern Avenue scattering panicked pedestrians in its path.

Two figures with hooded heads shouted obscenities from the open window of the cab. Perhaps a dozen other figures stood in the bed of the truck as it veered down the street, spraying dirty water from its wheels. All of them wore the sheets and shrouds of Klansmen.

"Holy Jesus," gasped E-Z. "That's all we need now. The Klan's throwing a costume party right in the middle of our little backyard barbeque."

DISPERSE, YOU BLACK DEMONS. CLEAR THE STREETS! blared a voice from the truck as it turned a tight corner around the firetruck at the gates of the parking lot. GET BACK IN YOUR HOLES, YOU LITTLE ANIMALS!

The truck came to a screeching stop barely fifty feet from where they stood, and E-Z put a protective arm around Aggie's shoulder as one of them approached the car.

"Where you goin', nigger?" he yelled.

"E-Z," she said. "Does that voice sound familiar to you?"

He looked at her, puzzled. She had never seen him so—what was it Aggie saw in E-Z's rigid features? Was it frustration? Anger? Fear? She'd never seen E-Z afraid before. And suddenly she was scared, too.

The Klansmen descended from the truck and stood like the pillars of Stonehenge in the street. The grim white specters took up their stations, cursing and laughing as the kids pushed and shoved one another to clear their path.

"Out of the car, nigger. You too, bitch," ordered the specter. "This is the kind of shit that brought this all down on our heads," sneered the figure from behind his mask. "Nigger with a taste for white meat."

They stood side by side in the mud that oozed around them on the ground, shaken and cringing under the stranger's scathing abuse.

One white-robed figure held the microphone of a portable PA system against his masked face and broke into demonic laughter. The amplified sound rolled eerily into the crowd.

"E-Z," she whispered close to his ear, noticing the sweat running freely down his face. "Does that voice sound familiar to you?"

"These aren't the kind of people I hang out with," he mumbled. "They're no friends of mine. Just be cool and we may get out of this."

Before E-Z could stop her, Aggie flung herself at the man with the mike and yanked the hood from his head.

"Jimmy Joe Wingate!" she shrieked. "My God, it's Jimmy Joe."

He lashed out, sheer rage contorting his unmasked features, and struck her across the face.

"You nigger-lovin' Yankee bitch!" he fumed. Blue veins blazed a visible pattern up his neck and across his forehead. His eyes were glazed with hate. He donned his pointed headdress and left her in the mire.

"You cowardly bastard!" yelled E-Z. "Is that your style? Beatin' on women and kids? How'd you like to go head to head with a man for a change?"

271

He flung himself at Jimmy Joe, swinging his fists, beating him to the ground.

Two of J.J.'s robed companions grabbed E-Z's arms and pulled him off.

"Get out of here, Aggie. Go get help!" yelled E-Z.

She hurled herself behind the wheel of her car while E-Z kept the Klansmen at bay and, throwing it in gear, she leaned on the horn and headed it back toward the great main gate of Arcadia.

"Lady," yelled a uniformed cop. "Move that car."

"Help me!" screamed Aggie. "I need help!"

It was only a matter of moments until the Avalon cops rounded up the rioters, among them Jimmy Joe Wingate and his sheet-shrouded crew.

It was nearly dawn when the firemen rolled up their hoses and rolled their trucks off the Arcadia campus. They'd managed to contain the fire to the auditorium and about a dozen first-floor classrooms.

Portable trailers furnished with paddle-armed student chairs and portable blackboards were brought on campus, and the staff that had been burned out of their classrooms were able to finish out the year.

And, after a brief period of hospitalization for a broken rib and hand, E-Z Jordon was promoted to the vacancy left by the incarceration of J. J. Wingate. He became Arcadia's first black assistant principal.

25

She walked along the beach, watching the sun rise beyond the hazy horizon, cutting a bright pink ribbon across the steel gray sky. Small waves lapped gently against her bare feet and a cool breeze ruffled her hair.

She'd have to work on her tan. It had faded in the corridors of Arcadia . . . just like so many things she'd left behind there.

She sifted through her recollections, as she'd sifted through the debris of the classroom that had been her second home.

They'd found no body where her room had been. Pride had faded into the dark, crawled back into the sewers and cesspools that had bred him.

There'd been little else she wanted to retrieve from that place . . . just the kids.

Why was it always the ones she lost that lingered in her memory? Why not the many who made it, the ones that won? Why could she not be satisfied to dwell on the many she had helped nurture to maturity and sensitivity and understanding?

What matter? She would never see any of them again. They would grow . . . or stumble and be left behind. But, wherever they were, they were no longer hers.

Even her gradebook had been lost. She'd had to rely on the word of each student in issuing final grades, and found most of them to be scrupulously trustworthy. To whatever extent it mattered from here on in, most everybody got what they deserved.

And what else was there to salvage from the ashes? Just the memories she choose to pluck from the chaos . . .

Sheila's great, sad almond eyes, Ernie's anger . . . Pete's helplessness and Becky's hopelessness . . . and all those hands in the air, waving to be recognized, anxious for attention. "Ms. Hillyer, Ms. Hillyer . . ."

The sun climbed fast, rushing to complete its appointment on the far side of another day. The gulls squawked discordantly and the ocean roared like a thousand hands clapping, tumultuous, overwhelming, but distant and remote as from another world or time.

And a flute . . .

Was it a flute? The sound piped forlornly from a nearly deserted drift of sandy dunes. Someone's radio no doubt . . . but where? The beach, midweek, in the middle of the day, was empty. For hours she'd shared this isolated strip of sand with a couple of young mothers entertaining their tots and a man on a morning run with his dog.

Then again, she heard it. She followed the sound.

He was shirtless and stretched out on the sand, his denims rolled up to his knees.

"Minstrel," said Aggie in amazement. "What are you doing here?"

He sat up, startled, grinning through his sandy-colored beard.

"Waiting for you," he replied.

"How'd you know where to look?" asked Aggie.

"You weren't at school today and you weren't home. Where else would you be?"

"And of the miles of possible beaches to choose from, you happened on the right one by mere coincidence?"

"No," confessed the imp. "Actually, I drove around a while until I found your car. Then I just hung loose till you showed up. Are you feeling better?"

"Better than what?" asked Aggie.

"You mean . . . well, I just assumed when you weren't in school . . ."

"I figure as long as I'm leaving, I may just as well use some of those accumulated sick days. It gave me a chance to settle some personal business, finish packing, saying my goodbyes. I find it all a little sad, you know?"

"Yeah, I know. I'm having the same problem. I can't wait to hit the road, but I'm having a hard time making a graceful exit. Can I offer you a dune?"

She seated herself in the sand beside him. "What are you doing out of school?"

"Ditchin', same as you," he said slyly. Then, as if he feared he'd been too bold with her, he added, "Ma'am, I wish I had a little grass to lay on ya, but they busted my dealer."

"One of the kids?" asked Aggie, concerned.

"Naw. The traffic cop that used to work the afternoon shift on the corner of Eastern and Regent Streets."

"You're kidding," gasped Aggie.

"I wish I was," said Minstrel, settled comfortably back into the warm sand. "When all the sources on the street dried up, you could always count on 'the man' to come though with the goodies. Why? Did you know him?"

"He changed a flat for me once. He struck me as super straight."

"Yeah, I guess he was, really. But I'm kinda glad they got him," said the young man earnestly. "He kept hoisting horse on me. I know he was dealin' it to a lot of the kids on campus, but I won't bite. I've seen a friend withdraw. But, man, he had access to the best grass."

"We should both be grateful we made it through school without getting busted. We should both take a lesson from that."

"You givin' it up?" asked Minstrel.

"Yeah," said Aggie soberly. "I think so. You know, I haven't even had a cigarette in the last three days, and I feel marvelous."

"You mean from not smokin'?"

"That's a part of it," answered Aggie. "Also, knowing I'm finally getting out of school. Instead of anxiety I'm feeling a kind of elation, a bouyancy that's like a natural high. It's a good feeling, to be in control of yourself that way."

"Sounds like you're trying to talk *me* straight."

"I'm hardly in a position to do that," said Aggie. "It took *me* a long time to grow up."

"I would, you know? If you asked me to, I'd never do dope again."

"For real?" she asked. "Why?"

"If I tell you, you'll only get upset again and I'm so glad you're getting happy I'd be the last person in the world to upset you again." He paused. "Are you for sure leaving?"

"Yeah," admitted Aggie. "Include me in the list of graduates this season. I've earned a sabbatical."

"What's a sabbatical?"

"A rest cure for teachers on the brink," answered Aggie. "It's when we've still got enough of our wits about us to go quietly, before they come to take us away."

"What are you going to do?"

"Now that I'm grown up?" she laughed. "I'm gonna hang loose, baby. I'm gonna travel as long as my savings hold out or I find a place to be. Whichever comes first. And I'm going to paint, if I can fit an easel into the car. Otherwise, I'll sketch. I'm as enthusiastic as a kid about to leave for camp."

"It's been a bitch this year."

"You figured that out too, huh?" said Aggie, shaking her head.

There was a silence which he jumped to fill before it turned to depression.

"Why'd you decide to be a teacher?"

"If you promise never to tell. It was a case of arrested development," she confessed confidentially. "Maybe it was 'cause I liked school and got some genuine satisfaction from knowing and doing and seeking, and wanted to turn other people on to that. I was a precocious child and an early bloomer, but incapable emotionally of facing the world outside . . . some kind of a Peter Pan syndrome. If you never leave school, you never have to grow up. But I'm ready now. And I feel like I've been reborn. I've always claimed to be a sun worshipper. I'm just gonna follow the sun . . . for as far as the highway unwinds before me," she said, shoving the mane of her windspun hair off of her sweaty neck.

"Our paths may never cross again," he said glumly.

"I have family in New York. I get back occasionally. Maybe I'll look you up one day," answered Aggie. "Matter of fact, you could look them up. I'll give you their address. My dad will love you. He's very musical . . . loves the classics. Just tell my mom you're a grand kid . . . on *my* side of the family. She'll get a kick out of you and feed you a fantastic meal," she chuckled.

"If I write you there, you'll get the message?"

"I'll get the message."

"Somehow, I'm not as scared any more," he whispered.

"Neither am I," smiled Aggie.

"Hey, Aggie," yelped Minstrel excitedly sitting up in a single motion. "You know what you were saying about not being able to fit your easel into the 'Vette? And remember I told you I wanted something small enough to park in the city and fast enough to get back here quick if something happens to my folks?"

They looked at each other and shook hands on the deal, laughing.

Epilogue

The next, the last time she saw Minstrel was at a great distance over the heads of the crowd that had assembled for commencement.

The marching band was seated beneath the sun that scorched the football field. Nearly seven hundred students of the senior class sat on rented chairs, sweating under caps and gowns in Florida's sweltering heat.

Oh, Arcadia, mused Aggie, you great brooding monument of taciturn tradition. You turn your stony face in silence as your sons and daughters reverently pass before you in final tribute.

She heard Bo Calloway's congratulatory remarks, and then the endless stream of somberly garbed students filed slowly toward the dais. As if on a conveyor belt they moved in orderly precision up one side of the flower draped risers and down the other in alphabetical order.

She waited patiently while Bo recited the lengthy list of names until Daniel Mitchell was called and watched with possessive pride from the remote recesses of the field as Minstrel stepped forth proudly.

Surely this was a time to celebrate, not to mourn. It was commencement, not a wake.

The strains of the Alma Mater followed her from the field.

Minstrel and the multitude would enter the world, equipped with their diplomas and their dreams to seek their own reality.

And so would she.

School was out.